WHO DID I MARRY?

SARA PUCCI

Storm
PUBLISHING

Ebook ISBN: 978-1-83700-011-1
Paperback ISBN: 978-1-83700-012-8

Cover design: Ghost
Cover images: Adobe Stock, Shutterstock

Published by Storm Publishing.
For further information, visit:
www.stormpublishing.co

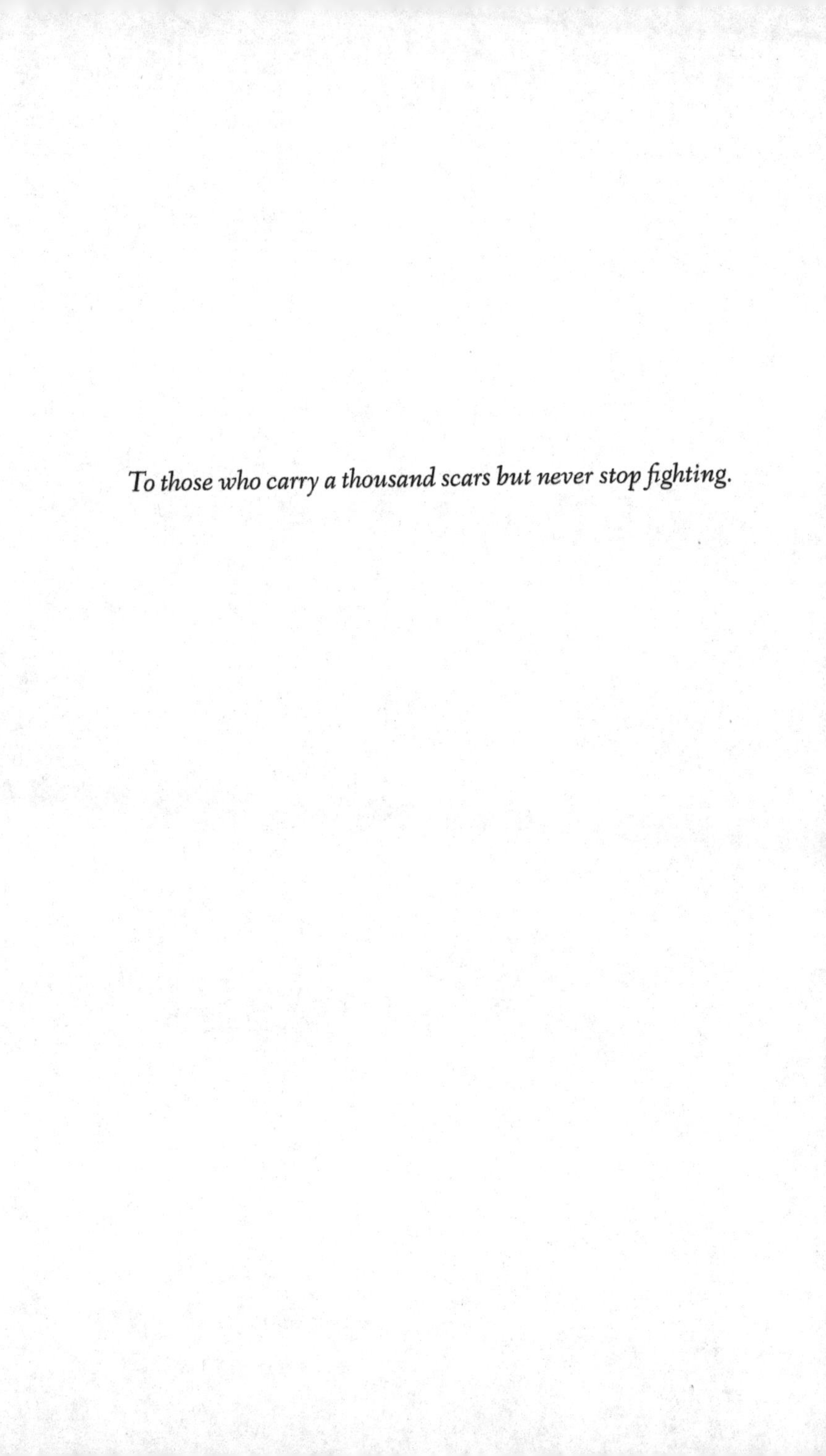

To those who carry a thousand scars but never stop fighting.

ONE

MADELINE

May 5, 3:00PM

For the past fourteen years, we've watched our daughter grow into a charming young woman.

Perhaps I should speak for myself. *He* isn't here right now. This isn't the first time he's been conspicuously absent. He's making a habit of it... just like our quarrels. *How long can we keep the truth buried? How long before the mask cracks under pressure?*

It's just a matter of time before he slams the door open, blurts out a weak excuse, and makes me feel small and inadequate in front of all these people. But I'm used to his outbursts. I can handle it for another day, especially on Charlie's birthday.

I'll make an effort to get through the party without seeming distant, while dodging the judging glances. Everyone always wondered how someone like me ended up with someone like him—how, almost fifteen years ago now, the low-class girl managed to make the high-class boy fall in love with her. It doesn't matter how long I've been with Tyler, or how much I show that my love for him has never had anything to do with his money; I'll never be considered one of them.

Luckily, because I don't want to be.

I wasn't born into their world, their polished lives, where everything is handed to you and nothing is earned. Even though I've known most of them since Charlie started going to middle school, they're all still random faces to me—parents of my daughter's friends, neighbors—giggling to one another, sharing secrets that only the richest people of New York can keep hidden and take to their graves. A part of me envies them—their ability to be cruel and, at the same time, shameless.

Guilt is unfamiliar to them. They can get away with so much, and their dirty money will cover it up forever.

The only person who remained humble, despite her wealth, was Tyler's grandmother. Sadly, she's no longer with us.

Invisible hands grip my throat, making it hard to swallow the last sip of merlot. I shift my weight to one side until my hip presses against the open doorframe of our kitchen, facing the backyard. Pop music plays in the background and for a moment I try to focus on the lyrics, to dissolve the negative thoughts spinning around my head, but it's hard.

Today, I shouldn't waste my energy in thinking over the what's, how's, and if's. The past can't be changed anyway. I might as well get drunk and try not to think about him.

I press my lips together and exhale. I should try to make my smile seem less forced or at least pretend that I'm not stuck in my head. The edges of my lips are trembling. *Maybe if I head over to the living room and make an effort to join a conversation, my shoulders will feel less tense and my stomach will stop hurting.*

My knuckles turn white as I grip the glass tighter, the wine tingling in my throat. I feel sick and I haven't even finished one glass of alcohol. Throwing up all my feelings would make me feel so much better. But it won't happen. *I can't lose control. I won't.*

Charlie chats with her friends in the backyard, smiling and fidgeting, surrounded by pink balloons and confetti scattered across the tiles and around the pool. The wind tosses her blonde hair as it blows toward the far wing of the townhouse—the guesthouse, as we like to call it—where Sadie, our maid, lives. Technically, it's just the other half of the double townhouse we bought and connected years ago, joined by an internal door near the back staircase. It's easier to call it guesthouse than to admit we don't really need the space, except for old furniture and storage. Luckily, Sadie has her own entrance, which means our paths rarely cross, and I prefer it that way. Her door, facing the backyard, is half covered by a sparkly birthday banner that stands out against the white exterior.

I narrow my eyes, trying to see through the gray curtains of Sadie's floor-to-ceiling windows. It's been a while since I've been in our guesthouse; recently, only Tyler has gone in to give Sadie her checks. Sometimes I wonder if she's hiding something. The interior of the guesthouse barely sees daylight.

The laughter of one of Charlie's friends pulls my attention back towards the pool as a sudden breeze drifts through the kitchen's sliding door and brushes against me.

Charlie's fingers wrap around her hair, her deep emerald eyes lock with mine for a second. My daughter's plump lips fall into a straight line before she blinks away, laughs almost too loudly, and refills her red plastic cup with more soda from the refreshment table. Her friends follow closely behind.

My fake smile fades like a smudged painting. I wonder if she just read me. I don't want her to worry. Tyler will show up soon and we can carry on with our day like a normal family living in an 8,000-square-feet townhouse in the Upper East Side.

My best friend Rose steps into the kitchen, her presence

shifting the energy in the room. Every time she's around, I feel relieved. Less lonely.

She's wearing an exotic flowery romper, with her brown waves swept to one side. "I'm going to steal a bit more of your wine if you don't mind?" Rose's smile turns into a smirk as she pours more alcohol into her glass, a red lipstick stain stamped on the edge.

I nod and set my glass down on the counter, crossing my arms over my chest as another gust of wind sweeps through, sending goosebumps crawling over my skin.

Sadie appears behind me, making me jump. Her hair—dyed bright red with brown regrowth—and piercing blue eyes create a stark contrast, accentuated by the heavy layer of foundation that she wears.

She approaches the fridge and carefully takes out Charlie's birthday cake, placing it on the cake stand on the marble kitchen island. The sweet, rich aroma of vanilla and buttercream makes my mouth water. The top tier of the cake is decorated with shimmering edible glitter, and the words *OFFICIALLY FABULOUS AT FOURTEEN* are scrawled across the second tier in bold icing, next to winky face and heart emojis.

Outside, the crowd of teenagers, arms raised to the sky, sing over the pop song blaring from the speakers outside. Charlie laughs while singing, her gaze darting to the ground every few seconds, her cheeks flushing with unease.

A chill runs down my spine as I catch Sadie's eyes scanning me from head to toe, her lips pressed tight, her eyes narrowing. For a few seconds, her eyes stare into mine, her jaw is clenched tight, her eyebrows rise to the top of her forehead as if waiting for a reaction or trying to send me a message. She then shakes her head slowly and walks away with a huff.

Rose's eyebrows arch. "What's wrong with her?"

I roll my eyes to the ceiling, taking a deep breath before responding. "I honestly don't know."

"You should confront her, you know. You can't be treated like trash in your own home"—Rose gestures around us—"I would fire her."

"My mind is somewhere else right now." My gaze moves back to Charlie; she's brushing her wet hair back into a ponytail while sitting on one of the sun loungers near the edge of the pool.

Rose follows my gaze, the tension in her brows relaxes when her eyes set on Charlie. "Gosh, I remember when her hands were the size of a teacup," she says, placing a hand on her chest.

A bittersweet tightness grips my stomach. "I know, she was so tiny." I still remember those nights when she would curl up in the middle of the bed between Tyler and me, her little body taking up more space than you'd think. I would die to relive those moments when the love between my husband and me was fresh, alive, and nothing would ever come between us.

It was just the three of us back then. Now it feels like someone is always pointing a gun in the back of my neck, ready to shoot. Our life has changed so much during the past few months and years... I don't entirely recognize Tyler anymore. I barely recognize myself.

Rose nods, locking her eyes with mine before her eyebrows reach the middle of her forehead. "Is he still at work?"

I nod. She knows the ins and outs of my life, the good and the bad. Sometimes I think it's a blessing to have a friend that knows everything, other times I wonder if it's a curse—because when they know too much, they hold the power to hurt you the most.

I sigh, glancing away. "He is. I should call him soon though, it's getting late."

Rose's lips compress. "I still wonder why you care so much about him. He treats you like shit most of the time."

My shoulders slump. She doesn't understand. How could she?

Rose isn't married, doesn't have kids. She doesn't know what it's like to have built a life with someone. I can't just throw that all away over a few arguments. Tyler works so hard for us, always making sure we have everything we need. Yes, he misses family events sometimes, but it's only because he's trying to give us a good life. And even though he can overreact at times, he always knows how to make me feel special, like I'm the most important person in the world. That's what really matters in the end.

"Try to put yourself in my shoes," I reply. "It's hard enough to explain how I feel right now."

Rose takes a deep breath. "I get it. I really do. But you need to prioritize yourself over him," she raises a glass in the direction of the pool, "for Charlie."

A small, strained smile appears as I nod. *For Charlie.*

Sometimes I wish that Rose was as blind as the people close to Tyler, the people who only know the angelic part of him, but it's too late now. When I first met him, Rose used to see him as this charming, kind man who wouldn't hurt a fly. But after I exposed the aftermath of his outbursts in every single detail to her—the broken furniture, the insults—her sympathy for me has turned into disdain for him.

How could I blame Rose? I would react exactly the same way if she was married and going through a tough period in her relationship. She would do anything to protect me and I would do anything to protect her. We have an unspoken pact, a promise we never had to shake hands for.

My thoughts are shattered by a familiar scream from the backyard and flames implode within me, followed by my heart leaping into my throat.

Charlie.

My eyes snap in the direction of the swimming pool. Party

hats, napkins, and clothes are scattered on the tiles. Three girls —one brunette and two blondes—pass an inflatable pink ball to each other in the water, swimming from one side to the other. Another group of teens chat by the edge of the pool. But Charlie isn't anywhere to be seen.

I break out in a cold sweat. A frantic drumbeat echoes in my ears, I feel my heartbeat increasing every second. I move my eyes frenetically, checking from one corner of the backyard to the other. I step outside, glancing around, searching for her, my mind racing with worst-case scenarios.

If anything happened to Charlie, I would never forgive myself.

Never.

Then I see her and a shaky exhale escapes my lips. A teenage boy with water dripping from his blond curls comes out from behind the greenhouse, carrying Charlie on his shoulders. She pinches her nose and closes her eyes, giggling, knowing he's about to throw her in the pool. As soon as they reach the edge, he tosses her into the water and Charlie lets out a gleeful shout.

The tension in my body disappears. It was nothing.

"Alright, everyone, it's time to sing," Rose says out loud, gesturing for the people in the backyard to gather around the kitchen island.

Charlie squeezes some water out of her damp dress and gestures for her friends to go inside. I follow as she steps in front of the cake, her green eyes sparkling with excitement as everyone starts singing "Happy Birthday" to her. I wish Tyler would show up at this very moment. But there's no sign of him. Even his family—his parents, Pam and Dave, and his sister Laura—are looking around, frowning, mumbling something to each other. I don't have to be a mind reader to know what they're thinking, because, for once, after all the time I've known them, we're all wondering the same thing: *Where the hell is he?*

Sadie quickly grabs the matches from the edge of the table

and lights the candles on the cake, her face frozen in pure indifference. The small flames reflect in her eyes, revealing nothing. Everyone around us starts singing, clapping in unison, me included, even though I can't stop staring at her.

Sadie steps away from the table, her eyes meeting mine. There's something off about her today, something she's carrying but won't reveal.

Manipulative women like her won't stay silent, unless disclosing whatever secret they're carrying is a risk for them.

Charlie closes her eyes for a brief second before taking a deep breath and blowing out the candles. For a few minutes, I see what joy looks like. But then her glance drifts with hope towards the fence that overlooks the back road.

Tyler's parents follow Charlie's gaze, his mother pointing at someone, her face lighting up for a second as she begins to wave. I turn to look, expecting to see my husband making his way in, but instead, all I see is a man in a gray oversized hoodie and a black New Era cap, staring at our backyard. His eyes are hidden by sunglasses, but even though I can't see exactly what he's looking at, I feel his heavy, oppressive gaze on me.

"Pam, darling, stop waving. It's not Tyler," Dave, my father-in-law, says to my mother-in-law, who is standing behind me.

I take a couple of steps forward, passing teenagers who are now running around the backyard, soaking each other with water balloons, while some of the adults savor their cake and chat about the latest gossip.

Beyond the fence, the man's figure is too rigid, almost like a statue. His skin looks pale; his lips are thin, almost invisible.

Then his arms move.

I come to a stop. I feel as though something is pressing down on my chest. It might be fear.

He pulls the hood of his gray hoodie up over his head; it swallows his face. I don't know why, but my breath catches. My skin prickles. And then—just as my heart starts pounding with anxiety—he slips his hands into his pockets and walks away.

I rush back into the kitchen, grabbing my phone from the counter.

This neighborhood has always felt safe. It's a laid-back residential area, with a few local cafes and a couple of boutiques on our street. Tourists tend to concentrate more in the direction of Times Square or the Empire State Building. But we're only ten minutes' walking distance from Central Park, so we do get random people walking around. We've never had crimes or drama happening on our street though.

Maybe the creepy man just wanted to see where the noise was coming from? Maybe he was just passing by and got curious? But I trust my gut and there was something strange about his presence.

At least he's gone now. If Tyler had been here, I wouldn't have felt so unsafe.

I phone him and it rings for a while, but he doesn't pick up. I try again, no response. The tip of my thumbnail presses against the index finger until the pain becomes unbearable. His voicemail greets me, I take a deep breath, tucking a strand of hair behind my ear.

"Hey." My jaw clenches. I don't want to sound too worried, too needy, but I haven't heard from him or seen him since he left for work this morning and, for some reason, I have a bad feeling.

"I..." I swallow, biting my cheek, fighting the urge of starting another argument. I almost feel guilty for feeling frustrated, I don't want to bother him at work, but he's missing Charlie's birthday. I guess all I want to know is if he can make it here before the party ends and whether he's okay. "I hope you're not too busy. Call me when you have a chance. I love you."

A heavy sigh escapes my lips as I fight to push down waves of disappointment; anger, sadness, and guilt churn in my stomach. I don't even know how it's possible to experience so many feelings at once, but here I am—burning inside.

I notice Sadie carrying a blue bucket with cleaning supplies in the direction of the front door, her hands covered by yellow gloves. The way she's suddenly walking so rapidly catches my attention. Then I hear the door slam shut, followed by the sound of her shoes tapping against the porch steps.

As I gather the empty wine glasses into a corner of the kitchen, Rose steps in, short of breath. Her pupils are dilated, her lips are parted, her chest is rising and falling far too quickly. She grabs my arm and pulls me into the corner beneath the staircase leading to the second floor.

My pulse quickens with worry. "What's going on?"

"There's—" Rose's hands start shaking and I hold them tight.

"Take a deep breath," I say. My heartbeat slows as Rose closes her eyes and manages to calm down.

"A man. Outside." Rose swallows, her breath carrying the smell of chips and wine. From the way she talks and moves, it's clear that she's had too much to drink. My mind drifts back to the scary man who was staring at me just moments ago. I'm about to tell her, *I know, I saw,* but Rose shakes her head as if she can suddenly hear my thoughts. "He's lying on the sidewalk. His—his shirt is stained with blood."

"Where?"

Rose pulls me by my wrist to the front of the house, just three steps away from the stoop. I catch a glimpse of a leg clad in jeans and a shoe peeking out from behind the green trash can. We take two more steps.

My breath freezes. A sharp whistle drowns every other noise.

The longer I stare, the more it becomes real, the harder it is to breathe.

I squeeze my eyes shut.
Charlie's birthday party is over.

TWO
SADIE

May 5, 4:30PM

One of the windows of the guesthouse frames the crime scene perfectly.

I inch one of the thick curtains aside, just enough to peek through. The music playing from the speakers suddenly stops.

Two police officers are crouched over the body, their faces grim as they study every detail of what appears to be a man's corpse. A few guests from the birthday party step closer reluctantly, some covering their mouths in disbelief.

It's difficult to make out what the police are saying just by watching their mouths move, but I can sense their suspicion by the way they scrutinize everyone around them. One blue-uniformed policeman whose shiny badge reflects the bright sunlight gets back on his feet and crosses his arms tightly, his posture stiff, while a woman in a black suit and leather boots rubs the back of her neck. Both wear guns holstered at their hips —weapons that could be similar to the murder weapon.

The siren lights on the two police cars continue to flash, casting red and blue hues over Madeline and Rose's faces. Their expressions show pure innocence and shock—or at least that's what they're trying to show. I've never seen Madeline's face turn so pale, like she's going to faint at any minute now. She stands still, paralyzed by the sight. Rose, on the other hand, is moving her hands frenetically while she talks to the officers.

"What's going on?" one of Charlie's friends asks. They move to the front of the guesthouse, pointing at the road ahead. I squeeze my fingers around the fabric of the curtain, ready to shut it if anyone turns my way.

Charlie shakes her head. "I don't know." She holds a party paper bag between her fingers and begins nervously tearing at the edges. "I—I think we should go inside. My mom will handle this." She pinches her lip with her nails and walks into the kitchen of the townhouse, followed by a bunch of teens.

My attention returns to the once quiet street. A blonde woman in her fifties appears out of nowhere and pushes the officers aside, crying and screaming like mad. She kneels over the body and covers her face with her hands. She's sobbing and shaking. The officers gesture for her to move away from the scene, but she won't.

Madeline takes a step forward, frowning at the woman. *Does she know her?*

One of the officers finally manages to convince the blonde woman to remove herself from the crime scene, and she steps away, black mascara smudged all over her cheeks. The policeman asks her something, but she doesn't respond. She just stares in front of her, arms hugging her chest, lips trembling, body shaking.

I squint, trying to see through the legs of the people moving around the body, straining to catch a glimpse of the victim. But I'll have to wait a little longer until someone shifts. I could go over and check for myself, but that would be a bad idea, and I'm not stupid. The last thing I want is to be one of the main suspects, and the longer I stay out of this mess, the better.

The sun seems to shine more brightly when the man I fell in love with three months ago appears on the other side of the road. But there's something strange about the way he's walking and looking around. He's staring at something miles away, in completely the opposite direction from the police examining the body. He walks slowly towards his wife in an odd, robotic way. It almost seems like he's forgotten where he is.

I wish I could knock on the glass and gesture for him to come inside so he doesn't have to be questioned by the police—especially if he's drunk. But he won't be able to hear me.

Madeline crosses the road and says something indecipherable to him; he slowly blinks, but doesn't seem to respond. He just stands still while she waves a hand and snaps her fingers in front of him, as if she's trying to wake him up.

The emptiness in his expression is attracting attention. The woman in a suit—presumably a detective—notices the way he's barely able to stand and cross the street. I watch her take out a small notepad and pen from her blazer pocket. Tyler shakes his head multiple times, raising a hand to shield his eyes from the sun. His movements are too uncoordinated not to raise suspicion. The detective takes him by his arm, walking him towards the police car.

My heart jumps out of my chest at the idea that he's going to be interrogated by the police as a murder suspect.

He's always so kind to me—I think of his bright smile, with perfect teeth that light up his face, his dark hair falling effortlessly to the right side, a little messy but somehow perfect, and his neatly groomed beard. Madeline's husband—Tyler—would never hurt a fly.

The only one who can make him go crazy is Madeline. And no one seems to notice it—except me. I live with them, I watch them, I listen to their conversations. I see it all, every detail, every shift in his mood, the way his smile fades every time she opens her mouth. He's a good man, but she knows just how to push him to the edge, make him snap. It's like she does it on purpose. She's always unhappy, always complaining, always finding fault with him—with everything he does. She never appreciates anything. She acts like the world owes her something, as if she has some right to be miserable while he busts his ass at work.

I could make him happy. I could be the one to give him peace. I would never treat him like she does. I could be everything she's not—understanding, grateful. I would never complain. Unlike Madeline, I know how to care for him, how to take care of things. She can't even clean properly, can't even cook a simple meal without ruining it. I've seen the messes she leaves behind, the meals that end up in the trash. She doesn't even try. She doesn't even care.

Madeline is the definition of a useless wife.

I know him. Tyler would never ruin the life and career he's worked so hard for by killing a random man.

My blood boils as the policeman picks up a blue bucket with cleaning supplies from the tiles near the house, glancing around. *I completely forgot about that. I'm such an idiot, but I couldn't think straight.*

I was heading out to clean and I saw the body lying on the floor. I panicked and went back inside the guesthouse. I was afraid the killer was going to attack me too. I rehearse my account of my actions.

I close the curtain and walk around the living room, my eyes searching the walls, the shelves, the artworks... anything that can give me inspiration. Inspiration to lie better. *This neighborhood has always been peaceful, it scared me to death to see something like that.*

My body sinks on the couch pillow, fingers caressing my chin. *I don't know anything.* My hands start trembling. *I swear.*

Sunlight spills into the living room, illuminating the bright red petals of fresh roses in a vase on the coffee table. The vibrant color shimmers through the glass surface, reminiscent of blood in a thriller movie.

Then, a thought strikes me—an image flashes in my mind. The one thing I'd completely forgotten about, the one thing that could ruin everything.

A camera, positioned directly above the front door of Tyler and Madeline's house.

THREE
DETECTIVE RYNN

May 5, 6:00PM

Something isn't right about Tyler Johnson.

His untouched glass of water sits on the silver table of the interrogation room. His pupils are dilated, his breath is shallow, and I can sense the barely contained nerves he is trying so hard to mask. I've seen this man at conferences on TV and he doesn't look like himself right now. It's like he can't access his usual manners, charm, and confidence. Or perhaps he was just performing on TV.

He twitches his fingers nervously. "I told you. I was at work. What more do you need to know?"

It's only been half an hour since he was brought to the station from the crime scene, where the dead body was found in front of his porch, but he's acting like I've been holding him hostage for days.

"On a Saturday?"

Tyler shrugs, his shoulders stiff. "I'm the CEO of Vertex Capital. I don't have set work timings. I come and go as needed."

People like him, with a public reputation to maintain, don't stumble into crime scenes with glassy eyes and erratic movements, refusing to speak to the police.

"Right. Do you have anyone who can confirm that?"

His response comes almost too quickly. "Of course. My employees."

Tyler's hands slide along the sides of his plastic chair. His movements are inconsistent, like he's not quite in control of his body. His eyes flick from the table to the door, then to the glass of water between us and back again.

I lean forward. "Why did you refuse to speak at the crime scene?"

He swallows. "I... I was shocked. I thought—I thought maybe I'd get in trouble if I said the wrong thing. I just... I just needed some time to process what I saw."

This excuse doesn't sit right. If he were innocent, he would have said something to protect himself. But it's like he's stuck between lies and doesn't know which one to pick.

I watch him carefully, studying his body language. His breathing has sped up in the last ten minutes. There's something hidden behind his eyes. *Is it guilt? Fear? Confusion? Or maybe it's something I can't see yet.* His strange reactions don't just reflect fear of being implicated in a crime, there's something more.

What is he hiding? And who is he trying to protect? Himself, or someone else?

"We believe that the murder victim has been dead for less than twenty-four hours. He had a head injury and a deep, fresh wound on his stomach. This murder seems planned; someone moved the body into the daylight when it was convenient, almost like a sick game." My nails tap rhythmically against the wooden table. "There was a woman at the scene. Blonde, in her fifties. She was crying over the body. Her name's Victoria Parker. Does that name mean anything to you?"

I notice Tyler flinch slightly when I mention her name. *He knows who she is. He must do.*

Tyler's jaw clenches. He briefly catches his reflection in the two-way mirror, then his gaze falls to the center of the table. "Have you—have you identified the body?" His voice cracks, as though he's asking more out of fear than curiosity. *Is he trying to buy time or is he genuinely nervous?*

I frown, trying to understand where he's going with this question.

Is he hoping we're as far away as possible from figuring all of it out?

"Not yet. We haven't found any ID, no phone—nothing to help us figure out who the victim is. But we believe that Victoria is the victim's mother. She's being interrogated in the next room right now. The point is—do you have any connection with the victim?"

Tyler's gaze connects with mine. His lips part as if he's about to say something—but then he stops himself.

"I have the feeling that you weren't just 'in the wrong place at the wrong time.' I can see it in your eyes. I'm going to ask you again: Did you know the victim?"

No response. He just stares into my eyes, his teeth biting his lower lip. He keeps adjusting his body on his seat as though he's trying to get comfortable. Once again, he looks like he's on the edge of saying something, but the words die on his tongue.

I press further. "You're not helping yourself by shutting down. Whatever happened between you and the victim—whatever you're hiding—you're not helping yourself. Unless you're protecting someone else? Someone you don't want to get caught. Your wife, perhaps?"

Tyler slams his fist on the table, making me jolt. He covers his ears with both of his hands, moving his body forward and back. Sweat drips down his forehead and his hands shoot up to his neck as though he can't breathe.

Something about what I said triggered him. He's either having a panic attack or he's acting desperate on purpose. But this doesn't explain the way his body keeps randomly moving. There's a question that keeps flashing at the back of my mind...

"Are you on drugs, Tyler?"

His eyes widen, the question a punch he didn't expect. He blinks rapidly, clearly trying to process the meaning behind it. "What do you mean? I—I'm fine."

My eyebrows arch. "It doesn't look like you are."

Tyler's breath catches in his throat. His face goes pale and he shifts uncomfortably in the chair. His hand hovers near the glass of water but stops just short of touching it, as if he is a marionette and someone else is controlling his movements.

"I've never done drugs in my life." His eyes dart around the room, avoiding mine.

"You're either dying from guilt or super high. Just tell me what's going on with you."

Tyler's entire body goes rigid. His chest rises and falls rapidly as if he's trapped in his own mind, fighting against himself—or a force that's strangling him. His hands are clenched tight into fists, a tremor runs through him.

I keep staring at him. I've seen this before a million times. People on the edge of telling the truth but unable to cross that line. I know the feeling—the hesitation, the fight against betraying himself... or others. Every time I interrogate someone guilty, the tension in the room rises. But I also know that the longer someone resists, the more likely they are to slip.

One wrong word, one wrong step and it's over. *Is Tyler the one who is going to fall?*

"We're going to do a drug test." I stand up. "And when your mind is less... foggy, we'll talk again about the body found outside your property."

Tyler doesn't resist as my colleague arrives and guides him

out of the interrogation room. His head drops low; he is unable to walk in a straight line.

FOUR

MADELINE

May 12, 10:00AM

Rays of sunshine seep between the branches of whispering pines at the graveyard.

Everything around us seems to hold its breath.

Warm wind blows my hair behind my shoulders. The strong scent of Tyler's cologne brings me back to times when our tears were replaced by smiles.

Rows of gravestones, each with different names and dates sculpted into them, stand side by side in neat lines, covering the small hill all the way to the bottom.

It's been a week since the man's cold body was found in front of our porch. Thinking that the police might know who did this to him makes me nauseous.

My husband was in shock when the cadaver was identified as someone close to him, a colleague, a friend. The police don't believe him. They think he's hiding something, especially since he was under the effects of scopolamine when he showed up at Charlie's birthday party—right when Daniel's body was found lifeless.

I always thought that his only bad habit was smoking weed, but now I realize that I've probably been blind to so much more.

I always believed what Tyler said. Every word, every promise. But I'm struggling to piece the truth together right now. Especially because he has twisted memories from the hours prior to his arrival at the party.

What has he done? Do I even want to know?

Charlie wraps her arms around my waist, squeezing gently, her blonde waves flying around her head.

"Are you okay?" I whisper as I follow my daughter's eyes glancing over the closed coffin. Colorful flowers surround a framed photo of Daniel in the middle of the grass.

She nods. I didn't want her to come, there was no need for her to, but she didn't want to be left home alone after everything that happened. And I hate to see her sad.

I caress her hair, gazing at Tyler standing by the edge of the engraved stone. His body is present but his mind clearly is somewhere else. Detective Rynn and two police officers are overlooking the scene from a distance, glaring at Tyler.

The officiant, a short, bald man in a black suit, steps forward. "We are gathered here to honor and remember Daniel," his gaze sweeps over the sea of mournful faces, "a beloved son, colleague, and friend."

A soft sob escapes from someone in the crowd, and I glance sideways to see Tyler's dad, Dave, dabbing at his eyes with a tissue. I scowl.

Why is he crying? Did he know Daniel too?

His wife, my mother-in-law Pam, stands beside him, twirling a strand of her hair around her finger. Tyler's sister's hands are clenched into tight fists, her arms crossed across her chest. Their eyes are looking at the raised coffin, but they don't show any sign of sadness. Their expressions hold the quiet emptiness of buried emotions.

The officiant steps back, giving a small nod in Tyler's direction.

He doesn't move. His body looks frozen in place, as if a ghost just stole his soul. But then he slowly steps forward, his polished shoes crunching against the gravel path.

Tyler takes a deep breath and unfolds a sheet of white paper, reading the words he wrote last night out loud.

"Daniel was one of the strongest guys I've ever known. We've been through difficult, confusing times together over the years."

He stops, letting his words sink in before continuing.

"I wish things went a different way..." His hands start shaking and he moves his gaze towards his family. Pam and Laura both shake their heads, their jaws look tight. But Dave's gaze falls to the ground.

I frown. Daniel was just Tyler's friend, a colleague. *What happened between the two of them? Did they know each other before they worked together? Did something happen between his family and Daniel's?*

The mourners suddenly turn backwards, distracted by the sharp tap of someone's heels. I recognize the woman right away from her platinum-blonde hair. Victoria Parker, the same woman who was crying over Daniel's body the day he was found in our porch, is walking on the path towards us, her eyes covered by big black sunglasses. A long black coat covers her slim figure, her hands are hidden inside the pockets.

I immediately notice Dave's face turning red, but he keeps his head lowered as if he can't face anything or anyone right now.

What is he afraid of? What is he so sad about?

Pam's right leg starts shaking, her foot taps on the ground. The rest of Victoria's friends and family slowly move towards her as she stands a few inches in front of the coffin; they whisper condolences and caress the fabric of her coat. She doesn't react, her face is fixed on the freshly dug grave. A chill runs through my spine. Victoria Parker was Daniel's mother, but something feels out of place.

I can't shake the feeling that something isn't right.

As if there's something hidden—something that one of us knows—that could make this awful situation even worse.

As soon as Tyler clears his throat, Victoria slowly removes her glasses, her eyes—framed by precise eyeliner—narrow into a squint. She throws her sunglasses in the direction of Tyler's family and I gasp, pulling Charlie to the side.

"What the fuck are you doing here?" she snaps, stepping quickly in front of Pam, her heels elevating her height. "You're not invited to my son's funeral. How dare you?" Her voice shakes with fury and I realize that something even darker is about to rise to the surface.

Detective Rynn steps closer to the women, moving her gaze between Victoria and Tyler's family, frowning.

Pam's left eyebrow arches. She doesn't move, doesn't blink. She acts like she couldn't care less about Victoria's words. "I came to pay my respects," she whispers.

"Pay your respects? Is that what you call it? You never cared about him." Victoria laughs nervously, but the sound is bitter, as if all her suppressed rage has finally erupted. "And Dave—*your* husband—pretended Daniel didn't exist. Tyler is the only one who cared, who showed up." She turns sharply towards Tyler, her voice rising, full of accusation. "But I bet you didn't say anything either, did you? To protect your rich family."

Tyler shifts uncomfortably, his eyes dart to the ground for a moment, then back up to Victoria.

My head spins with questions that I'm unable to process fully. *What is this about? What happened between them? Between Victoria, Pam, and Tyler's family? What are they holding back?* I step towards Tyler, my chest tight with confusion. "What's going on?"

He doesn't look at me; instead, his eyes flick to his mom and dad and then back to the ground. It feels like he's not just avoiding my question but trying to avoid the truth altogether. Tyler exhales sharply, like a man who's been holding his breath for far too long. "It's not the right time for this," he mutters, running a hand through his hair. "Victoria..." He pauses, looking at her like he's trying to read her—trying to find a way to fix things that he knows can't be fixed.

But Victoria isn't done. She presses forward, her voice cracking. "Oh, it's the right time. It's *exactly* the right time. Dave and his precious family have been hiding everything for years—keeping Daniel out of sight, out of *their* life, all because of their reputation." She turns to face Tyler. "Just when you were supposed to be at your grandma's Will reading. Your sister's set up nicely with the old house, but were you worried about having to share the money with your half-brother, Tyler?" Victoria shakes her head and says between gritted teeth, "And now my son is dead."

Pam flinches at Victoria's words, but her face remains cold as ice. She stands perfectly still, like she's waiting for the storm to pass, or for someone else to intervene and stop Victoria's accusations.

My mind spins with questions as I try to decipher what's going on. But the more I try to make sense of it, the less I understand.

Tears stream down Victoria's face. "Shame on you. Your family couldn't risk the scandal. Daniel was an inconvenient truth that didn't fit into your perfect little world. Back in the time you would've called him a *bastard*."

My eyes widen. I gaze at Tyler, his face burning red. Detective Rynn intervenes, "Hold on a second. Mr. Johnson, is Daniel your half-brother?"

"Finally someone speaks the truth." Victoria wipes away her tears. "You should look into this, Detective. The Johnsons don't share their secrets with anyone who wasn't born with their last name."

I swallow as her words kick in; I feel like a complete outsider.

Why didn't I know about this? I'm Tyler's wife. How could I not know he had a half-brother?

Dave steps forward. "Enough, Victoria, let's pay our respects to Daniel in a decent way."

"Shut up, Dave," she responds, crossing her arms. "Daniel couldn't even visit you, you wouldn't let him. You, his father, treated him like a mistake. Like a secret. I lived with his questions, his loneliness, while I was trying to bond with you. He loved you, Dave—he wanted to know his father, but you made it impossible for him to even get close. I hate you for what you did to him."

Victoria spits on one of Dave's black shoes and storms off, leaving everyone speechless, unsure of how to recover from the venom she's just left behind.

FIVE
MADELINE

May 12, 12:00PM

The silence between us feels deafening. Tyler puts his seatbelt on and types letters on the car's GPS screen.

"My family and I are going to sign some paperwork for my grandmother's estate," he says. "I'll drop you and Charlie at home, then head over to meet them."

Victoria's words rumble in my ears. *Just when you were supposed to be at your grandma's Will reading. Your sister's set up nicely with the old house, but were you worried about having to share the money with your half-brother, Tyler?*

"You're going to pretend we didn't just walk away from your secret half-brother's funeral? Don't you think that's, I don't know, a little more significant than whatever paperwork you're dealing with?" I can't hide the shock in my voice.

Tyler grips the steering wheel harder as he turns on the engine. I watch his jaw tighten, his muscles flexing beneath his skin. "We had legal complications with Grandma's will and it got delayed. It's family business. It needs to be completed."

"No grief, no shock?"

He sighs. "I don't know what you want from me. What do you expect me to say? I barely knew him."

"But in the funeral you said things—"

"Forget what I said at his funeral. I had to say things I didn't really feel to stop Detective Rynn thinking I killed Daniel."

I glance at the rearview mirror. Charlie's eyes are glued to her phone, scrolling through social media, her thumb nervously picking at the skin around her nail—a habit she always falls into when she's anxious, overwhelmed. This isn't easy for her. Watching Tyler being taken away by the police under the effect of some sort of drug, seeing Daniel's body in front of our house —it's too much. All I want for her is a normal life.

"How am I supposed to feel about all this?" I snap.

"Just act like we've got everything under control." Tyler takes a turn on our street.

I shrug. "Don't we?" I blink rapidly, my mind racing to make sense of his words.

What is he hiding? What else does Tyler know that he's not telling me?

"Why haven't you told me about Daniel?" I already know what he's going to say. He's good at avoiding uncomfortable conversations.

Tyler's eyes narrow as he glances at me, his voice colder than ever. "You don't need to be involved in everything."

My jaw drops. "Involved in *everything*? We're married! You hid a half-brother from me for all these years. And Charlie..." I stop and glance at the rearview mirror. Charlie is wearing head-phones, loud music spills out of them. "She doesn't deserve to go through this situation."

He scoffs, his tone dripping with sarcasm. "Oh c'mon. Don't be dramatic now."

I bite my lower lip. "I'm asking *why* you and your family

kept this secret. Was it to conceal a scandal? Like Victoria said? Is it true that Daniel wasn't allowed to visit your father?"

The car jerks slightly as Tyler accelerates down the busy road. My hands are balled up in my lap, my fingers dig into my palms as I stare out the window, trying to focus on anything but this. But I can't let it go. "You still haven't answered me."

His gaze flickers to me for just a moment, irritation flashing across his face. "We had to protect our reputation. You wouldn't understand how important that is even if I tried to explain it to you."

"Why? Because I grew up poor, and having half-brothers isn't exactly a surprise to me?"

"No. Because you've never had to worry about losing everything because of someone else's mistakes. My father shouldn't have cheated on my mother, but he did. And my mother forgave him. You can imagine how that would've affected my career. Now, the news will eventually come out, and I'll have to protect myself at all costs." He pauses at the traffic light, glancing over at me. "I don't expect you to understand. We come from completely different worlds, and your family situation... well, it's nothing like mine."

His words cut deep into wounds that have never fully healed. "That's so low of you," I reply. Anger flashes through my cheeks, tears fill my eyes. *My family has nothing to do with this, why does he have to remind me about my past?*

He slams the brakes, bringing the car to a screeching halt in front of our townhouse. My body lurches forward, my heart races as I turn to face him.

"Go home, Madeline," Tyler says insistently. His cold gaze remains locked on the road ahead. Charlie gets out of the car and runs towards our neighbors' house, waving at one of her closest friends who is sitting on her front stoop.

I push the door open and slam it behind me, feeling the

force of his side-eye like an arrow in my back. There's no point in turning back to fire Tyler a last look, the sound of his car wheels confirms his departure, leaving behind the echo of our unresolved issues.

My keys jingle as I walk towards the house; the heart-shaped keyring Charlie bought me for my birthday last year slips down my finger. I halt just before the three steps to the porch, a strong tension pulls my muscles.

Light seeps through the unlatched door.

Sadie must have left it open. But since Daniel's murder, I don't feel comfortable knowing that the front door of my house has been left unlocked.

The creak of the wood of the porch stairs tightens the knot in my stomach; the sound of my pulse thumping is like drums playing in my ears. I gently push the door; it groans as it opens.

When Sadie is home alone cleaning, I'm greeted by either the sound of the vacuum echoing through the house or her favorite singer's voice drifting from the speakers.

But today the house is holding its breath.

"Hello?"

No response.

I crouch down at the edge of the sofa, my fingers retrieve the smooth wooden baseball bat we keep hidden there in case of emergencies. Gripping it tightly, I straighten up, my eyes move quickly from one corner of the house to the other.

My heels tap against the stairs, my teeth bite my lips. A suffocating quiet surrounds me as I walk into the bedroom. I stare in horrified shock at the remains of whatever the intruder —or intruders—scattered all over the place. Papers and documents are spread across the bed and strewn all over the floor. It looks like someone was searching for something more valuable than jewels or expensive clothes.

"What the hell...?" My eyes dart from the bed to the floor.

Blood rushes to my ears as I hear a faint sound. My skin prickles as I slowly back up towards the walk-in wardrobe. I pull the door shut, darkness enveloping me.

Turning on the light is not an option—I don't want to be found.

My back slides down against the cold wall until I reach the wooden floor, settling into a seated position. I nearly drop my phone as I unlock it. With trembling fingers, I dial the police and bring the phone to my ear, struggling to slow my breathing.

"911, what's your emergency?"

"There's someone in my house." My voice is barely a whisper. "Please send someone. 158 80th Street, I... I'm hiding upstairs, in the wardrobe."

"Ma'am, I need you to stay calm. Officers are on their way. Can you tell me if you saw anyone?"

I shake my head even though they can't see me. "No, I—I didn't see anyone."

"Is another member of your family present in the house?"

"No, only me." The thought of Charlie walking through the front door right now terrifies me. My fingers tighten around the phone as I search for Tyler's name in the contacts.

Please come home. Someone broke in.

A thud makes me gasp. My entire body stiffens.

Whoever is in the house isn't leaving. But what are they looking for?

"Ma'am, is there a lock on the wardrobe door?"

My eyes dart to the knob. *No lock.* My heart sinks.

"N... no." My voice is now trembling as badly as my hands.

"Okay, that's alright. Stay as quiet as you can. You're doing great. The police are only a few minutes away."

I can hear the stairs creak.

Oh God, they're coming up.

Tears blur my vision as I bite down so hard on my lip that I draw blood. My heart thuds painfully in my chest, it's so loud that I fear the intruder might hear it. I clutch my phone tighter, my knuckles turn white.

The footsteps seem to have stopped.

I squeeze my eyes shut and place my hand over my mouth. Every breath I take feels like a huge risk. A man's voice breaks the silence.

"It's gotta be here. Nobody just vanishes with millions without leaving a trace."

I widen my eyes. Through the slats in the wardrobe door, I watch as he steps into the bedroom. I swallow hard, hanging up on my phone call with the police; I'm terrified that the intruder might hear it.

Pages rustle, flipping rapidly. Then another voice cuts through the silence, coming from a phone on speaker; it echoes in my bedroom. "There has to be proof there. Something, anything!" I can hear the man pacing back and forth.

"You think his wife knows something about it?" the intruder asks.

My brows furrow. *Who is this man and what is he looking for?*

"I don't care if she knows or not," the man on the call replies, "you're the only one I trust who's been working for him. Find something to bring him and his company down!"

My heart races. This man is here because of my husband and there's no way he will easily find whatever they're looking for. When Tyler hides something, he does it well.

"I'll check the closet, maybe he stashed something in there," the intruder says. Steps draw closer, I press my hand even harder on my mouth, trying to suppress any breathing sounds.

If he opens that door, I'm going to be a dead woman.

The wardrobe door handle slightly bends before the piercing noise of sirens suddenly makes the intruder step back.

"Shit! The cops!" the man whispers in panic.

"Damn it, go! Now! Take all the documents you found with you!"

Papers rustle as the intruder hurriedly gathers them. His footsteps pound down the stairs and the door slams. I release my hand from my mouth.

He's gone.

SIX

DETECTIVE RYNN

May 12, 12:30PM

The sky is cloudless above the Johnsons' house; the red brick facade stands bold in the harsh midday sun. The house looms behind a wrought-iron fence in a neighborhood that has barely experienced crime before.

Madeline's call was unexpected. An intruder could change everything in our investigation into Daniel's murder, and the spotlight could shift in a new direction. *But would it be the right direction?*

At the funeral, I really thought I had managed to read most of them: Tyler, Madeline, Victoria, and Tyler's family. But the more time that passes in this case, the more I realize that the majority of these people carry secrets they don't even share with each other.

Daniel Johnson could have been killed by his half-brother Tyler to enable Tyler to claim more of the inheritance left by their grandmother—their father's mother. And of course, Tyler is greedy; I got that vibe from him. But that can't be his only motive. There must be more to this story.

I step up the porch stairs and reach for the front door. There's no sound coming from inside, all I can hear is the distant hum of passing cabs and the occasional murmur of people on the street.

The handle turns easily between my fingers. Pushing the door open, I step into the foyer, my eyes scanning the surroundings. Anthony, my work partner, follows quietly behind. The Johnsons' home is immaculate—every shelf is spotless, the floor gleams under the chandelier, and the kitchen is pristine, with not a thing left out on the counter. I guess their maid is doing a good job. But part of me wonders if she's just trying to lay low by being the model employee.

Anyone could be a suspect right now.

As I move further into the house, my hand hovers near my holster. Then I hear footsteps running down the stairs. But the tension in my muscles releases when I hear her voice.

"Detective Rynn?"

It's Madeline. She reaches the bottom of the stairs but still clings to the railing like she's about to faint. "The man is gone," she says, swallowing hard and glancing around with wide eyes.

I narrow my gaze. "Are you sure?"

"I heard him run out the back door as soon as he heard the sirens. Your car, I mean."

I gesture towards the couch. "Take a seat and tell me everything you heard."

Madeline nods and sits, her hands pressed tightly in her lap.

"I... I heard him talking on the phone with someone," she says, swallowing again. "He was looking for something."

"What did he say?" I lean forward slightly.

"I think he was one of Tyler's former employees. He was talking about money, but... I didn't catch it all. I was focused on trying not to breathe too loudly. He almost opened the wardrobe door. Thank God you came in time."

I nod, my mind already piecing things together. *A former*

employee? Was this break-in about Tyler? My thoughts spin. There's so much I still don't know.

I glance towards the stairs. "Where's your daughter?"

"Charlie's hanging out next door with a friend." Madeline tilts her head slightly to one side, but for some reason her cheeks flush. She frowns and glances outside the window, her eyes scanning the surroundings. Does she feel anxious that her daughter might be in danger? What is she thinking?

There is something about Madeline that gives me the feeling she's not being entirely truthful, somehow she brings this aura of mystery everywhere she goes

I wonder if Madeline is making the whole intruder story up to shift suspicion on to someone else, someone who might not even exist. *Could she be trying to distract us from something worse? Maybe making us believe she's the innocent one?*

I can't jump to conclusions just yet. I need proof. All we know right now is that Daniel and Tyler share the same father; that Daniel's mother, Victoria, is unhinged; and that Tyler and Daniel were both expecting an inheritance from their grandmother—a money pot Tyler can't touch because of some clause.

It's strange how everything seems to be connected.

Anthony runs a hand through his long curly hair. "Did they steal any jewelry?"

I turn on my heel and head towards the open kitchen, letting Anthony take the lead with the conversation. He usually hangs back, quietly observing, probably because he's still new to this job.

Framed photos of Madeline, Tyler, and their daughter, Charlie, line the cream-colored walls. They look happy—like the perfect family. But everyone knows that doesn't exist.

"I'm not sure," Madeline responds, her voice tight. "But he was going through my husband's papers, his documents. He left a mess in the bedroom."

Anthony nods, jotting down notes. "I'll head upstairs to have a look." I hear him slowly walk upstairs.

I walk back to the living room, eyes on Madeline. "Where's your maid?"

She blinks. "Why do you want to know where Sadie is? The intruder was a man—"

"Sadie has access to your property, so we'll need to talk to her. She might have seen the person breaking in. And there might be a connection to Daniel's murder too. We need to gather as many clues as possible to get to the bottom of this."

Madeline hesitates for a moment, then nods, tilting her head toward an interior door a couple feet away. "I think she's home."

The distance between the Johnsons' house and Sadie's current accommodation is literally only ten steps away through the connecting door.

I knock at her door and moments later she appears. Sadie isn't what I expected—she's young, probably in her early twenties, with a baby face half-hidden behind strands of mousy red hair. There's a nervous energy about her—the kind that makes you wonder if she's hiding something or just terrified of everything.

"I'm Detective Rynn," I introduce myself. "I need to ask you a few questions."

Sadie clutches the edges of her satin dressing gown, her nails scratch the fabric like she's trying to rip it on purpose. "What is this about?" she asks, furrowing her brow.

"There was a break-in at the Johnsons' property about an hour ago, and we're wondering if you've seen anyone suspicious." I glance over her shoulder. All the lights in the guesthouse are switched off, the curtains drawn. The floor looks spotless, but there's a pile of clothes near the armchair—a crumpled sweater, a pair of jeans—arranged in a way that looks rushed. Like someone tried to leave in a hurry.

"No. I haven't seen anyone," Sadie says, placing a hand on the door as if she's ready to slam it in my face.

"I see. Also, I meant to ask you—"

"This isn't the right time," she interrupts, her jaw clenched.

I raise an eyebrow. The girl certainly has an attitude. "We found a bucket with cleaning supplies near the porch when Daniel's body was found. Did you notice anything suspicious while you were cleaning the area?"

I see her swallow. "No."

"So, you want to tell me that the body magically appeared in front of the Johnsons' house?"

Sadie crosses her arms. "What do you want me to say? I didn't kill him, if that's what you're implying."

I take a deep breath. "Something tells me we'll find the murder weapon around here, though."

She scoffs. "I'm done with this."

I stop the door with my hand, just enough to keep her from slamming it in my face. "I'm going to get a warrant to search your property," I point a finger at her, "and when I find whatever you're hiding, you'll have a lot more to explain."

Sadie smirks. "You shouldn't waste your time looking into me. You should look into them instead."

I follow her gaze and turn towards the road. The woman who I believe is Madeline's best friend—the same woman who stood beside her when the body was found and tried to explain how and when she saw him—just stepped out of her red convertible. Madeline rushes outside and hugs Rose.

A voice calls out from the Johnsons' backyard door. "Detective Rynn."

Anthony approaches carrying a stack of papers; a frown is etched into his face. "I found something, in front of the house."

I glance at Sadie, her eyes flicker nervously, before looking back at Anthony. "Lead the way," I say to him. My adrenaline surges in response to this potential breakthrough. I follow

Anthony to the porch. He points at the top of the Johnsons' front door, where a tiny camera is aimed at the road stretching horizontally in front of it—right where Daniel's body was found.

"That's not working." Rose, Madeline's best friend, steps beside me, arms crossed over her chest.

My eyes narrow. "How do you know?"

Rose shrugs, her shoulders rising in a nonchalant gesture, and glances at me as if she's challenging me with her gaze.

As if she's speaking directly into my thoughts: *You will never figure this out.*

SEVEN

SADIE

May 13, 2:00PM

Tyler stares at a blurred yellow stain on his office wall.

I can vividly remember when that happened.

It was a day when he was upset with Madeline about something, and he threw a porcelain coffee mug at the wall. It took me a while to remove the marks from the rug. I didn't even notice the dry coffee residue he's looking at right now.

"Is there a way you could remove this?" he asks. His tone is a little too detached for my liking. I glance at the stain and then back at him, noting the tension in his jaw. "I can try, but it might take a few attempts. Or I can just quickly paint over it."

"I don't care how you do it, just get rid of it." Tyler's skin brushes against mine as he steps out of his office. Goosebumps rise all over my body as our skin touches. An electric shock—not everyone gets to feel it. I consider myself lucky. As I bend over to grab the spray and cloth to try and remove the stain, I glimpse Madeline through the window—she's talking with her daughter, Charlie, outside.

Charlie's eyes are watery, she's clearly upset about something. Madeline takes her head between her hands and pulls her forward into a hug. Sometimes I feel sad for Charlie. Growing up in a messed-up family is not easy.

I can relate. Family issues are among the reasons I moved out of home in my early twenties. I couldn't stand seeing my parents drowning in alcohol daily. I couldn't stand how that home smelled, how I didn't get the chance to grow up in a normal family. I had to take the lead when I was fifteen or we would have ended up on the street. My parents weren't working and they were pushing me to support the family. I was afraid they would kick me out if I didn't. So, I did what I had to do. I started selling drugs at my school, until I almost got caught. Thankfully, after years of jumping between dealing and part-time jobs, I saw the Johnsons' ad online; they were looking for a maid—accommodation provided.

And that saved me. He saved me. I will always be grateful because, thanks to Tyler, I get to live normally now. Or at least until the police start putting more pressure on me, like I'm some sort of criminal.

I had no choice but to act.

React to someone else's selfish actions.

I clench my jaw and scrub the stain, trying to think about anything other than Daniel's lifeless body.

My therapist used to say that we should all accept each other's flaws. That no one will ever be perfect. But there are many narcissistic people in this world.

Speaking of which, how can I get past Victoria Parker's egotism?

That woman has been tormenting me since her son was tragically murdered. She keeps sending me messages on social media asking if I can help her find out who killed Daniel. She described how Madeline is opening but ignoring her messages, and told me that she tried to call Tyler multiple times but she thinks that he has blocked her number.

I tried to explain to her that I'm just their maid, but she won't stop harassing me. Detective Rynn's visit yesterday was enough. I don't want any more surprises.

Some people have no boundaries, but she better stay inside her fence. I don't know what I'll do if she ever dares to show up at my doorstep...

"Everything okay here?" Madeline steps into the office, her hands hiding in the pockets of her jeans.

I nod. "Yes."

Her eyes brighten. "Good. I just wanted to check in. Tyler's been... well, he's been *stressed* lately, you know, with his company and... the investigation. I really hope we never have to deal with any intruders again. We replaced the outside camera this morning." She sighs. It's almost theatrical—like she wants me to feel sorry for her.

I raise my eyebrows, placing the spray and cloth back inside my bucket. The wall is now evenly white. I can't wait to see Tyler's happy face. Madeline glances over Tyler's framed certificates like she's trying to make herself a part of his success. "I've been thinking a lot lately about how I can help people beyond my clients. You know, it's not enough to only talk to people who can afford private therapy. Don't you think?" Madeline pauses, waiting for me to respond.

I blink, forcing myself to stay still. *Right. Because she's so good at helping others when she can't even help herself.* I wonder what she thinks when she jumps into her role as a therapist—occasionally, of course, whenever it suits her.

Why work full-time when your husband is a millionaire, right? I swear, sometimes I wish I could snap right back at her. But I keep my mouth shut. *Especially since I've seen what I've seen...*

She continues, oblivious to my indifference. "I've been considering adding a new service to my therapy practice—something like workshops or free group therapy for people who don't have the resources to access help otherwise. I think it could really make a difference. Don't you?"

I can't help but roll my eyes internally. The irony stings. "Sure, why not?" I respond, my gaze sliding to her outfit. Madeline always wears secondhand clothing. She believes that she's helping the Earth by buying used stuff, but the truth is that she only makes her husband feel more ashamed of her. I can see it in Tyler's eyes sometimes, the way he tries to hold his thoughts back to avoid another fight. The calm, carefree way Madeline carries herself warms me from the inside, like I'm burning in hell. *How can she think about her career when there's a murder investigation going on?*

"This is fucked up." The four words tumble downstairs like stones. I can feel Tyler's energy from here, and it is not good.

Madeline blushes. "Excuse me." She holds to the railing as she makes her way to the second floor.

I slide into the storage space right beneath the staircase, hoping to hear their conversation. "The man who broke in... he took all my stuff!" Tyler's voice rises.

I hear something breaking; it sounds like glass. My heart races.

"What stuff, Tyler?" Madeline's tone betrays her frustration.

"Important documents, damn it!"

"Are you involved in something illegal at work?"

There's a pause. I can visualize Tyler's face. *How Madeline makes his blood boil. Every. Single. Time.*

"What makes you say that?" he asks.

"The intruder... he was talking on the phone with someone. He was saying that 'no one could vanish with millions.'"

"And you think I stole money from someone or something?"

Steps echo from the floor above. Perhaps she's getting closer to him. Or farther away. "You tell me. I heard the man saying he used to work for you."

"You shouldn't trust a stranger's words. I mean, it's pretty obvious he broke in here looking for cash."

"Jesus, Tyler. You're such a bad liar." Madeline starts yelling. "There were papers detailing debts piled up—your debts! From your company! Just tell me what you did!"

"Those debts are old and all paid for."

Thick silence stretches between them.

He shouldn't trust her. She's probably making up words from the intruder, words that were never actually said.

Madeline is a great liar, an excellent manipulator.

"What about your grandmother's Will?" Madeline suddenly changes gears. She really wants to have a go at him. She really wants him to get mad.

"Nothing has been sorted yet." He seems to respond without hesitation.

"Your grandmother didn't leave you an inheritance? Is that the issue?"

"Enough with your questions, Madeline. Christ, I feel like I'm being interrogated by you too."

"You don't share anything with me, and I can't stand it."

A door bangs. Footsteps race down the staircase.

I swallow nervously and rush into the kitchen, opening the fridge. I try to act casual, like I'm just going about my business, not spying on them—like I always do. I grab vegetables and start chopping carrots on the counter, but I stop as soon as I hear Tyler's phone vibrating on the coffee table in the living room. I place the knife on the cutting board and quietly step closer to the wall connecting to the living room.

Tyler whispers in half sentences. "It'll be soon... Our anniversary is only three months away..."

I frown.

"Yeah, that fucker's death is messing things up."

I can't see myself right now, but I'm sure that my whole face has turned red.

If only I knew what Tyler is thinking... but I can't read his mind. Besides, nobody knows what's happening backstage in other people's lives. Some people lie to break you, others tell the truth to do the same.

Is Tyler lying or telling the truth to the person on the other end of the phone?

There's another crucial question that may never be answered: Why is Tyler counting down to his anniversary when he said he wants a divorce?

EIGHT

MADELINE

May 13, 4:00PM

His ego is bigger than this whole fucking house.

I want to scream at the top of my lungs; to rip out the anxiety that's punching my stomach restlessly and throw it at him; to make him feel, for once, what I feel and what he has never felt.

But I know how this works; I know he's going to make me feel worse. I know he'll find an excuse, and I know that my words will bounce back, leaving him untouched while I'm left bending under the weight of a situation that I shouldn't be a part of.

So, I'm going to pretend that I'm not bothered. For as long as his difficult mood lasts, at least. I sit on the couch, a book resting on my legs.

Tyler checks himself in the mirror of the foyer, his suit clings perfectly to his broad shoulders. His tie matches the dark-brown shade of his expressive eyes. He's the opposite of me—he always makes sure he leaves home looking his best: expensive suits, polished shoes, ties, outfits that should represent a dependable man. But I know that beneath all the fanciness, it's an illusion. Inside, he's full of insecurity masked by pride.

I never truly understood why he needs to work his ass off like this, even on evenings, weekends. I have never asked to live in an expensive house on the Upper East Side or to own two luxurious cars when the subway brings you everywhere in New York City without worrying about traffic.

He always said that earning money makes things easier, but I don't believe that. Happiness and health come first; they are the basis of everything.

I often question whether I'm genuinely the cause of his explosive behavior, as he claims during our arguments, or if he's simply speaking in anger without considering the impact of his words. Do I somehow provoke his rage, or do his insecurities drive him to act the way he does?

As a therapist, I can see the roots of his behavior clearly, his rage seems to be a manifestation of insecurity more than anything else. The main issue is that his anger blinds him to the consequences of his actions.

I've tried asking Tyler if he'd be open to couples therapy, hoping it might help us understand each other better. But he just scoffed at the idea, dismissing it as pointless. It felt like he was saying my job and everything I believe in is a joke.

It sucks knowing that he doesn't even consider it an option, as if our relationship and my work don't matter to him at all.

Since starting his cryptocurrency company, Tyler's priorities have shifted, bringing the tension in our fourteen-year marriage to the surface. There are moments when holding his hand, randomly kissing, or having sex feel like forced gestures to keep the peace between us.

I count to five in my head as I inhale and again as I exhale.

"Going to another meeting?" A storm brews within me, my hands fidgeting.

He clenches his jaw and stays silent as he sits on the small velvet bench to slip on his shoes.

Maybe I should stop trying to communicate when he doesn't want to? Maybe I should focus on understanding his point of view, while hiding the fact that his reactions wear me down?

I gaze into his eyes; they darken with anger. It's as if a shadow falls across them, revealing a deeper part of his soul; a part that I'm afraid to confront.

I cross my legs, gazing out the living room window, watching a bird flutter around the branches of a tree. I wish I had the freedom to fly away when things get tough.

This is yet another day where Tyler's silence shadows my thoughts, making me wonder what I did wrong this time.

He rushes out of the house in an instant, jumps into his car, and speeds off faster than he should.

Maybe I should go back to my therapy studio. I haven't been there since Daniel's body was found. I thought I needed to be close to my family, but maybe it's time to get out of this house. Get some fresh air. Talk to my patients. It always helps me to help them—it gives me a sense of purpose again. Maybe I'll find a little peace in it. But then again, what if it's too soon? What if being around people only makes my anxiety worse? I've been hiding here, in the quiet, trying to numb the weight of everything that has happened. But I can't keep avoiding life forever. If I don't go back, I'll just keep spiraling.

A sudden sound near the front door makes me gasp. It's a soft, fleeting rustle, almost too quiet, like a mouse just sneaked in.

I step closer to the entrance and see a small piece of folded paper lying on the floor. As I reach for the note, a sense that something is off hits my gut. As I gently unfold the paper, the message inside sends a chill down my spine:

There's nothing worse than a whore living in the house of a liar.

The back of my neck tingles as I slowly stand and peek through the keyhole of the front door, scanning the street. None of the people walking by seem suspicious.

But then it hits me.

Sadie.

I squeeze my eyes shut before I open them again and storm back through the house. My slippers slap against the pristine floorboards. The sound starts and stops as the rugs change under my feet; the edges of the carpets snatch at the toes of my slippers. The connecting door to the guesthouse is shut, but light shines through the gap at the base. I knock on the white wooden door multiple times before Sadie finally unlatches the door.

"What is it? I'm not working today." Her leopard-print pajamas are wrinkled and her clothes are scattered on the floor in the corridor just behind her.

"Did you write this?" I ask, showing her the note stuck between my fingers. Her brows furrow and she instantly shakes her head.

"There's no reason for me to threaten you with a note when I can just say what I think to your face."

I bite my tongue until it hurts. "Right."

"Anything else I can help you with?"

"No." I spin around and walk towards the backyard door, rereading the handwritten note.

The thought of someone watching us, or me, turns on an alarm in my head. *What's going on? Is Tyler doing something sketchy?*

The camera. I almost forgot. We plugged in a new one to replace the old one that wasn't working properly.

I open the app and rewind a few minutes to watch the footage.

A man with a black New Era cap, sunglasses, and a denim jacket stands frozen in front of my door for two minutes. Then, without a sound, he slips a note under the door and rushes off, glancing sideways to see if anyone has noticed him. A shiver runs down my spine.

I recognize him. I know that face, but I can't place it.

Where have I seen him before?

My pulse quickens as I try to remember. I zoom in on his face: two moles on his left cheek, very thin lips, pale skin. I pinch my chin and suddenly it comes to me: *Charlie's birthday party.*

NINE
MADELINE

May 20, 9:00AM

While birds chirp melodic songs, my face rests on the memory foam pillow. I watch the birds as they flit between the branches outside my window.

The soft silk blanket caresses my skin, rays of sunshine warm my face, the sound of the neighbors' kids chatting awakens my senses.

I used to be that kid, too, waiting for my stepdad to get the car running early in the morning, moaning about life as I hoped not to be late for class again. When I was fifteen, I had the worst period of my life and my parents never knew. My classmates bullied me continuously, filled my days with insults, not only at school but also on the streets, calling me the ugliest kid in that small, closed-minded town I once *had to* call home.

I was one of those girls who wanted to disappear into the shadows so badly, hiding from everything and everyone, buried by the shame of my circumstances. I lost count of how many times I used to wish for a "normal" life.

My parents never knew because they wouldn't help in the

way they were supposed to. They were always either making chaos or making no effort at all. Despite all these years, I still bear scars from my past. The pain of not being appreciated.

That's the reason it became crucial for me not to look insecure or beatable. I can't stand the thought that someone could look at me and think, *she's so weak.*

It's important for me never to lose my sense of self because of other people's opinions. Even though I'm married to a rich man and living in a multi-million-dollar house in one of the best neighborhoods in NYC, I've done a lot of charity work over the past few years, offering free therapy sessions to regular clients who had money issues and volunteering at shelters for those who couldn't afford help. It's not about proving anything to anyone, but it truly makes me feel good to help others.

Those who deserve it.

I'm going back to work next week. I must keep my mind away from the issues at home. I keep thinking about that man slipping a note underneath our front door. I haven't told anyone about it except Rose and, of course, Sadie. My family is going through enough right now.

Sometimes I feel like I'm an imposter. Keeping things from people close to me, lying to myself. The truth is, I'm just as vulnerable as the clients who sit across from me.

I have to hold on to the side of Madeline that everyone seems to like. I've built these layers of protection to convince myself and everyone else that I'm in control.

Until I bleed.

"Good morning, beautiful," Tyler whispers, rolling on to my side of the bed. He's not wearing a shirt; his warm feet touch mine for a moment before moving up towards my legs. He hates the chillness of my skin.

"Morning." I force a smile, trying to push away my thoughts. Tyler's skin slowly heats up mine as he wraps his arm around my waist.

He caresses the skin around my belly, his index finger tracing patterns under my top. His eyes lock on to mine intensely. "What's on your mind?" Tyler's hand slowly moves beneath my shorts.

I hesitate. I'm not entirely sure I'm up for this. I keep thinking about the New Era cap man. The way he was spying on us at Charlie's birthday...

"You seem a little tense," Tyler murmurs, not taking his gaze off me.

My cheeks warm up. Until two seconds ago, sex was the furthest thing from my mind, but now... I must admit, it doesn't seem like such a bad idea. My husband has the power to silence my thoughts with a single, magical touch.

"I suppose I am." I match his gaze with equal intensity, the depth of his eyes teleports me to a universe where all problems disappear.

As Tyler moves closer, the scent of sandalwood and earthy musk fills my nostrils.

"Relax." His breath tickles my ear. My heart starts pounding like a wild animal trying to break free, and I try to do as he says, releasing the tension of my shoulders into the softness of our bed.

He moves on top of me in an instant. His muscular arms cage my body and I swallow. *What if he can read me like an open book and he sees the fear and vulnerability in my gaze?*

What if he finds out my deepest secret?

I brush off those thoughts as soon as they hit my mind. He's not focused on reading my thoughts right now—Tyler has never been an empath.

"You know I can't resist your body, your sexy curves." His warm breath brushes my neck. "My irresistible wife..."

Tyler kisses my neck; gentle shivers run down my spine. His touch gradually ignites a spark deep within me, making the negative thoughts that woke me up suddenly disappear.

"Do you want me?"

Words get caught in my throat. I pull his face against mine, biting his lower lip.

Tyler's hands move in a matter of seconds from my neck, down my trembling arms, and under the fabric of my top. His fingers release the lace of my satin bra. He knows the power he holds over me, the way his touch drives me to the brink of madness.

The room is soon filled with our mingled moans, and the scent of our sweat. I lose myself in his taste, in the heat of his touch while he pulls my hair back, my neck curving on the pillow.

And then, in a burst of intensity, our bodies shake simultaneously, both trying to catch our breath.

I glance at his satisfied smile as he slips out and heads to the bathroom. A wave of realization hits me. Our physical connection has always been the anchor in the storm of our arguments—holding us steady despite all the screams, tears, and smashed plates.

The faint sound of water dripping from the sink stops and Tyler walks back to bed. He pulls me close and places his head on top of my shoulder, shutting his eyes. Maybe we're fooling ourselves, holding on to this idea of intimacy while ignoring the mold forming in the walls around us.

A hazy image of the note I hid inside my bedside table flashes in my mind. It feels like an evil ghost is haunting me.

I pull away from him slowly, unwilling to disturb the fragile peace we've created. Tyler doesn't say anything, he just nods, his grip loosening as I slip out of bed.

As I step downstairs, I find Charlie sitting cross-legged on the rug in the living room, sketching something in her journal—always locked with a key—placed on top of the coffee table.

When I walk in, she pauses and looks up, holding the pencil mid-air. Charlie is wearing white pajamas covered in red hearts.

"What are you drawing?"

"Nothing." Charlie closes her journal, locking it. I'm surprised by the way she furtively avoids my gaze.

I try to smile, sitting on the sofa in front of the coffee table, but a sense of unease gnaws at me. "Are you okay?"

The way she's holding her journal suggests that there's something important hidden beneath that cover. Something she doesn't want anyone to see. Charlie and I are pretty close, and we usually talk about everything—the good and the bad. But the one thing Charlie never opens up about is boys. She doesn't seem to be interested, which seems a bit strange at her age. Unless she's secretly writing love letters to a boy at her school or in the neighborhood in her journal, which would be a cute thing to do.

I sit down on the couch in front of her.

"I'm worried about him going to jail," she whispers.

The weight of her fears presses down on me, and it's hard to push it aside. "Who? Your dad?"

Charlie's cheeks flush bright red; for a moment, she freezes. Her eyes dart away and she bites her lip. "Yes. What if they find some evidence against him?"

A cold knot tightens in my stomach. "Don't think like that, honey. The investigation will be over soon. You'll see, I—"

But Charlie is not reassured. She cuts me off before I can finish. "But—"

"Charlie, I don't want you to worry." I place a hand on hers. I feel her fingers twitch under mine.

Her eyes drop to the floor; her expression reveals her conflicted feelings. "Okay, I will try."

I take a deep breath. "I promised you I would always protect you, remember? Whatever happens, I will always do everything I can to make sure you're happy. I mean it, Charlie."

She doesn't look at me. She just nods while her fingers fidget with the hem of her sleeve. For a second, I wonder if she believes me or if she can hear the cracks in my voice that I'm desperately trying to hide.

But I know this much: *I can't let her see how scared I am.*

My breath catches as a rustling sound comes from the hallway. A letter lies on the wooden floor.

Icy fingers wrap around my heart. *Is that man back?*

I walk towards the door, my hand trembling as I grab the letter. The name *Tyler Johnson* is printed across the front in bold. The word *Confidential* is stamped near the edge of the envelope.

I break the seal and unfold the paper, my breath hitches as I begin to read.

My hand covers my mouth, and I struggle to make sense of what's real anymore.

As if I had dared to believe there would be no more secrets from the Johnson family.

TEN
DETECTIVE RYNN

May 20, 9:45PM

The board in front of me is covered in photos, maps, and notes —scattered pieces of a puzzle that refuses to fit together.

I rub my temples and push my elbows down on the desk. The clock ticks loudly. It's almost 10PM.

The door slowly opens behind me. Anthony walks into the office carrying a blue folder between his fingers. I can already tell by his facial expression that there's something on his mind.

"Please tell me you found something," I say, lying back on the chair.

"I did actually. It's not much, but it's a start." He pins two photos on the board underneath the pictures of Madeline, Tyler, and Sadie. The two distinct faces of Victoria and Rose.

My brows furrow. "I'm missing your point, Anthony."

His fingers circle the photos. "There's a thread here some-where. I think we should interrogate all of them."

The legs of my chair scrape against the floor as I push myself up, my mind racing as I try to find the angle I'm missing. I lean over the desk, placing my weight on my arms, crossing them in front of me. "Why do you think Victoria has something to do with her son's murder?"

"Do you remember when I interrogated her the day we found the body, while you were questioning Tyler Johnson in the other room?"

I nod, keeping my gaze on the board in front of me. "You think she was lying about something she said?"

"Well... no. But she wouldn't explain why she was in the area on the day of the murder, until I found a restraining order against her from a while back. From Tyler's dad, Dave."

I tilt my head back. "Well, I can't say I'm surprised. She sounded like she really hated the Johnsons at the funeral. Do you think she knew Dave was going to be at Charlie's birthday party?"

"I believe she wanted to see him, to speak to him, to confront him. I don't think she's over Dave. Behind all that hate she must still love him. She seems to be someone who begs for her lover's attention, if you know what I mean. But that's not everything."

I raise an eyebrow.

"We know that Daniel's body was moved that day. He didn't die on the sidewalk in front of the Johnsons' property. What I find suspicious is that the road right in front of their house was closed off on that day, so that no cars would pass through. That seems too coincidental, don't you think?"

"Where are you going with this, Anthony?"

He places his hands on his hips. "Guess who works in the City Services Department?" He points at the photo of Rose pinned to the board.

My stomach drops, blood rushing to my face. "Rose?"

Anthony nods. "She's been working there for years. She's got the kind of access that could make a closure like that happen. It's too coincidental."

"But that doesn't make sense," I argue, shaking my head.

"Rose was the one who called us. She was the one who found Daniel's body on the street. What about the people who walked by?"

Anthony shrugs. "Maybe the body was well hidden by the killer, but someone else moved it to make sure it was found. And whoever that was, they would have made sure there were no cars passing by before they did what they had to."

I pause, the gears turning in my head. "Victoria?"

"Or Sadie," Anthony adds. "Whoever moved Daniel's body wasn't doing it to help the Johnsons. I'll tell you this much: Rose isn't the type to put them at risk. Whoever did this hated them—wanted them to take the fall. Cancelling the birthday party would have raised too many questions, so whoever moved the body had to lay low. And, of course, the front camera wasn't working that day, and the only ones who can control it are Madeline and Tyler..."

I pinch my chin as I think through the details. "Each of them has secrets," I murmur, stepping closer to the board. "I think you're right. We need to interrogate them all and get a warrant to search their houses. The autopsy showed that Daniel died from the wound to the back of his head. He could've been pushed on something pointed—maybe the corner of a table, or something else. But there's also the additional wound on his stomach, likely from a knife or something sharp, probably to ensure he would bleed out and never wake up. The murder weapon is still out there, and one of them has it. I'm sure of it."

"They weren't smart with the body, so there's no way they've hidden the weapon well enough either."

"Let's hope you're right. Something tells me they aren't going to make this easy."

ELEVEN

MADELINE

May 25, 10:30AM

Today is my first day back at my therapy studio since the murder of Daniel Johnson and, sitting here alone, I can't help but reread that letter again. It's as if somehow its meaning might shift if I just read it one more time.

Each time, I search for something new, a clue I missed before, a hidden message that might change everything.

But nothing does.

Dear Tyler,

I am reaching out as your lawyer to provide important information regarding the terms of your late grandmother's Will.

You are set to inherit a total of $5 million, but there's a clause that will delay the process. This inheritance is contingent upon you remaining married to your wife Madeline for a full fifteen years from the date of your wedding.

*Your grandmother believed that a supportive and loving relation-
ship is the foundation of a successful life, which is why she
included this clause.*

*I must also address your recent inquiry regarding what would
happen if you were to divorce before the fifteenth anniversary of
your marriage to Madeline. Any attempts to dissolve your
marriage prior to that date, which is three months from now, will
result in the loss of your inheritance. Therefore, your dispute will
not be considered at this stage.*

Kind Regards,

Laura Johnson

How could he? The question circles in my head like a
relentless predator stalking its prey. I thought we were real.

A knife twists in my stomach, reopening wounds that I
thought had started to heal.

I can't help but think about the words in that letter, now
stuck in my memory forever. I've read it so many times—trying
to search for something to absolve Tyler. Something to lessen
the betrayal.

But there is nothing. He's just a liar.

It's as if someone has hit pause on my heart, instantly
freezing all my tumultuous feelings. *None of this was ever real.*

I'm caught in a spell, just one of his pawns. *Has he ever
truly loved me? How long have I been living a lie?*

Tyler clearly thinks I'm an idiot, that I'm so blindsided by
his love that I would've never figured this out. And his family
sent this letter to *our* home. *Did they deliberately send this letter
home so I would find it?*

But he's never been so wrong.

I remember how I felt the day I heard him talking to Sadie

after one of our arguments. "I need to divorce her, this isn't healthy," he had said. I could barely breathe as I listened, standing at the guesthouse door, my heart pounding in my chest. It was as if the future I imagined with him had just shattered. I couldn't understand if I was angry, hurt, or just numb. Maybe all those feelings tangled together.

Facing the truth has always been hard for me, so I acted like I hadn't heard Tyler say that he wanted a divorce. *Sometimes, he says things he doesn't mean when he's angry, right?* That's what I told myself, over and over. It's just anger talking, just a moment of frustration. But then he asks his lawyer—his sister, of all people—what would happen to the money if he divorces me. That's different. That changes everything.

It's not just a passing comment anymore. It's not something said in the heat of an argument. He's serious.

I feel the walls closing in around me. *I can't lose him. I can't.* I can't imagine my life without him, without us. I will do anything, *anything*, to keep this family together. Because I still love him. I love him like I did when I was a teenager, before life got complicated, before everything became a constant battle. And Charlie—she deserves a *normal* family. A home where everything isn't falling apart.

At the same time, I won't let him walk all over me. I won't be a doormat for him to wipe his feet on. He will never, ever get that damn money.

I'm going to demolish his castle built of lies once and for all. I will fight for us. For our family. But I'll do it on my terms. No one is going to take me for granted—not him, not anyone.

I lean back on the chair in my therapy studio, letting out a heavy sigh.

My life feels like an overheated blanket. I could burn anytime.

Just as I'm about to sip my tea, a knock on the door pulls me away from my thoughts. Instinctively I hide the letter in the first drawer of my desk. My first client isn't due to arrive for another twenty minutes, but maybe he is early.

"Come in." I stand before my desk.

The door creaks open and a woman wearing a long maroon jumpsuit walks in; her makeup is heavy and precise, as if it's been applied by a professional.

Victoria Parker.

She scans the room as if she has been waiting for this moment all day long. Finally, her blue eyes, framed by big yellow-rimmed glasses, fall straight into mine. "Hello, Madeline."

I swallow, trying to act casual. I've been avoiding her calls and messages on social media since her son's murder, and I bet she's here to seek answers—answers that I don't have, and even if I did, I wouldn't give them to her. She gives me stalker vibes. I get that her son died and that she wants to find the killer to achieve some closure, but harassing people isn't the answer.

"Victoria. How can I help?" I try to keep my tone professional while I double check that my phone is securely in my pocket, just in case I need to call the police. The way she overreacted at her son's funeral makes me think she's unstable, but how could I blame her? She lost her son.

Victoria sits down slowly on the small couch that's usually occupied by my clients. "I thought I might show up here since you aren't answering any of my messages."

"I'm really sorry about everything you're going through. I can't imagine how you must feel—"

Victoria interrupts, her body going rigid. "Dave *ruined* my life."

My pulse quickens as a rush of questions floods my mind. Wherever Victoria is going with this, it can't be good. If her hatred for Tyler's father is the reason she's not grieving her son's death, what does that say about her?

I force myself to remain composed. If she's here because she wants to process her emotions, I can help. As long as she doesn't start to point the finger towards me or my family. "It sounds like Dave's actions have caused you a lot of pain, and you're feeling like it's affecting everything, even your grief. I can imagine that feeling overwhelmed by everything must make it harder to process your son's death."

Her lips are tightly pursed in a straight line. "I don't think you know who the Johnsons really are, Madeline. They promise, but they never deliver. Dave used to tell me he would break up with Pam to be with me."

I cross my arms. "I know that there's a lot more going on with the Johnsons than I realized, Victoria. I didn't know Tyler had a brother, for a start. But I have to admit, I'm curious—why are you bringing this up now, especially after your son's death? Why is this situation weighing so heavily on you at this moment?"

She shakes her head. "All the lies. I want to know who killed Daniel. I guess you're feeling a bit betrayed, like I do, with the situation involving your husband's company."

I can feel the color draining from my face. "What are you talking about?"

"I hired a private investigator to look into the Johnsons. Apparently, Tyler promised his clients huge returns, convincing them to invest their savings in his company, and it was all a scam. You two should talk."

My brows furrow. I struggle to believe her. It sounds like she wants to turn everyone against each other. "Why are you telling me this?"

The temperature in the office grows cooler. Victoria's expression hardens, her eyes narrow as her fingers dig into the armrest of the couch.

"Because"—the warmth in her voice vanishes and she leans forward slightly—"these past couple of weeks have been suffocating for me. I want revenge. For my son's murder, for the life I was denied when Dave shut his door on my face. That asshole has a restraining order on me."

My heart races. "I don't have anything to do with this, Victoria. And I want you to stop investigating my family."

"You're one of them now, your hands are covered in blood too."

A chill runs down my spine and I clench my jaw. "I want you to leave, now."

Her eyes narrow and she pulls a small, sharp knife out of her pocket. "Not so soon, Madeline." She gets up and inches closer; I quickly step backwards until I'm pressing against the wall. Victoria motions to slam the knife into the wall next to me but stops halfway. She leans in so close to my face that I can smell the stench of her cigarette breath, hot and sour against my face.

My heart beats so quickly that I bet she can hear it too.

"You have a daughter, don't you? Beautiful girl. Must be what, fourteen years old now?" Victoria pushes her body backwards and walks around the room.

A wave of nausea hits me. *This woman is a psycho.* "Leave my daughter out of this."

"If you want me to do that, tell Dave that I want compensation for the pain he's caused me, or I will never stop digging until I find out who the hell killed my son. Understand?"

"Don't you dare threaten my daughter," I say through gritted teeth. "You'll get your money. But this"—I tilt my head to the knife in her hand—"this isn't going to get you any closer to finding your son's killer. So, back off."

Without a word, she returns the knife to her pocket. "I'll be waiting," she whispers before she walks towards the door, leaving the room as quickly as she entered.

TWELVE
SADIE

May 30, 10:00AM

My hand brushes against something unexpected in the pocket of Tyler's trousers as I'm about to put them into the washing machine.

It's rough and crumpled—a napkin or a piece of paper perhaps. My fingers curl around it and I pull it out, finding what looks like a receipt.

The ink on the thin, small scrap of paper is smudged, but I can still make out the details. It's a receipt from a store, dated just a few days ago. The total amount catches my eye; it's far more than I'd expect for a simple purchase.

Flash drives: 5 units, VPN subscription, Anonymous burner phone.

My mind is conflicted; I'm torn between the desire to crumple the receipt, throw it in the nearest trash can and forget about it, and the need to uncover what Tyler is hiding. From what he said to Madeline the other day, it sounds like he has done something wrong at Vertex Capital, his company, and he needs to cover it up with something. Money.

I place the receipt in my uniform pocket and start the washing machine. Walking towards the kitchen, I find Charlie sitting on the sofa, watching a reality show on TV. Madeline has finally gone back to work, and I bet she's having a great day.

Especially since I gave Victoria Parker her office address.

If Victoria wants to find out the truth, she needs to speak with other people. I'm not looking for her.

I open the fridge, taking out eggs, bacon, and bread. "Would you like French toast for breakfast?" Charlie doesn't move her eyes from the TV screen, but I catch a faint nod.

As soon as I close the fridge door, Madeline's best friend Rose shows up in front of the backyard door. She slides open the glass door, smiling. I'm used to her showing up unexpectedly, but Madeline isn't here, so I'm not sure what she wants.

"Beautiful day today, huh?" Rose drops her bag on the counter. "How are you?"

"Fine, thanks."

"You don't have to lie to me, you know." She rests her arms on the counter, leaning forward, her eyes piercing into mine. "I know what you did. I saw you doing it. I'm just wondering: why?"

The air feels too thick to breathe. I freeze, my pulse races. "What are you talking about?"

"You don't have to pretend with me. Just know the only reason you still have this job is because Madeline thinks it's best to keep the peace with her enemies. Unfortunately for you, I disagree. I will keep an eye on you."

"What's your problem, Rose?" My voice is too loud. I don't know why I'm even asking. I know what her problem is—it's me.

"Keep your bravery for Detective Rynn when she knocks at your door again, won't you?" Rose flashes me a quick wink, the corner of her mouth curling into a mock smile. "Anyway, I came to visit Charlie." She walks away and sits next to Charlie on the sofa, hugging her. She whispers something in Charlie's ear that makes her laugh.

Rose is totally unlike Madeline, in fact she's her total opposite, but she still touches my nerves. Where Madeline is careful, Rose is a tornado. She doesn't care about diplomacy, about playing nice.

I've been around intense people like her before. The kind of people who thrive on fear. They like seeing you squirm, just for the fun of it. They know exactly what to say to rattle you, and somehow they always seem to know where you're most vulnerable.

I can't let Rose have that power over me. Not again.

The way she made it sound like I'm only here because I'm being tolerated... It's all a game, I mean, I know it is, but I don't know the rules. And that scares me.

I force myself to shake it off. Focus. Get a grip. She can't touch me if I don't let her. No one can. I've got to keep my head in the game, keep my distance.

And for God's sake, don't show any weakness, Sadie. Don't let them catch you.

I crack the eggs into a bowl and whisk them, adding a dash of milk and a sprinkle of cinnamon. As the pan heats up, I dip slices of bread into the mixture and then place them on two plates on the kitchen island.

Charlie walks towards the kitchen island and pulls out the two stools underneath; her posture is a little tense.

"What time is your mom back?" Rose asks, sitting on the stool beside her.

"In the afternoon, probably," she murmurs in a low tone of voice.

Rose picks the bread up and takes a bite of the toast. "This is good, Sadie. Good job!"

I don't look up at her. I can't, not with that fake cheer in her tone. Instead, I turn to clean the grease on the stovetop. Rose's smile is too wide, too forced. It feels like she's trying to get me to admit something, or maybe she wants me to play along with this little *everything's fine* game. I won't.

I wait for the two of them to finish eating before I go back to the guesthouse and turn on my laptop, scrolling through the flood of posts on social media. An intriguing article about *"The New Era Of Cryptocurrency"* has sparked a lot of likes and comments. Hundreds of readers seem to have an interest in something I will never really get my head around.

Vertex Capital, under the leadership of CEO Tyler Johnson, the son of Pam Johnson, has recently sealed an innovative agreement with Fortis Investments, one of the most well-known investment firms in New York City, marking an historical moment for the cryptocurrency sector.

Tyler Johnson said at a recent press conference, "This partnership represents a major milestone for Vertex Capital and we hope it will be a permanent game changer in how individuals and businesses interact with digital currencies."

As I continue scrolling and reach the comments section, the excited tone of the article dissipates.

It's a scam! Don't trust it! They're going to steal your money for a currency that doesn't exist!

Keep your money safe—don't fall for this!

Remember the last crypto bubble? This is just another way for them to profit while we lose everything!

I swallow hard. *How can a promising agreement between*

two companies provoke such a backlash? Is Tyler really involved in a scam?

The problem is that I have no idea how this world works. I would probably be the first person to fall for a scam like this. Especially if Tyler is running it.

I close the laptop, leaning back. The thought of manipulating people's money for profit is *so wrong*.

The man I love wouldn't do that—would he?

THIRTEEN
MADELINE

May 30, 3:00PM

Liam Wilson is my last client of the day.

The afternoon sessions are my favorite. I hate the morning rush of clients who inevitably leave coffee stains on the expensive turquoise-velvet couch I bought. Removing those marks has become a regular chore, and it seems like I'm always scrubbing away fresh spills every few sessions.

The start of the summer heat in New York City seems to get thicker every year. I hold the edges of the white porcelain sink in my office restroom, and I can't stop tapping my square-shaped, pink acrylic nails against it as my stomach contorts. My anxiety has been sky-high since Victoria showed up this morning.

What does she really want?

A knock on the bathroom door pushes away my thoughts, my focus snaps back to reality. I open it cautiously, unsure who my receptionist has let into my office. Liam is never early.

Rose is standing there, dressed in a bright yellow sundress, flip flops and sunglasses.

My eyebrows rise. "Rose? What are you doing here?"

Rose doesn't usually come to visit my office. She likes to spend her afternoons getting tanned at Coney Island, usually while reading a romance novel.

"I was having breakfast with Charlie when I saw your message and I couldn't stand still." She glances around my office for the first time. "Victoria was here?"

"Yeah, she pulled out a knife. It was scary."

Rose shakes her head, staring at me with a serious look. "You have to talk to Tyler, I don't think Victoria's problem is with you—I believe it's with the Johnsons."

My hand rubs my face as I shut my eyes for a moment. "I know. I don't know how to handle this anymore..."

Rose looks thoughtful, but then her face shows a hint of regret. "Where's the letter?"

"Top drawer of the desk."

She rushes over and pulls it out, reading through the words. I follow, crossing my arms to my chest.

"Unbelievable," she mumbles.

"I know." I sigh, glancing at the clock above my desk. "My client will be here any minute. I'll text you later, okay?"

"Okay. Let me know if you need me." Rose waves her hand and steps into the corridor, the sound of her flip flops fades into the distance.

A flame spreads through my chest as I tuck the note back in the top drawer of my desk, out of my sight.

Just as I'm about to switch my phone to silent mode, a text from Tyler pops up on the screen.

Can we talk?

My brow furrows.

I'm about to see a client. What's up?

Tyler's reply arrives almost immediately.

> I just want to say... I know I haven't been around as much as I should be. I promise I'm going to make a real effort to take more time off and be present with the family. You and Charlie deserve that.

I take a deep breath, hoping his words hold value. Is this a good time to tell him about the letter? It probably isn't. Unless he already knows that I've seen it and he's kissing my ass.

> Thank you. Your message means a lot to me. I love you, speak to you soon.

Despite Tyler's history of breaking promises, the sincerity in his message makes it hard not to hope that this time will be different. The way he expresses his love, even in texts, only deepens my feelings for him.

Sometimes I wonder how I'm still stuck in that honeymoon phase even though fourteen years have passed by.

I spray perfume on my neck and wrists, remove the invisible dust from my black suit, and step into the waiting area. The vibrant pastel-blue walls of my studio help ease my anxiety; I truly adore my little sanctuary. Here I can finally breathe freely and think clearly.

I started my therapy studies years ago with Tyler's help. It was a long and complicated journey balancing my business with the demands of Charlie, who was just a newborn. Tyler was working alongside his grandma at the time and his long hours kept him away for most of the day.

Every night, after Charlie was asleep and the dishes were washed, I'd sit at the kitchen table with my textbook and notebook open, the hum of the old fridge the only sound in the apartment. We were living in Queens back then, and our apartment windows were so thin that the distant sirens, car horns, and street chatter below felt like they were happening right inside. It was exhausting, but I don't regret it one bit.

Looking around my studio, I can see the traces of those late-night struggles in every achievement. It's been five years since I officially launched "Harmony Therapy–Madeline's Studio."

A small corridor connects my office, the en-suite bathroom, and the lobby where my receptionist welcomes my clients. "Liam Wilson is late," Sarah says and types something on the computer, her hazel eyes focused on the bright display. The reception desk at Harmony Therapy is pastel green and reflects the tranquil ambience I aim to create for my clients.

I nod and stare at the empty white-leather sofa in front of the desk. I typically have a fifteen-minute rule for late arrivals, but I'm happy to make exceptions when I can.

"I'm so sorry, Madeleine." Liam suddenly bursts in. His skin is glowing as if he's wearing foundation, or perhaps it's sweat.

"No worries, let's go to my office, shall we?" As I head there, I hear Liam's footsteps following along.

The scent of fresh lavender envelops my office, emanating from a sound machine hidden in the corner behind the curtains.

"At least I made it," Liam exclaims, raising one arm in triumph. His vibrant smile lights up his face as though he's a fifteen-year-old who just won a football competition.

This is only the second session I've had with Liam Wilson. The first one was a few days before the murder happened. He seems to be a sweet man, even though he asks personal questions.

"You sure did. Why don't you sit and tell me how your week has been?"

"Of course," Liam exclaims, settling into the velvet chair, passing his fingers through his ash-blond hair. "My week has been... kinda slow. I'm still trying to find a job so I'm keeping myself busy in the meantime. I went running."

"It sounds like you've been staying active, which is great—both physically and mentally. Running can be a good way to clear your head. But it also sounds like you're feeling the weight of the job search. How has that been affecting you, if at all?" I ask, crossing one leg on top of the other.

He pauses for a moment, his green eyes staring into mine. "Well, it's hard you know. I mean, I have to pay the rent and stuff." Liam clears his throat and shifts on the chair before carrying on. "Hey, I have to ask... with everything going on lately, how *do* you manage to keep your head straight? You seem so... calm. Not a lot of people handle stress like you do in your situation. I mean, you must have some tricks, don't you?"

My lips part but no sound comes out. I'm confused by his answer. *Maybe he doesn't want to talk about his problems so he's trying to dig into mine? But why does he suddenly sound so nervous?* "We all have our challenges, but it's about staying grounded. Learning when to let go and when to focus on what you can control," I respond.

"Do you ever feel like you're... holding back? Like you could have been something more? You know, beyond just being Tyler Johnson's wife? With the murder investigation all over the news, I don't blame you if you're looking for an escape."

I force my smile to stay intact, but it's a little colder now. *Of course he knows about the investigation, who doesn't?* Tyler's reputation doesn't help on these occasions. It's impossible to have some privacy, to hide from the media. "I'm perfectly happy with my life, thank you. I'm not looking for more than I have."

My phone vibrates on the shelf by my side, the screen lighting up with Tyler's name. I completely forgot to turn it off, but I feel relieved that I have an excuse to come out from this conversation. It was getting out of line.

"Excuse me, I have to take this." I stand up and walk to the opposite corner of the office.

I frown as I press the green button on my phone. He's never called me in the middle of a session before. "Tyler?"

"Madeline..." His voice is shaky. "Detective Rynn called, she—"

"What—what did she say?"

"She wants to interrogate us. All of us. You, me, Sadie, Victoria, Rose... even my family! I can't believe this! I haven't done anything, I told her already, I—"

I swallow as my legs go numb. Tyler is panicking on the other end of the phone, but I can't hear anything else but a whistle.

Someone is about to sink.

FOURTEEN
DETECTIVE RYNN

Case report date: June 6, 2024

Reporting officer: Detective Rynn

Location of interrogation: Police Station, interview room #2

Subject name: Madeline Johnson

Case: Murder investigation of Daniel Johnson

<u>Transcript summary</u>

Detective Rynn: "You mentioned that the camera at the front of your house was broken. When did you find out it wasn't working anymore?"

Madeline Johnson: "I don't know, a few days before Charlie's birthday, I guess. We never needed it, until... well, until Daniel's death."

Detective Rynn: "That's a bit of a coincidence, don't you think? The camera fails just when you might need it the most. Do you have any idea how that happened? Or was it just a faulty camera?"

Madeline Johnson: "I—I don't know. It was working fine before."

Detective Rynn: "Let me ask you something. Do you feel safe in your area?"

Madeline Johnson: "Yes."

Detective Rynn: "Even when you know that there's a killer out there, possibly targeting your family?"

Madeline Johnson: "I—I meant I usually do. But I do keep an eye out nowadays."

Detective Rynn: "After Daniel's death and the break-in, did you notice anything unusual around your house? Strange people, cars, anything at all that seemed out of place?"

Madeline Johnson: "Actually, yes. There was this man—he was staring into our house at Charlie's birthday and he slipped a threatening note underneath our front door a few days ago."

Detective Rynn: "A man? You never mentioned him before?"

Madeline Johnson: "I must've forgotten. But I've got a video recording from the new camera we had installed and a hand-written note."

Detective Rynn: "I see. We'll look into this; however we believe that someone close to your family murdered Daniel. Is there anything else you want to tell us that might help the investigation?"

Madeline Johnson: "Victoria Parker threatened me in my office. She had a knife."

Detective Rynn: "A knife? What did she say to you?"

Madeline Johnson: "It was one of those small folding safety knives. She demanded money from us. I told her that we'd give it to her, but only if she left our family alone. She agreed and then walked away saying she'd be waiting. It was terrifying."

Detective Rynn: "Thanks for letting us know. We'll talk to Victoria Parker. I want to speak to you about Rose, your best friend. Last time I saw her, she shot me a threatening look. She seems to be very protective of you. Why is that?"

Madeline Johnson: "She's always been that way. She wants to look after me, that's all. Rose has been there for me since I was young, and she's helped me through difficult periods."

Detective Rynn: "I see. Would she help you run away from a murder?"

Madeline Johnson: "What? No."

Detective Rynn: "We know about her job, Madeline, and we found out that she gave the order to close your road for maintenance on the day of Charlie's party. Next thing we know, a dead body was found on the street. A bit suspicious don't you think?"

Madeline Johnson: "That is ridiculous. It's her job. You'll have to ask her about it."

Detective Rynn: "We will, Madeline."

Madeline Johnson: "You know what? I'm done here. I told you everything I know."

Case report date: June 6, 2024

Reporting officer: Detective Rynn

Location of interrogation: Police Station, interview room #2

Subject name: Sadie Kelsey

Case: Murder investigation of Daniel Johnson

<u>Transcript summary</u>

Detective Rynn: "How long have you been working for the Johnsons?"

Sadie Kelsey: "Over three months."

Detective Rynn: "And how are you finding it?"

Sadie Kelsey: "Okay, I guess."

Detective Rynn: "Do you like working for them?"

Sadie Kelsey: "The pay is good and the accommodation works for me. I like Tyler."

Detective Rynn: "And Madeline?"

Sadie Kelsey: "I'm not a fan of her. She's too much sometimes."

Detective Rynn: "Is she hard to work for?"

Sadie Kelsey: "It's not that. She's just too much for Tyler. They fight all the time because of her."

Detective Rynn: "Would you say their marriage can be... toxic?"

Sadie Kelsey: "Yes."

Detective Rynn: "We found your cleaning bucket next to Daniel's body. How did it end up right by the body?"

Sadie Kelsey: "I—I... Okay. I did see the body, but it freaked me out, so I dropped the bucket on the ground and ran to the guesthouse."

Detective Rynn: "You saw the body? When exactly did you see it? Why didn't you call the police immediately? Why run off to the guesthouse?"

Sadie Kelsey: "I—I didn't know what to do! I was just in shock and I was afraid the killer was still nearby. I—I didn't think straight. I saw him a few minutes before the police arrived."

Detective Rynn: "You didn't think to check for a pulse or try to help him?"

Sadie Kelsey: "I didn't want to get involved in something I didn't do."

Detective Rynn: "So you ran because you didn't want to be blamed?"

Sadie Kelsey: "No! I wasn't thinking straight! I just... I was scared, okay?"

Detective Rynn: "And after you ran to the guesthouse, what did you do there?"

Sadie Kelsey: "I just stayed inside, and then I saw Rose and Madeline through the window finding the body, then the police arrived and—"

Detective Rynn: "So one of your windows faces the crime scene?"

Sadie Kelsey: "Yes."

Detective Rynn: "Interesting. You suggested we investigate Madeline and Rose last time I talked to you. Why did you say that? Do you know something else that we should be aware of?"

Sadie Kelsey: "It's just a gut feeling—"

Detective Rynn: "We'll see about that."

Case report date: June 6, 2024

Reporting officer: Detective Rynn

Location of interrogation: Police Station, interview room #2

Subject name: Victoria Parker

Case: Murder investigation of Daniel Johnson

Transcript summary

Detective Rynn: "Why did you threaten Madeline Johnson with a knife?"

Victoria Parker: "Detective, that family destroyed my life. My son is dead because of them!"

Detective Rynn: "How can you be so sure that one of them killed Daniel?"

Victoria Parker: "Trust me, Detective. All they care about is money. Daniel was going to receive a portion of the inheritance from their grandmother. The timing of his death can't be a coincidence."

Detective Rynn: "We looked into the Will and found a clause that prevented Tyler from receiving the money until a specific event in his life occurred. So, that can't be the reason."

Victoria Parker: "What was the clause?"

Detective Rynn: "That's private information that I'm not allowed to disclose. Victoria, why were you in the area when Daniel was found?"

Victoria Parker: "My son wasn't answering my calls, so I thought he was at Charlie's birthday party."

Detective Rynn: "I'm confused. Why would you think that?"

Victoria Parker: "Daniel was supposed to meet Tyler that morning, but when I went to his apartment, he wasn't there. So, I thought that perhaps Tyler had finally decided to include Daniel in the family. I was so wrong."

Detective Rynn: "Were Tyler and Daniel close?"

Victoria Parker: "No, they weren't. But I have the feeling that Tyler was trying to pull Daniel into his shady business dealings or something like that."

Detective Rynn: "I see. We'll look into this. In the meantime, stay away from the Johnsons."

Case report date: June 6, 2024

Reporting officer: Detective Rynn

Location of interrogation: Police Station, interview room #2

Subject name: Rose Logan

Case: Murder investigation of Daniel Johnson

<u>Transcript summary</u>

Detective Rynn: "We found out that you made a request for the road in front of the Johnsons' property to be closed for maintenance on Charlie's birthday. Can you explain why?"

Rose Logan: "That's my job. I was told to make that request."

Detective Rynn: "Rose, we know you're the manager. You're the one in charge."

Rose Logan: "It's standard procedure—road closures happen all the time for maintenance. It wasn't anything out of the ordinary."

Detective Rynn: "How long have you known Madeline?"

Rose Logan: "A really long time. Years. Madeline is my best friend."

Detective Rynn: "Would you kill for her?"

Rose Logan: "Only if I had to. Self-defense is allowed in this country, isn't it?"

Detective Rynn: "It is. Why do you ask?"

Rose Logan: "No reason."

Detective Rynn: "Do you know something we don't, Rose? Any idea of where the murder weapon is?"

Rose Logan: "You're the detective. You're supposed to figure it out! If you don't know, then how the hell am I supposed to?"

Case report date: June 6, 2024

Reporting officer: Detective Rynn

Location of interrogation: Police Station, interview room #2

Subject name: Tyler Johnson

Case: Murder investigation of Daniel Johnson

Transcript summary

Detective Rynn: "Glad to see you clean this time around, Tyler. Let's talk about the morning of Charlie's birthday. You said you were working, but Victoria Parker said you were supposed to meet with Daniel that morning. Did you meet him?"

Tyler Johnson: "I was supposed to meet him for business purposes."

Detective Rynn: "So? Did you go to his apartment?"

Tyler Johnson: "No, I sent him a text message. I cancelled."

Detective Rynn: "You cancelled the meeting, why? Do you have any proof of this?"

Tyler Johnson: "No, I sent a message from a cheap phone that I no longer have access to."

Detective Rynn: "A burner phone, huh? Is this how you handle the scams going on at your company? We know, Tyler.

We've been watching. We're just waiting for the right moment to bring the hammer down on you. But right now, Daniel's murder is my priority. So, tell me—what are you hiding?"

Tyler Johnson: "I'm done talking without my lawyer present."

Detective Rynn: "No problem, Tyler. Just remember—you can try to swallow the truth, but sooner or later, it's going to choke you."

FIFTEEN
MADELINE

June 10, 9:30AM

A candle flickers in the kitchen, casting shadows on the peeling wallpaper.

My tiny, bare feet rest on the dusty floor as I sit in a corner next to the dirty chimney. Time is suspended; the surroundings seem too peaceful and quiet. The ceiling is full of mold that seems to spread as I gaze at it.

Where is Mom?

I trace shapes in the dust on the floor. I draw a house, a dog, and three bodies. My mom and I.

I don't want to draw him with us, even though I know I should. My mom always says how great he is. She laughs at his jokes, even the ones that aren't funny. I don't understand why she thinks he's so funny. He's mean. Mom says he's my new dad now, but I don't see him that way. He's not like the dads I read about in books or see on TV. He's big and loud, with a rough voice that sometimes makes me want to pretend to play hide so I can keep out of his sight. His face is always a little red and he never smiles like Mom does when she talks about him.

He's got thick brown hair that always looks messy and greasy, like he just rolled out of bed, and he wears these strange clothes that look nothing like what Dad used to wear. When he's at home, I must sit quietly and not make a fuss or he'll get grumpy. I see him sitting on his big wooden chair, watching TV and yelling at the screen when the people on it do things he doesn't like.

Sometimes he talks to Mom in a way that makes her sad or worried. On good days, they speak quietly and I try to listen, but I can't hear most of the words. It feels like they are sharing secrets, things I'm not supposed to know. When I ask Mom about it, she tells me not to worry, but it makes me wonder if something is wrong with me or if I did something bad.

Mom says Dad is in a better place, but I can't see him, so it's hard to understand. I think he must be up there playing with the other angels in the clouds.

I wish he could come back and be here with us again. I don't understand why he had to leave, but I know he would make everything better if he was still here.

Suddenly our stepdad storms into the kitchen and he looks mad. His blue eyes look like the sky when it's all gray and cloudy, like when it's about to rain.

He yells really loud and the whole room shakes. It makes my tummy feel funny, as if many butterflies are flying inside me.

I hide my arms behind my back, nervously scratching at the skin around my nails to mask my fear.

I watch as he throws a steak knife—it lands with a thud in the center of the kitchen table.

It's kind of strange, but I don't feel anything.

It's like when you know something terrible is going to happen and you just get used to it.

Behind him, my mother's eyes begs him to stop. His wide eyes take in the horrifying scene; we will never be able to forget it.

My heart races, but the noise of falling bricks drowns it out—our home suddenly collapses.

I sit and keep my head between my knees, holding my teddy bear tightly.

Just as I attempt to scream at the sight of a massive stone hurtling towards my mother, I find myself in the garden, the house vanished.

Gone as if it never was, as if it never truly felt like a home.

I jolt awake, my body covered in cold sweat. What's left of the nightmare of my past spins through my mind. I sit on the edge of the bed and sip water from the crystal glass on the bedside table. The sunlight streaming through the window lifts my spirit and promises a better day ahead.

One breath at a time.

My hands tremble slightly as I set the glass down. I draw my knees to my chest, burying my head in the space between. With closed eyes, I attempt to regain control.

I thought I had put all that behind me. I want to be the person I pretend to be for everyone else, confident, strong... the Madeline who has everything under control. But I feel stuck in that old kitchen with the same fear and confusion; the truth is, I'm still afraid of the same things I was as a little girl. Maybe some wounds never really close.

I wish Tyler was here to comfort me. I wish I could just lie in his arms and feel the warmth of his skin against mine, but he's already at work. Every time tears find me, I have to hide the pain and carry on with another day in my solitary battle.

Tyler promised that he would be more present, that he would make an effort to be there for me. But I'm not surprised he's still absent. He's probably thinking about how to get out of the mess he made within his company—a part of his life that he keeps secret from me. At least we're going to have dinner together tonight. As a normal family.

I could lie and say that Tyler and I will figure it out like we always do, but the truth is that we never really solved our problems. He never wants to communicate.

There have been days when I've burst into tears in front of him, overwhelmed by the need to speak my mind, to yell, to tell him to fuck off. But I never yelled for long. I can't. He won't let me. He raises his voice higher until I can't hear myself anymore. I've always been so scared of the idea that he might leave me—I would rather hurt myself and swallow my pain than risk pushing him away.

The silence after our fights has become a suffocating routine. I keep my feelings bottled up, sealed, my fear of abandonment overriding my need to talk. To shout. Each time I bite back my words, I feel a piece of myself fading away, replaced by a weak version of me that I wanted to leave in my childhood. But I've convinced myself that my efforts to be a good wife are worth it to keep the peace, to keep him.

Deep down, I know this isn't healthy. The black hole between us seems to grow larger and deeper with each day that goes by. Now Tyler's involved in something shady at work and, with the murder and the inheritance clause too, everything feels off. And I can't help but wonder: *is there any chance these things are connected?*

I'm waiting for the right time to use what I read in the letter to my advantage. *You were trying to get the money and then abandon me, how dare you?*

The police are probably focused on trying to find the murderer, but I'm well aware that it's only a matter of time before they knock at our door. When we came back from the interrogation a few days ago, Tyler was going mad.

I can still hear the crash in my mind—Tyler raising his arm and smashing the beer bottle into the sink. Glass scattered across the counter and I gasped, paralyzed for a moment.

His face was red, a vein in his forehead pulsed as his hands clenched. I could tell it wasn't just the interrogation that had set him off—it was something deeper, something darker.

"You know what the problem is?" His angry voice echoed through the house. *"You always want to talk. You contribute a pitiful five percent to this family with your shrink business. I do everything while you sit around listening to people cry all day, whenever you decide to get off your ass and go to work. You're lazy, and you can't even see it."*

Tyler's words stung, but what really bothered me was the look on his face. He was looking at me with disgust. I tried to speak, to calm him down, but the words wouldn't come. I don't know if I was more scared of his anger or of what this meant for us.

Then he took a step closer.

My heart started to race, every second felt heavier. With each step, my lungs seemed to contract, making it harder to breathe.

I couldn't think straight.

But Tyler didn't scare me as much as my thoughts.

Because the longer I stared at the sink filled with pieces of glass, the more I wanted to grab a fragment of glass and slice the skin of his neck.

SIXTEEN
CHARLIE'S JOURNAL

June 10

My mother cooked lasagna tonight.

She has never been a great cook, but she wanted to make an effort for him. I wasn't sure why she even bothered. He always complains about her cooking and insists that she should let Sadie do her job.

I was sitting at the kitchen table when Dad walked in. He kissed Mom on the lips. She smiled, but I could tell there was something going through her mind.

She was bent over the oven and his eyes locked on to her like he was checking every little imperfection. He straightened up, grinning. "Wow, look at this! My beautiful blondie really outdid herself."

Mom didn't look at him at first. She just rolled her eyes and I could see her face turning a little pink. "Oh, stop it!" she teased, but I know she was pleased to hear that comment. You never know how he might react. Maybe she didn't even believe he was being genuine. Sometimes, I feel like I don't even know him. It's like there are two versions of him—this charming, affectionate guy who sometimes shows up and brings us unexpected gifts, and then this stranger who yells and breaks stuff.

He pulled her closer, his hands on her arms, and I could see the way he softened for a second. He moved a strand of hair from her face, just like he always did when he thought he was being sweet. He kissed her forehead, and his fingers started making circles on her skin.

"Your skin feels a little dry," he said, looking at her like he was some kind of expert. "Are you still using that cream my mom gave you? I have to say, you really should use it more."

I saw her tight smile. She didn't say anything right away, just shifted back a bit. She fidgeted. Her hands went to her sides. I could see her trying to hold it together.

"Yeah, I've been using it. I guess I just don't always remember to apply it as often as I should."

Dad tilted his head back. "You know, it's these little things that make all the difference," he said, like he knows everything about skincare. "Imagine how radiant you'd be if you really took care of every detail."

He always tries to find something to fix in her. Even when things are fine, it's like he doesn't accept her for the way she is.

I could see the way Mom's eyes dropped, like she was shrinking under his scrutiny. I don't think he even noticed how much it bothered her—how much it made her disappear.

And I thought, just for a second—if he keeps looking at her like that, she'll start believing she isn't enough. I know how that feels.

I don't think Dad even noticed me at first. I was setting the plates on the table, and when I finally said, "Oh, hi, Dad," I felt like I was acting too well somehow. I didn't expect him to even look at me. His eyes were glued to his phone, and when he did look up, a crease appeared between his brows.

"Did you have a good day?" he asked. I wasn't sure if he actually cared. He didn't look at me as he spoke. He sat down at the table, still not meeting my eyes.

It's like we both agreed not to talk, almost as though there was an invisible wall between us. We'd fallen into the same game—just ignoring each other, letting the silence fill the space that used to be full of words. I didn't know what had happened between my dad and me. But I guess that when someone is constantly absent during the time you're supposed to grow together, you grow apart.

I watched him as he leaned over his plate, inspecting the lasagna like it was some kind of crime scene. His face was scrunched up with skepticism. "Hmm, not bad," he muttered. It wasn't exactly a compliment, but it wasn't a total insult either.

Mom tried to lighten things up by talking to both of us at once. She seemed almost desperate, like she was trying to make us forget that our family is being investigated for murder and that my dad is also a fraud. But Dad wasn't really paying attention.

His fork was already halfway to his mouth, and I could tell he was about to start with the critiques.

Finally, he spoke. "It's alright... But you know, you could use a bit more seasoning. And maybe a different blend of cheeses. And did you really have to use ground beef? I prefer sausage in my lasagna."

Mom's face froze. I could tell how much his words stung. No matter what she did, it was never enough for him. It wasn't the first time he'd done this—picked apart something she had made real effort with. It always seemed like she couldn't get anything right in his eyes.

I stayed quiet, keeping my gaze on my plate, trying to drown out their conversation. I didn't want to be caught in the middle, but part of me just wanted to scream. I knew it wouldn't matter—it wouldn't change anything.

Mom tried to hide her frustration, but I could see it in the way her hands grasped her fork. She forced a smile, but it didn't feel real. "Right, noted," she said.

I took a bite of my food. I liked it, but I wouldn't complain even if it was bad.

But then Dad kept complaining. I could see Mom's shoulders droop as she listened, her confidence eroding with every word he said.

"You seem so ungrateful every time I do something for you," she said quietly.

I wanted to say something, but I knew better. This was between them, and I was just a spectator, watching the same thing happen again and again, almost every single day.

Dad rolled his eyes. "Here we go again," he muttered. "I can't say anything to you. It's called constructive criticism. But you always think you don't have to improve on anything, that you're perfect, right?"

He's always been like this. Before we hired Sadie, I used to help Mom clean the house, and every time, there was something wrong. The dusting wasn't thorough enough. The floors still had some dirt on them. It was like no matter what Mom and I did, we couldn't do it right. Even when we were walking down the street, he would find something to point out: "Watch out, you're cutting off people's paths." It's like I could never catch a break. Even when Mom just wanted to relax, there was always something. "Why don't you exercise more?" or "You should eat healthier."

It's exhausting.

Mom had worked so hard to make that lasagna, even though cooking isn't her thing. She just wanted to do something nice and he couldn't even let her have that. The moment he sat down, he started picking it apart.

And then came the part that always cuts the deepest. "Thanks for cooking. But this lasagna sucks," he said. I could see the hurt in Mom's eyes, even if she tried to hide it. "I bet Charlie would've done a better job."

My heart was pounding in my ears and I could feel the blood rushing to my head. I could barely breathe.

It all happened so fast. One second, I was sitting at the table, *trying to finish my dinner, and the next, everything exploded. Dad's face... I've never seen him look like that. His eyes were so full of rage.*

He yelled something—I don't even remember what it was—and then, without warning, he punched the wall.

I gasped, my hands trembling as I pushed my plate away from me. I could feel the heat of the room, but it was suffocating, too. I wanted to scream, but no sound came out.

Mom didn't move. She didn't say anything. She just stood there, eyes wide, frozen like a statue. Her hands were shaking by her sides.

I wanted to look at Mom, to say something—anything—to make it better, but I couldn't. I just stayed there, feeling like I was drowning in the silence. I could see the tears in her eyes, even though she didn't cry. I could see it in the way she held herself— so stiff, so broken. But I didn't know what to do.

I couldn't take it. I slammed my fork on the table, and I could feel the heat rush to my face. My cheeks burned with anger; I wanted to scream and tell him the truth. My voice trembled and I almost told him.

But I made a promise, so I kept the secret.

Our secret.

SEVENTEEN
MADELINE

June 15, 11:00AM

I often have the feeling that when Liam looks at me—he *really* looks at me.

His eyes keep wandering from my hair to my chest to my legs and sometimes it seems as though it's hard for him to maintain eye contact. It makes me blush, but at the same time, it doesn't annoy me. A part of me likes being admired, especially by a good-looking man like Liam Wilson. It's nice to feel good in my own clothes without being judged for the way I look.

Liam's gaze feels softer than Tyler's critical glare.

His casual white shirt is unbuttoned halfway down his chest, revealing his toned muscles. I swallow; the thought of seeing him without his shirt makes my heart race. At least this therapy session is giving my mind something else to focus on aside from the problems at home.

Shaking myself back to reality, I smile and extend my hand. He takes it immediately; his palm is warm and a little sweaty.

"Hi, Liam. How are you today?"

I close the door behind us, gesturing for him to sit on the sofa. I sit in front of him, crossing my legs.

"Better than usual. You know, I've been thinking about our last session a lot." Liam sighs.

I had almost forgotten about our last session. But, now that I think about it, it was awkward.

"What's on your mind?" I lean forward slightly, searching his light-green eyes.

Liam looks down at his hands, twisting his fingers together in his lap, his knuckles are white. He takes a breath, his lips parting as if to speak, but the silence stretches for a while longer before he finally opens up.

"I've been thinking that sometimes... people do things for a reason. You know, they don't just wake up one day and decide to hurt someone, right? So, I was wondering if Tyler has ever mentioned me?"

I'm confused. *Why would Tyler talk to me about Liam? Do they know each other? And why does Liam keep trying to peek into my life?*

"Liam, I'm here to help you explore your thoughts and feelings, not to involve myself in your personal matters outside of the therapy room. Why do you want to know about my husband anyway?"

He smiles, but there's something unsettling about his expression. "I used to work for Tyler and he fired me." Liam raises his hands as if he didn't do anything wrong.

I can feel my cheeks flushing—this conversation is inappropriate. Liam doesn't seem to be here for the right reasons.

He lowers his arms and shakes his head. "People like Tyler think they can control everything. Push people around. But he doesn't realize that people like me... we don't forget. And when you've been pushed enough, you can find ways to make people remember you. Make them feel the same way you felt." Liam's voice turns cold and suddenly I feel uncomfortable in my own office.

I swallow, trying to keep my legs from shaking nervously. "I feel like you want to tell me something. I need you to be honest with me. What's really going on?"

His lips part as if he's about to say something, but then his mouth becomes rigid. I thought I could read Liam, but I was wrong.

What if he is only here to access Tyler—to gain information about his company or to try and get his job back?

"You're a good therapist, Doc. Real perceptive." He shrugs. "But I have nothing against you. I'm just sharing my frustrations, that's all."

"Then why are you asking about my husband so much? This doesn't feel right. If you want to get your job back, therapy isn't the place for that."

Liam doesn't flinch. In fact, his smile widens. It feels like he's enjoying this, like he couldn't wait for my reaction. But then his gaze drops to the coffee table.

"You're right, I didn't mean to make things awkward. I just hope you're okay. You know, with the investigation and all."

I study Liam's body language. Something is off. His mood shifts too quickly. You can't just switch gears like that. No client has ever openly asked me about my personal life, especially not in this way. And he's pushing—crossing a line. I keep my expression neutral, but internally I'm on high alert.

As the sunlight moves across the room, it catches Liam's face. Something in the light catches my eye. He's wearing foundation. It's subtle, but beneath the layer of makeup, I spot something else concealed beneath—two moles on his left cheek.

My heart skips a beat, a chill runs through my spine. I recognize him now. *I know him.* A wave of nausea rises in my chest. Liam is the man who was watching me at Charlie's birthday party... the man who slipped the note through my door. The man with the New Era cap.

What does he want from me? From my family? Questions spiral in my mind.

"Madeline, are you feeling okay?" He leans his head to the side.

I nod. "Yeah, sorry, it's just warm here. Our session is over. Will I see you next week?"

Liam looks at me intensely. "You sure?"

I force my breathing to slow, my pulse still races beneath my skin. *I can't let him know that I've figured it out. Not yet.* I don't know how much he knows, what he's seen, or how far he's willing to go. One wrong move and he'll see through me. So, I do what I do best. I play it cool. I keep my face impassive, my posture open, as if I'm still just a therapist listening to a troubled client.

I nod, smiling.

EIGHTEEN

SADIE

June 15, 2:30PM

My eyes are on him.

I tell myself not to look. I shouldn't look. But I do.

He's sitting on the couch—laptop balanced on his lap, legs resting on the coffee table.

Tyler's shirt clings to his shoulders, the fabric is transparent enough to show the outline of his abs underneath.

I should focus on cleaning the floor. The mop is laid against the door frame, waiting to be used. Meanwhile, I'm just standing behind the staircase, observing him. Daydreaming of what we could be if Madeline was out of the picture.

His skin is illuminated by the glow of his laptop and his forehead creases with concentration as he navigates the internet. I wonder what he's reading, whether he's worried about the online comments about Vertex Capital in the same way that I am.

If Tyler's company ever shut down because of his wrongdoings, I would lose this job and I can't afford to lose it.

To lose him. It's been a while since we sat and talked. He used to moan about Madeline to me all the time, but I guess that with the investigation he has other priorities. Still, even though the detective made it clear that I'm a suspect too, all I can think about is Tyler.

He could save me eventually, get me out of trouble. He would understand.

Tyler's eyes flicker up and they catch me standing there like a freak. "You okay, Sadie?"

I don't respond right away. I inch closer and sit down on the edge of the couch, closer than I probably should. My knees brush against the side of his hips, and my breath catches for a second. He blushes, his lips forming into a straight line. I force a smile. "Yes—I mean, sorry. I know I should stick to my duties. I just... have a lot on my mind. Detective Rynn interrogated me."

He closes the laptop and places it on the coffee table, Tyler's feet fall to the floor. But his legs are still brushing mine.

His brows knit together. "I heard. Sorry about that. I'm happy to give you a raise for the inconvenience."

Is he trying to shut me up with money?

It feels like he's trying to throw cash at me to make this uncomfortable moment go away, like I'm some problem he wants to solve with a transaction. I shake my head quickly, my fingers curl around the edge of the couch. "I don't want more money. I just... feel a bit lonely here, you know? Away from my friends. It's different."

He leans back, his eyes not leaving mine, although his face seems more relaxed now. Maybe he's pleased he doesn't have to pay me more given the issues he seems to be having at his company. "I get that. Do you want to talk about it?"

There's a part of me that wants to laugh. I'm dying to talk to him about anything, really. About him, about me, about this weird, dizzying electricity between us that's been building ever since I walked through the door.

But I can't. I can't just spill everything out like that. "What do you do when you feel lonely?"

Tyler shifts slightly on the couch, his hand running through his hair. "I keep myself busy, try to learn new things, spend time with my family—"

"But sometimes Madeline is a bit much, isn't she?" I interrupt him, instantly regretting my words. The heat of regret rises in my chest, but it's too late to take my words back.

His eyes widen for a fraction of a second. Then his cheeks flush. "Every marriage is hard. Ups and downs."

I swallow, trying to keep my cool. "Sorry," I murmur, dropping my gaze to the floor. "I guess I thought you two were going to split up. I was just worried about my job, that's all." The lie tastes bitter on my tongue, but it feels safer than admitting what's really on my mind.

"Don't worry. Your job is safe."

I want to ask again—*are you divorcing or not?* Is that what Tyler's hinting at when he says my job is safe? Or is he just telling me what I want to hear? It's probably better if I don't push it too much.

"Would you like to watch a movie with me in the guesthouse tonight?" The question comes out a little too shamelessly, a little too eager, like I'm a different person than the one who's been hiding behind the door. But if I don't say anything, Tyler and I will never be able to bond.

His lips part, but no sound comes out. My palms are suddenly clammy. I shouldn't have put myself in this position. I shouldn't be so forward. But I have to take advantage of these rare moments where Madeline is working.

"I—"

A knock on the door stops Tyler from finishing the sentence. "Police," a woman's voice calls out. "Open the door, please."

I recognize that voice.

It's Detective Rynn.

I glance at Tyler. His expression shifts to shock. "Did you do anything? Do you have anything to do with my half-brother's murder?" he whispers to me frantically. "I swear to God, Sadie," he hisses.

Why is he angry at me all of a sudden?

I shake my head, overwhelmed by a wave of panic. "I didn't... I didn't!"

Another knock, louder and more insistent this time. "This is the police. Please open the door."

Tyler's eyes roll to the ceiling. "Great. Just great. Go open the door then and see what they want," he orders.

I walk to the door, my hands shaking. When I open it, Detective Rynn and her partner are standing there; their expressions are serious.

"Good afternoon, Sadie," the tall man—I think he's called Anthony—says. "Is Tyler Johnson here?"

I glance back at Tyler, who is still sitting on the sofa, his arms crossed, his gaze fixed on me. His body language signals: *Don't let them in.* His silence is more intimidating than any words he could say in this moment.

I turn back to the officers, trying to muster a reassuring smile. Even though I want to defend him, I can't. They've probably already seen him through the living room windows. He will hate me for this, but I have no choice.

"Yes," I whisper, my voice trembling.

The officers exchange a brief glance and they both walk in, turning to enter the living room. I close the door behind them, afraid of what they're going to say. Hopefully they're just here to share a new lead on the killer and then they will leave us be. Tyler and I have a conversation to finish.

Tyler finally stands. "Hi, are there any updates on my half-brother?"

Anthony takes handcuffs out of his back pocket, pulling Tyler by his wrists. My hand covers my mouth in shock.

"Tyler Johnson, you're under arrest for the murder of Daniel Johnson, you have the right to remain silent. Anything you say can and will be used against you in a court of law. You have the right to an attorney. If you cannot afford an attorney, one will be appointed for you. Do you understand these rights?"

I barely process the words in my mind, the world around me is blurring.

They think Tyler killed Daniel? No, that can't be it. It can't be...

My stomach churns. Tyler frowns; his mouth opens as the handcuffs click around his wrists. "This is a mistake. You don't have the right—"

"You have the right to remain silent, Mr. Johnson," Detective Rynn interrupts as they guide him towards the door.

A jolt of shock courses through me. "Tyler..." I call, feeling my stomach twist.

"Sadie, I haven't done anything!" Tyler shouts from the porch as they guide him towards the police car. "I would never harm anyone!"

What's happening?

I'm left in the doorway, frozen. My mind races through a thousand questions with no clear answers.

I wonder how Daniel must have felt when his heart stopped beating—when his body finally surrendered to the pull of death.

My mind shifts. I think about all of them. Every single suspect.

How genuine were Victoria's tears? Madeline and Rose wove that excuse about the camera not working so expertly. Rose always seemed unaffected. Was it apathy?

I think about Tyler's dad. I wonder if his guilt started rising the moment he realized—really realized—that the son he'd rejected, pushed away, had never been given the chance to be anything more than a mistake, the product of an illicit affair. *Is that guilt eating him alive or doesn't he care? Did Tyler's family always know what really happened?*

I can't believe it's Tyler... *Tyler.*

My hands stop trembling, but I can't shake the feeling that something else is clinging to them—something I can't wash away.

Blood.

NINETEEN

MADELINE

June 17, 10:00AM

My breath catches in my throat as the heavy wooden doors
creak open.

Everyone in the courtroom follows the sound with their
gaze. They stare at Tyler, perceiving him either as a criminal or
with pity.

Two police officers walk him to the defense table, where
his sister and lawyer, Laura, is already waiting. His head is
slightly lowered as if he's trying to shrink away from everyone's
gaze; his dark hair is messy and his beard has grown in the
forty-eight hours since his arrest. He wears an orange jumpsuit;
a tiny, long chain connects his wrists and ankles. As he sits right
in front of me, I place a hand on his shoulder, but he shakes
it off.

"Whoever framed him will pay. My son would never do
this. *Never*. It's only been a month since that body was found,
they have to keep digging," Tyler's mother Pam says. She sits
beside me shaking her head in disbelief. She has no doubt that
her son is innocent. Over the past two days, she has written

several social media posts about the "corrupt system" and how successful people always take the blame.

I swallow, nodding. The last couple of days I've been lying on the couch at home, sleeping, eating junk food. I couldn't sleep in our bed without him. I turned the TV on sometimes, just for background noise. Charlie looked after me like I was her child, and I felt so guilty that I couldn't process the situation in a different way for her. I don't want her to carry the weight of our family's mistakes. I wonder if Tyler is mad that I didn't come to visit him. But my emotions got the best of me.

Sadie is sitting in the corner behind me at the edge of the public gallery, her hands squeeze a napkin on her lap. The way she looks around with worried eyes makes her somehow suspicious. But I wonder if that's the role she's used to playing—the innocent young maid who's afraid of losing her job.

I look around the courtroom. At least Liam Wilson is minding his business today.

A woman in her early fifties sits behind the prosecution table going through papers. My stomach contorts when I see Victoria shaking her legs restlessly, her eyes fixed on the judge's bench. I can tell from her expression that she wants to get this over with; that she doesn't want to be here; that sharing the space with Tyler's family is making her feel uncomfortable.

A bald, short man wearing a court coat walks behind the judge's bench, moving the microphone slightly closer to his mouth. The public stand up for an instant and Charlie squeezes my hand, pressing her lips together. The man bangs the gavel, silencing the whispers coming from the rest of Daniel's family.

"Court is now in session, please be seated," he announces, moving his eyes side to side. "Good morning, everyone, my name is Justice Herman. The defendant, Tyler Johnson, is present for the initial hearing on charges of the murder of Daniel Johnson. How does the defendant plead?"

Laura stands up, her gray suit makes her look older. "Your

Honor, at this time, we enter a plea of not guilty on behalf of the defendant."

Tyler's right leg shakes beneath the table; he pinches his lower lip with his nails.

The prosecutor rises up. "Your Honor, Daniel Johnson was killed on the morning of May 5th. We have evidence that Daniel was found in front of the defendant's home with a head injury and a stab wound to his stomach. Tyler Johnson admitted that he sent a message to Daniel from a burner phone asking to meet him on May 5th, the morning of his daughter's birthday, and then cancelled. This suggests that the murder was planned in advance. Your Honor, we checked the surveillance footage in front of the victim's house and it clearly shows Tyler Johnson entering and exiting Daniel's building within the span of an hour on the morning of May 5th. Tyler Johnson and his family always treated Daniel differently. None of them cared about him. I believe that Tyler Johnson is *not* innocent. We are asking for him to be held without bail until the trial."

I scratch the palms of my hands. Tyler's mother gasps at the prosecutor's words; she covers her mouth in shock.

I wonder what she's thinking, I wonder what everyone else is thinking. There's no evidence of a knife or whatever weapon they believe killed Daniel. *But what was Tyler doing at Daniel's apartment on the morning of Charlie's birthday? Was that why he never responded to my texts? Is he really capable of killing someone?*

Laura's eyes widen. She raises her hand, standing quickly. "Your Honor, we respectfully disagree with the prosecution's assessment. Tyler Johnson has no criminal record and the reason he went to visit Daniel Johnson that morning was to discuss a potential business partnership. Tyler arrived at his house, but Daniel wasn't home. It's likely that by then Daniel was already dead. There is no real evidence to suggest that

Tyler had any involvement in the crime. We respectfully request that bail be set at an amount within Tyler Johnson's means and that he is allowed to remain under house arrest while awaiting the next hearing."

"No!" Victoria's voice echoes through the room. "He took my son's life and he should be locked up." Her lips tremble, betraying the pressure she seems to be feeling at not being in control of the situation.

The judge bangs the gavel once again. "Order in court."

"Mom, what's happening?" Charlie whispers.

"I don't know yet, honey."

"The court has made its decision. At this stage, while there are suspicious circumstances and evidence is being reviewed, the direct link between Tyler Johnson and the crime is still being established. The court orders that Mr. Johnson is to be placed under house arrest until the trial date. Until then, Mr. Johnson must refrain from any contact with potential witnesses and must stay within the confines of his home unless permitted by the court for specific reasons, such as medical or legal matters."

I bite the inside of my cheeks.

This isn't over.

Rage transforms Victoria's face; she inches closer to the judge's bench, clenching her fists by her sides. "Are you fucking kidding me? Are you giving him special treatment because he's a millionaire living on the Upper East Side?"

There's a collective inhale from the courtroom. Tyler shifts in his seat, his jaw tense. He looks at Victoria like she's his worst enemy.

The gavel comes down again with a bang. "This court will reconvene in one month. This matter is adjourned."

I feel lightheaded at the idea of having him imprisoned at home.

Anthony and I recently found out that Pam Johnson, Tyler's mother, is now taking charge of Vertex Capital, at least while her son is under house arrest. And since the murder weapon is yet to be found, I must find out if he hid it at work.

I'm certain it won't be easy to speak to Pam Johnson. I saw the way she was glancing over us with disgust in the courtroom, like she was going to make us pay. But I'm not scared of withdrawing her son's secrets from their vault.

With a deep breath, I grab my badge and head out the door, stepping into the police car. I put my sunglasses on and turn on the engine. The busy streets of New York City are filled with pedestrians hurrying along the sidewalks, dodging each other. I'm glad I'm not one of those pedestrians—it makes me nervous just thinking about pushing through the endless crowds of tourists. It's crazy how there's no off-season for tourism in this city.

As I drive towards the East Side, I swear at one of the cyclists cutting through. A skinny guy wearing a helmet and sunglasses turns and raises his middle finger. I don't get it—is he on a suicide mission?

Jesus.

As soon as I turn onto Fifth Avenue, I spot a parking space in front of Vertex Capital.

I smoothly pull into the spot and kill the engine. The towering glass building that houses Vertex Capital stands before me; its sleek, modern design makes it look like it's the real deal, but everything I've heard so far suggests that the company is steeped in fraud. But we have no real proof yet, only rumors, despite what I told Tyler. I exit the car, straightening my blazer and smoothing my trousers. The low heel of my boots clicks confidently on the pavement as I walk towards the entrance.

Inside, the bustling lobby is filled with abstract, ugly artwork. Employees rush, sip coffee, yawn, and complain on their phones. The young, blonde receptionist glances up, her smile widens slightly as she breathes in.

"Good morning. How can I help you?" she asks politely.

"Good morning, my name is Detective Rynn. I need access to Tyler Johnson's office."

"Mr. Johnson's office? May I ask what this is about?" she asks, glancing at her computer screen while she clicks on something with the mouse.

"It's an ongoing investigation. If you can't let me in, I'll need to speak with someone who can grant me access."

She hesitates for a moment before picking up the phone. "One moment, please."

Actually," I stop her with a quick smile, "I'd prefer if you didn't call anyone just yet. I'm sure you understand, there are certain... details that need to be handled discreetly." *If Pam knows I'm here, she will probably rush to hide the evidence.*

The receptionist blinks. "I'm afraid I'm not authorized to—"

"I'm sure you understand," I cut her off, "I don't have the luxury of waiting for approvals and calls to be made. I'm conducting an official investigation and you're required to grant me access to Mr. Johnson's office. Now." I raise my eyebrows. "Please, show me the way."

I sigh in response to the delay. "I'm sure you're aware that obstruction of justice is a serious offense. We wouldn't want to make this difficult for anyone now, would we?"

The receptionist's bright-red lips part, but words are slow to emerge. Then she smiles and nods. "Of course. Follow me, please." She leads me to a gray, modern elevator with mirrored walls that reflect us as the doors slide shut. As the doors open, a massive office space spreads before me. The floor is polished marble and the walls are adorned with certificates celebrating the employees of the year and other achievements. A few employees in suits are working at laptops on their desks, their eyes move horizontally—too focused to care if there's police on the premises.

She guides me down a large corridor until we reach a closed white door with a shiny gold plaque stating, *TYLER JOHNSON, CEO*, mounted on the door.

"This is Tyler Johnson's office, Detective. Just so you're aware, his mother, Pam, is in charge of the company during his absence." She opens the door and gestures me to walk inside.

"Thank you." I flash her a grateful smile. She nods and walks away, closing the door behind her.

My eyes move around the room, curious. The office is way too clean and feels unused. A large desk dominates the center of the room. Shelves mounted on the wall are lined with books and awards fill the edge of the desk; a large window offers a panoramic view of the city skyline.

I move towards the shelves, my fingers brush over the spines of books and the edges of awards. They're primarily boring trading books and prizes and medals from conferences.

Everything seems ordinary so far.

A quick glance over my shoulder to look through the glass wall confirms that the corridor is empty. With a sharp intake of breath, I grip the desk drawers, the cool metal is cold against my clammy palms. The top drawer contains a mess of pens, paper-clips, and clear sticky notes; I close it and open the second drawer.

A framed photo, an old, expired ID, and several bank statements slide between my fingers, then my hand brushes against something unusual, something that shouldn't be there. A hidden drawer is cleverly concealed at the bottom of the one I just opened.

My heart skips a beat as I carefully slide it open, revealing a stack of papers, some covered in small printed text, others hand-written.

I quickly grab the papers and scan them using the printer on another desk in the corner of the room. I type my email quickly so that I have digital copies with me, hoping to finish everything before Pam shows up.

Some of these documents are handwritten by Tyler Johnson, detailing each brick of the company he managed to build with his own hands. But the more I read, the more the words blur and my head starts spinning as I land on sentences that explicitly reveal a fraudulent scheme.

Target demographics: young investors seeking quick returns...

Utilizing social media influencers for credibility...

Create urgency through time-limited offers...

Projected gains based on artificial inflation and market manipulation...

Create false testimonials...

Guaranteed returns of 300 percent within three months...

Exit plan: Liquidate all assets and disappear into obscurity...

In three months, once the bulk of the investments have been drained, pay off disgruntled investors using Grandma's inheritance—manipulate investors to keep them at bay until then.

Vertex Capital, once painted in shades of ambition and pride, is now exposed as a deep, dark abyss of greed and manipulation. Tyler Johnson has been running a fraudulent scheme in the heart of New York City. Those rumors aren't just rumors anymore.

It doesn't matter what he thinks he's achieving by doing

this. If he thinks that money will fix everything. The inheritance from his grandmother won't cover up the fact that he's an absolute liar. But one thing is certain: in two months, a lot of things can happen, especially if he does receive that money. If he doesn't, well... it looks like his empire will burn.

A bank transaction grabs my attention. My eyes widen as I read through the details. Ten thousand dollars was transferred from Pam's account the day after Tyler was arrested. My eyebrows shoot up when I see the name of the recipient.

Henry Herman.

"These fuckers," I whisper in disbelief.

What would the outcome have been if Judge Herman hadn't been bribed? One thing is certain: Tyler probably wouldn't have been placed under house arrest. He may not have a criminal record yet, but he's still being investigated for murder. Only white-collar criminals usually get the privilege of house arrest. Or millionaires, I guess.

The murder weapon isn't here, but the evidence I've found is a step in a positive direction. I can feel it.

TWENTY-ONE
MADELINE

June 20, 10:30AM

The mug's ceramic surface feels smooth against my fingers—the comfort of its heat contrasts with the breeze coming from the coffee shop AC.

The walls are decorated with nostalgic black-and-white photographs of old cityscapes.

Rose and I picked a table next to a window overlooking one of the busiest city streets. I like to come here and get distracted by staring at people hurrying by, making up stories in my mind about where they're going, who they're meeting, why they're rushing.

Across the tiny table, my best friend is sipping her coffee, waiting patiently for me to tell her about all the craziness that happened at the hearing.

Her long brown hair falls in tiny waves around her shoulders, next to a delicate gold necklace that shines gently as she moves.

Rose's past shadows our conversation. She was once stuck in

a complicated relationship too, and though she rarely talks about it, the experience has left an indelible mark on her heart, and she doesn't want me to go through the same thing.

But is our life about to get really messed up, or is Tyler going to be declared innocent after all?

People have rough patches, don't they? But relationship troubles don't make people kill someone. Tyler could've gone to visit Daniel on Charlie's birthday for business like he said, not to kill him.

I should be there for him. Isn't that what marriage is about—going through the worst storms together, holding on until you can see the first colors of a rainbow fading into the sky?

But as soon as I think this, an image of Tyler appears in my head. I remember how his inner demons quickly spread through our townhouse when he gets angry; I remember the sound of his fist hitting the wall, leaving an imprint of masculine fragility on the wallpaper. *Is it normal to feel so small and terrified in your own home? To walk on eggshells, constantly second-guessing yourself to avoid triggering another scene?*

We have had so many beautiful moments together though. It's strange to think about how Charlie came into our lives; she was a great—but unexpected—twist of fate.

I was only nineteen, caught in the excitement of my new love story with Tyler, who is three years older than me.

We spent rainy days watching movies in his studio apartment and sunny days in the Hamptons at his family's home.

Thanks to his grandmother's real-estate investments, his parents were, and still are, wealthy, and though he tried to make money in his own way when he was younger, their support was always there in the background. And then one day, after just a few months of dating, I found out I was pregnant. The news hit me like a hurricane.

I remember sitting on the edge of the bed, staring at the

positive pregnancy test, my hands shaking so much I nearly dropped it. The idea of becoming a mother at that age was overwhelming. I felt as though I was teetering on the edge of a cliff, the ground beneath me shifting precariously.

The first thoughts that rushed through my mind were about Tyler. *Would he stay? Would he walk away from us, from me?* Our relationship was still so new.

But that day, he took my hand and promised we would face life together, with "our baby."

Tyler and I made the choice not to have any more children, to give Charlie our undivided attention. We wanted to ensure she never felt overshadowed or neglected. Sometimes I wonder what it would have been like to have a larger family and I know it's not too late to have another child if we wanted to. But it isn't the right time to discuss it, at least not until I face the consequences of Tyler's hidden schemes.

Rose's eyes search mine, filled with silent solidarity. But she doesn't know what it feels like. She wouldn't understand.

I take a deep breath. *Am I being too quick to perceive Tyler as innocent? Or am I clinging to the memory of a man who no longer exists, hoping that things will go back to how they were?*

I loved the idea of him that I had in my mind. And that's the problem. Love makes me believe that anything can be fixed, that one day Tyler will wake up and be exactly how I imagine him. But that person doesn't exist. It's just a fictional character I create when I need to excuse his actions.

What am I going to do now?

The thought of leaving him feels like stepping into a black hole. But staying feels like having to climb Mount Everest.

It's exhausting.

Maybe Rose is going to help me see what I can't see on my own.

"I don't know how it got this bad." I feel ashamed of saying that he has been arrested, of saying out loud that the person who is supposed to love me and take care of me is destroying me with his secrets and lies.

"It's not your fault," Rose says gently, but I know her. I know that she has always hated him and there's nothing worse than your best friend hating your partner. "You can't control how he behaves. It's up to him to stop being a child and admit that what he did was wrong."

I sigh, sipping my latte, licking my lips as I savor its taste. "We don't know if he's going to jail yet." I shake my shoulders, passing a hand through my hair. "I still feel like I should have done something. Maybe I should've spoken with Laura before the first hearing, to know what I could do to help. Instead, I just couldn't face it. Maybe if I had done something, things wouldn't have gotten so bad."

Rose reaches across the table, placing her hand over mine. "You've done more than enough. You've tried to make it work. But you can't keep sacrificing yourself, Madeline. It's not healthy. You have to think about Charlie in these difficult times."

I nod, biting my inner cheek to keep my tears from spilling. "I just... I don't understand how we got here. He wasn't always like this. We used to be happy. And now every day feels like a battle. I'm afraid to set off his temper now that he's stuck at home. He keeps saying that he didn't do anything, although he went to see him that same morning. I wonder how Daniel's body ended up in front of our porch..."

Rose's eyes narrow slightly. "Think about what's best for you and your daughter. You should leave him."

I look down at my mug, tracing its abstract design with my finger. "I'm scared all of this is hurting her too much."

Rose leans in closer, shaking her head. "You're a great mother. You're doing everything you can to keep the walls from falling down."

"I'm so scared Rose," I finally admit. "And, despite everything, I'm so in love with him. Sometimes, I look at him and I still have butterflies, like when we first hung out. I know it sounds strange to still feel so crazily in love after years of marriage, but it's impossible for me to feel otherwise, even if he upsets me and hurts me deeply. I keep hoping that, somehow, we can fix this. That he'll fix his attitude and our family can be happy together."

Rose squeezes my hand. "Just take it one step at a time. He has to go through the trial first. Just try to keep your head above water during all of this."

I nod slowly. Rose is right. But it's easier said than done. "I know you're right. I wish I could stop feeling like this and think clearly."

"It's hard," Rose says firmly. "But you're not alone. You have me, and I'll always support you no matter what you do."

Tears prick at my eyes and I blink them away. "Thank you, Rose," I whisper. "I don't know what I'd do without you."

Rose blushes and smiles; her grip on my hand tightens, but her smile flattens as soon as my phone starts buzzing. Within a couple of minutes, my screen is flooded with calls and messages from Tyler.

I feel strong enough not to take the calls or respond to the messages with Rose by my side. I need some space right now. I glance at the screen, Tyler's name flashes repeatedly.

"What does he want now?" Rose asks, her brow furrowing.

Rose knows how controlling my husband can be at times. She's always been very honest when it comes to telling me how she feels about him. However, I've had the feeling for a few years now that she's trying to push me away from him.

"He's trying to convince me to believe him." I scroll through the messages, each one a variation of the same message. But I'm not sure I can face him so soon after seeing how the police officer clicked the electronic tag around his ankle.

With a sigh, I silence my phone and slip it back into my bag, feeling proud of myself for not letting his sweet words get to me. I always struggle to ignore Tyler when he's trying to get my attention. "I think I need a break from all the husband talk," I say, placing my hands on my head and running them through my hair.

Rose nods in understanding, her smiling expression is supportive. "Let's make plans, then. We'll do something just for you to take your mind off everything."

"Should we walk around Central Park?" I suggest, forcing a smile as I meet Rose's gaze. It's a small thing, but fresh air helps.

"A walk is always a good idea," Rose agrees.

As we step out on to the crowded sidewalk, Tyler keeps trying to get in touch. I knew that having him home was going to be hard for me. He's bored, confused, alone... but I can't be incarcerated as well. I need to breathe.

Come home please, I need to talk to you.

Each word pierces through my motivation to distance myself from him.

Where the hell are you?

His anger seeps through the screen. But then he apologizes and begs for forgiveness.

I'm so sorry about this, but you have to believe me, I would never kill anyone. I don't deserve you. I'm a horrible husband.

My steps slow down as I read his messages. Part of me is desperate to believe that he wants to make things right. But the other part holds its doubts.

Rose notices my hesitation. "You don't have to respond to

him right now. He's at home doing nothing all day, let him cope on his own for once," she orders, snatching my phone from my hand. "Keep your eyes on the road ahead. We'll deal with Tyler later."

"You're right. He could still be found guilty and it's better for me to keep my distance."

TWENTY-TWO

SADIE

June 20, 6:30PM

Tyler stares at the black TV screen in front of him.

His shoulders are arched. Tears burnish his eyes as he caresses his forehead with his fingers like he does when he's trying to fight off a migraine.

My heart sinks at the sight. I'm not sure what he's feeling right now. *Is he sad? Is he angry?* It's hard to tell. Anything I say could lead to either anger or guilt.

But I can't leave him on his own like this. I care too much. Much more than his wife, apparently.

I cross the room to sit beside him on the edge of the sofa. "Are you okay?"

I've never seen him cry before. He never shows off his feelings like this; he likes to appear like a strong man when inside he's just as fragile as anyone else.

Tyler looks up at me. "I swear to God," he whispers, his voice choked with emotion, "I didn't touch him."

I reach out to touch his hand, but then I shrink my arm back. I don't want to upset him even more. Seeing him like this makes me want to burst into tears too. I wish I could take a bit of his sadness away. He just looks so lost. *How can someone so kind, so... normal be caught in something like this?* I don't even know if I believe it. But then, who am I to say what's true or not? I'm just the maid, I don't know what happens outside these walls, at least, I'm not really supposed to...

I take a slow breath. I'm not supposed to get attached either. I know that. But here I am, my heart aching with every minute that ticks by. "I'm sure there must be a way to fix this..."

He takes a shaky breath, burying his eyes in his hands. "I... I got involved with some people I shouldn't have. Daniel was just trying to help..." He runs his hands over his face. "But then things started to fall apart..."

"What do you mean?"

"Daniel was helping me with a business deal. It was supposed to take me out of debt, but it fell through at the last minute. I went to his place that day to talk to him, but he wasn't there." Tyler looks anguished. "I have foggy memories about that day."

I want to trust him. I want to believe him, but this doesn't make any sense.

"When you say that you got involved with the wrong people, what do you mean by that?"

"Some of these people... they think I'm running a scam by letting others invest in my digital currency," he whispers. "They're after me, and I think they killed Daniel. It's all my fault."

"Tyler, we need to find out who killed Daniel so you don't end up in prison. I can help—"

He interrupts, shaking his head. "You can't, they know where I live," he confesses. "There's this guy who was really pissed when I fired him a while back, his name was Liam, I believe he's the one who broke in. I think he wants a large sum of money from me."

"How much money does he want?"

"We don't have that sort of money..." he whispers.

The sound of the door opening breaks the momentum of the conversation. I don't have to look up to know who it is. The sharp click of her heels on the hardwood floors is unmistakable.

I don't want to move from the couch, but I can sense Madeline's eyes on us before she even says anything. A long pause, filled with a silence that somehow screams louder than words. Then—"What's going on here?"

I finally glance up at her and I see it—the flicker of confusion, suspicion, maybe even something darker behind her eyes. She stands in the doorway, arms crossed, staring at us. "Don't you have some cleaning to do, Sadie? The dishwasher needs unloading."

Her words are clearly a dismissal, not just of me but of the space between her and her husband. *I'm just the maid. The servant. Not someone who's supposed to sit beside her husband, offering quiet comfort in this time of need.*

"I—I'll take care of it," I mumble, getting up and heading towards the kitchen.

Charlie descends the stairs slowly, looking worried at the sight of her dad's face. I open the dishwasher and start taking the plates out, overhearing the conversation in the living room.

"Everything's okay, honey," Madeline reassures her daughter. "How about we order some pizza and have a movie night?" she suggests, trying to make this situation more normal for Charlie. "We could make it a family pajama party."

She's pretending for Charlie's sake, but I wonder if Madeline believes Tyler. *Does she still see him as her husband, the man she's always known? Or has the weight of these accusations already started to chip away at her image of him?*

I pick up another plate, gripping it a little too tightly. It feels almost like a performance. They're acting, pretending they can still be a family in the middle of all this mess. But I can see the cracks—Madeline's forced smile, the way Tyler's eyes never quite meet hers. They're becoming strangers in their own home.

"Okay, what movie?" Charlie asks.

"Sit next to me, we can choose together," Tyler says. His voice is softer than I expected. He hasn't been very close to Charlie lately. The change in his demeanor catches me off guard. Meanwhile, Madeline is quickly typing something on her phone, her eyes scanning the display, perhaps she's ordering the pizza.

Charlie hesitates for a moment, but then she crosses the room and sits beside him, sinking into the cushions. Tyler places an arm around her shoulders, pulls her close, and kisses the top of her hair. "I'm sorry about this situation and being so distant lately, I'll make sure I cherish these moments at home with you. My family."

Charlie blushes. She looks up at him and for a moment, I see a flicker of hope in her eyes. "Thanks, Dad. Should we watch a fantasy movie?"

"Sounds good." He takes the remote and turns on the TV. Madeline smiles at the sight of the two sitting close together and joins them, sitting next to Tyler. He gives her a quick kiss on her lips before turning to the screen.

Tyler catches my stare and looks away, his jaw tightening. A chill runs down my spine and I take advantage of this moment to try and make things less awkward between us. I step inside the living room and ask, "Do you need anything before I go to pick up the clothes from the dryer?" I try to keep my tone casual.

Madeline shakes her head, smiling, but then I hear her footsteps following me to the laundry room. I try to ignore her as I move clothes from the washing machine to the dryer.

"Question," she says, walking slowly towards me, arms folded across her chest. "Did you clean the porch on the morning of Charlie's birthday?"

My eyes narrow as I start folding the clothes. "Of course, as usual. Why do you ask?"

"I'm just wondering how you didn't find Daniel's body before Rose and I did."

My jaw tightens. "Whoever moved the body there must've done so after I cleaned the porch."

Madeline's head tilts slightly. "How do you know it was moved?"

I shrug. "Everybody knows at this stage of the investigation. Detective Rynn told me while she was interrogating me."

She punches the top of the washing machine, making my heart jump. I look at her face turning red. Her fist stays there for a second, pressed into the surface; the impact vibrates through my bones. I jerk back.

Why is she reacting like this?

"Don't fuck with me, Sadie. You knew where Daniel's body was. I saw you on the camera. *You knew.*"

Madeline had lied: the camera had never been broken. It had been watching and she was waiting for the right moment to expose everything.

She lied to the police, but so did I.

TWENTY-THREE
CHARLIE'S JOURNAL

June 25

I stared at the clock: 4:30 a.m.

I glanced at my dad lying beside my mother, their bodies not daring to touch. His breathing was slow and steady, lost in dreams he wouldn't remember in the morning. Moonlight filtered through the thin curtains, casting soft shadows across their bedroom.

The clock hands ticked, growing louder with each second, dying. Screaming.

I tried to fall asleep. I sighed and turned multiple times, got up, drank some water, and returned to bed, but nothing helped shake off the tornado inside me. It was all too much. The house was overflowing with so many secrets that I felt claustrophobic. Dad has a black bracelet around his ankle and it beeps if he steps outside the fence surrounding our home. I couldn't believe my ears when he got arrested. I thought that I was living in a nightmare and I would wake up soon, and everything would go back to the way it was. I was wrong.

As I watched her sleep, Mom's face was illuminated by the moon's faint glow. Her eyelids kept trembling every few seconds. I wondered if she was having nightmares like she always does.

I should have just woken her, asked her what was going on, what was next, when I could have some normality back in my life—if ever. Yet, a part of me hesitated. I knew she would pretend she had everything under control and reassure me that Dad wouldn't go to jail forever, that this was about to be over soon.

But what if this isn't all just paranoia fueled by fear and suspicion? What if I am right in thinking that this won't end well?

I have always been paranoid. I wouldn't be surprised if this was another episode of overthinking.

But what had Dad been doing at Daniel's apartment that morning? How had Daniel's body ended up in front of our porch anyway? This is all so confusing. I hadn't even known that Daniel—the unwanted son—existed. I could see it, though— Dad's rage directed at someone innocent, or perhaps at someone who only wanted to be included. He can be sweet at times, like when we watched a movie the other day. The three of us, as a normal family.

On the good days, Dad is kind, attentive, and caring.

In March, he took me to the amusement park and he insisted on riding the Ferris wheel even though he's afraid of heights. He held my hand the entire time, laughing, screaming. We played paintball together with my aunt, his sister Laura.

But he can switch just like that.

My feet descended the stairs, awakened by the cool tiles that gave me goosebumps. The sliding glass door overlooking the backyard opened with a soft click and I stepped out into the quiet stillness of the night. The early morning breeze felt refreshing.

Without thinking twice, I peeled off my nightclothes and slipped into the water. The cold shocked my system but cleared my mind in an instant.

I didn't want to think about anything right then. Everything felt different underwater. My worries and fears were suspended in the cold, clear blue... away from the chaos of the world. As my lungs started to burn, I pushed myself to the surface, breaking the water with a gasp.

The night air sent shivers across my skin, but the rays of sunshine on the horizon chased away the chill.

My attention moved towards the guesthouse as the light in the kitchen turned on. I couldn't see anything except shadows through those thick curtains. The water gently lapped against the pool's edge as I emerged, my body shook as I grabbed a towel left on a sunbed.

Wrapping it around myself, I paused to gaze at the clear sky. But a metallic noise made my neck crack towards Sadie's accommodation again.

Her shadow filtered through; I could see an arm rising, she was holding something in her hand.

Something sharp, like a kitchen knife.

I swallowed, short of breath.

It's a new day, and with it comes the lies.

TWENTY-FOUR
MADELINE

June 25, 9:30AM

"Honey, what are you doing out here?" I shake Charlie's shoulder.

She is wrapped in a towel, her hair wet, wearing a bright yellow swimsuit.

Did she sleep here all night?

Charlie blinks, disoriented, and glances at me, confused. The sun is blinding her eyes and she places a hand on top of her forehead, casting a shadow over her face, trying to adjust to the daylight. I hope she's okay; this is unusual for her. She left her journal on the side table right next to her and as soon as she sees me glancing over it, she pulls it to her chest, protecting it from unwanted eyes. I wonder what she writes in it; *does she use it to reveal her emotions, to let everything out?*

"I couldn't sleep." Charlie sits up and pulls the towel tighter around her.

I can't help but frown. "You could've caught a cold. Why did you sleep out here?"

Her tousled hair and the dark circles around her eyes suggest that she didn't sleep at all last night.

She shrugs, trying to play it cool, but I can see that she's not okay. "I just needed some fresh air to clear my head."

I sit down on the edge of the sunbed, reaching out to brush a strand of wet hair from her face. "Is everything okay, love? You seem... strange. You know you can tell me everything, right? If you want to talk about what happened with—"

She interrupts me, clearly forcing a smile. "No. I don't want to talk about it. I'm fine, Mom."

I would give Charlie the moon if I could reach it; I remember gazing at its silvery light from the dusty bedroom window of my childhood home in a town near the New Jersey border. My past and Charlie's are very different, and I want to be as different from my mother as possible. I want to be there for Charlie in every moment, supporting her dreams and celebrating her achievements, standing by her through her first heartbreak and first kiss; bad grades; mood changes during puberty; and all the other fun stuff.

"Come inside then. I'll make us something to eat." I stand up, offering her my hand.

"No thank you."

My lips press into a thin line. "Charlie, talk to me."

She gets up quickly from the sunbed, clutching her towel tightly around her. "I guess all the lies are starting to annoy me at this point. When will this end, Mom? How can you remain so calm with everything that's going on?"

I sigh. "I have to remain calm, Charlie, I have no other choice than to try and keep thinking positively. I'm doing this to protect you—"

"Whatever," Charlie exhales loudly, cutting me off. I knew this conversation was going to come up at some point. She's the type of kid who is always calm, quiet... but she's not stupid. Charlie is very smart, and she notices *everything*.

Tyler appears at the kitchen door facing the backyard and takes a step outside. He looks at us with a confused gaze and walks towards Charlie. "Charlie..." His tone of voice is soft, understanding. He puts a hand on her shoulder. "I know things have been hard for you too. But we're all in this together, alright?"

Charlie shakes her head and raises her eyebrows. She turns to her father and a frown line appears between her brows. "How can you say that if you don't even care about me? You barely talk to me."

I can see the pain flicker across Tyler's face for a second. He clears his throat. "That's not true. I care about you more than anything in this world." His voice is shaky. "But it's been hard, okay? There's a lot going on right now and I'm doing the best I can. We all are."

Charlie crosses her arms tightly over her chest. "You've always been like this. You and I have nothing in common, that's the truth."

Tyler's face hardens, but there's something in his eyes that tells me he's fighting to keep it together. "I know I haven't been there like I should have, but I'm still trying. I'm still here."

She smirks. "You're here because you can't go anywhere. Being 'here' isn't enough if you're not actually *present*." Her gaze falls to his ankle.

"Alright, Charlie, enough now. Let's go inside and have some breakfast together," I say, gesturing towards the kitchen door.

Tyler scratches the back of his head, then his jaw tightens. "What do you want me to do to fix this? Tell me and I'll do it." His eyes plead with Charlie, but we both know the answer. He doesn't want to hear that fixing something like this is hard, almost impossible. Whatever happens, Charlie will never forget that Tyler was under house arrest—no matter how old she is— just like she will never forget the fights between Tyler and me, the outbursts, the broken things. It's too late for that. But perhaps it's not too late to start over, if she wants to.

"I'm going to my room." Charlie abandons the conversation midway and Tyler can't help but roll his eyes to the sky.

His face hardens and he switches into defensive mode. "I can't believe she talked to me like that, you know? Teenagers are so hard to deal with."

I step closer to him. "I don't blame Charlie, this is hard for her too."

Tyler shakes his head, frustrated. "Yeah, but she shouldn't behave this way."

"What way, Tyler?"

For a moment, we stand there in silence. He looks at me. "I'm not sure that Charlie believes I'm innocent."

A knot twists in my stomach. "Don't think that way."

His eyes narrow and he takes a step towards me, his head tilting to one side. "Do you believe I'm innocent, Madeline?"

My face burns. He scoffs, shakes his head, and gazes to the side for a moment before looking back into my eyes. Tyler's face becomes rigid, his eyes narrow. "Fuck you!" he says and walks away.

TWENTY-FIVE
MADELINE

June 25, 12:00PM

Even though I haven't answered his question, he knows.

Tyler knows I don't think he's innocent. Lies, anger, and secrets follow wherever he goes—how could I think he's an angel?

He doesn't seem worried about his actions though, maybe because he has always felt safe.

Since he was a little boy, Tyler had the stability of a present family who, no matter what, always put him on a pedestal and loved him unconditionally, protecting him from any issue—major or minor. He would blink and, just like that, the problem was gone.

Tyler and I are too different and even though I have secrets too, I never let my mistakes weigh on anyone else.

I always tried to remind him that we grew up in two different environments and that these experiences shaped the woman and man we are today, but even though we ended up together, it doesn't mean that we must think in the same way too.

After we argue, I always seek him out to feel safe, to know that he's not going to abandon me one day. Tyler, on the other hand, wants space—for one, two, sometimes three days. This has always made me extremely anxious and weak, leaving me to beg for his attention and love, hoping that one day he will care about my feelings too.

We fell in love at a train station fifteen years ago. The weather was so humid that day that even though I'd straightened my hair I looked like a frizzy mess. Tyler was late and I was sitting on a bench, observing the strangers coming and going from Grand Central Station.

The station was alive with a symphony of footsteps and voices, each person wrapped in their own world. Businessmen in crisp suits and polished shoes hurried past, their briefcases swinging in rhythm with their strides. Tourists in casual attire paused to take in the grandeur of the station, their eyes wide with wonder as they snapped photos.

Even though that date with Tyler was my first date ever, I didn't feel nervous or scared. I knew that no matter what, I would always be myself, and I couldn't wait to build a family of my own, leaving the drama of my family behind me forever.

I was partially right. I had my beautiful girl one year later and I married Ty right before she was born. I have never regretted having Charlie at such a young age, but more than once I felt like something was wrong about staying with him.

I lost count of the many times before Charlie was born when I would return home and find Tyler high, unable to respond to my questions right away.

Sometimes I feel strangely nostalgic for those times. At least Tyler's behavior then was less cruel than it was during the times when I was in tears and he just shook his head in disappointment, calling me a child begging for attention.

"Go and run crying to Rose now," he still says every time he sees me cry. "You're being ridiculous. Do you have to cry every time we have an argument?"

When he is in that mood, there is no hope for any gesture of love or reconciliation.

He has never seemed to feel bad seeing his girlfriend—and later his wife—cry. Tyler has treated me like trash over and over again. And I've allowed him, I've kept everything I wanted to say inside, transforming my words into tears.

The truth is, I was scared then and I still am. If I speak the truth, I will leave him. If I react, he could break some furniture or yell at me so loudly that I end up feeling small—desperate to hide away from everything and everyone.

But I can't stand the woman that I've become with him. This scared, submissive version of myself must die. I want to stand up for myself; I want to reclaim the dignity I've lost over the years of our marriage. No more begging for love, no more crying in silence.

Determination flashes in my eyes. I have to confront Tyler, demand answers, and refuse to be treated this way any longer. *I deserve better. Charlie deserves a mother who is strong, not broken.*

My footsteps are heavy as I approach the kitchen door and move towards the living room. Tyler is lounging on the couch, eating noodles, absorbed in a football game.

My phone vibrates in the pocket of my trousers. My fingers hover over the screen, swiping up to open the message. It's from Detective Rynn. Her words make my blood boil.

> Hi Madeline, this is Detective Rynn. I discovered that your husband's family has made a payment to the judge, which could be an attempt to ensure that Tyler received house arrest instead of jail time. You should consider speaking with his lawyer about this as it could have serious implications.

I should be more surprised really, but I'm not. I'm furious. *Does Tyler ever think about us?* We have to live in this mess too, and he's making it worse by scheming behind my back.

We could have been a team, Tyler and me. Instead, sometimes I feel like we're rivals and the only person I can count on is Charlie.

Tyler should not be here; he should be in jail. Even if he didn't kill Daniel, why does he have the freedom to roam around our big house when a normal person would be held behind bars?

"Hey, wanna watch the match?" Tyler calls from the living room, not even turning to look at me.

"No thanks," I reply, running up to our bedroom.

Tyler pauses the game and follows me, noticing the flat tone of my voice. "What's wrong now?"

He steps in front of me in the corridor, blocking my way. I hold up my phone, showing him Detective Rynn's message. "How long were you going to keep this from me? And why do your family think they can get away with paying the judge?"

He grabs my phone from my hand, his brows curving. "Has that bitch been snooping through my stuff in my office?"

"She's a detective, Tyler. She wasn't snooping, that's her job." I gesture around, unable to keep my hands from moving; I'm overwhelmed with frustration. "And then you wonder why I have doubts about you. You keep so many things from me. If you think I'm going to stand by and let this continue, you're wrong. All your secrets will come out when you least expect it."

He passes my phone back. His hands curl into fists and his face hardens. "What are you going to do, huh?" Tyler grabs my arm, his grip is tight around my skin. "You're not going to say a word about what's been said within the walls of this house, understood?"

I swallow, shaking my arm away from his hand. "This isn't healthy, I don't want to be around you." I walk into our bedroom and shut the door, turning the key to the right. My back rests on the wood, my body slides to the floor. I glance over at my arm, pain pulsing through my skin. *I lied. I am afraid of this side of him.*

Would he be able to kill if someone made him angry enough?

"Are you willing to ruin years together for something like this?" he shouts from the other side of the door; the handle moves downwards a few times before he kicks the wood.

"Leave me alone," I beg, staring at the big canvas hanging over the bed. It's a painting of us: Tyler, Charlie, and me. A happy family. *Who is this family?*

"If you like to play the victim, why have you never left?" Tyler groans. He doesn't like to lose. It's always his rules or nothing.

"Because..." I start, but I'm unable to finish the sentence. I don't even know the answer. He's giving me hundreds of reasons to let him go, but I still don't.

I can hear Tyler's sarcastic laugh through the wall. "I'm not the crazy one here."

My jaw clenches, adrenaline and anger push me to stand and open the door. A vein is popping on Tyler's forehead, his fists clench like he's ready to punch the wall. *Or me.* He rushes inside the bedroom, turning to the right.

I'm not afraid of him. *I don't want to be at least.*

"Do you want to leave?" His threatening tone reverberates through the walls. The wardrobe door swings open as he pulls my white luggage out, unzipping it. He gestures towards it. "Go!"

I cross my arms, not daring to drop my gaze.

He steps closer. "I said, go! Leave!" he yells at the top of his lungs, pointing at the stairs leading downwards.

My body falters at the tone of his voice. "I'm not going anywhere," I respond calmly.

He scoffs, shaking his head. "You're pathetic."

I shiver with tension. "Maybe. But at least I'm not a convict."

Tyler's eyes darken. His gaze falls on my desk in the corner of the bedroom. Without thinking twice, he grabs my laptop and smashes it against the wall—the screen shatters into a thousand broken pieces and keyboard letters scatter across the floor. He breathes heavily.

"I'm not a killer," he hisses before storming out of the room.

I hear the front door slam shut and the house falls into the silence I was craving. My heart pounds in my chest as I stare at the pieces of what used to be my work laptop. *What has he done?*

I sink to my knees, gathering the pieces as I begin to cry. To really sob like I haven't for a long time.

Outside, the sky darkens with anger, matching the hurricane in my bones. Thunder rumbles in the distance, each crash makes me jolt.

I'm not used to thunderstorms. How did I get used to the chaos within these walls?

TWENTY-SIX

MADELINE

June 25, 1:30PM

The rain has stopped, but humidity fills the air.

"Shit!" Sadie's voice makes me turn to the slightly open window. I glance downstairs just in time to see her jerk her hand back and pull the shears away from the potted plant in the backyard. Her fingers are slick with blood.

I freeze as her face twists in pain. She wipes her hand on her dress, leaving a stain of dark red behind.

Without thinking twice, I rush downstairs and walk outside. The ground is still damp and the stone tiles of the backyard are covered in a mix of water and gravel.

"Sadie, are you okay?"

She ignores me, turning quickly to head straight for the guesthouse door, not sparing me a glance. Her footsteps are quick, but I follow her, my heart racing.

With one hand pressed to the handle, she pauses and looks back at me. There's a hard edge to her eyes now, a wall that wasn't there before. "I'm fine. You don't have to follow me around."

I frown. "You're bleeding, I—I just want to help—"

"I don't want you in here," she interrupts. "This is my private space. It's in the contract. You know that."

My lips part, I'm caught off guard by her sudden coldness. This isn't her home. It's a guesthouse that belongs to Tyler and me. We can come in whenever we want to if we decide so. The constant mystery of keeping the curtains shut all the time, along with her rude behavior, is really crossing the line. But as much as I want to stomp my foot, I know that Sadie has something on me. She knows things that she shouldn't. And I can't let her spill whatever information she thinks she knows. I have to keep things friendly, play along with her control game.

Until there's only one way left—mine.

She unlocks the door slowly, never breaking eye contact, as if to emphasize that there's no room for negotiation. "I'll take care of it. You don't need to worry," she finally says before shutting her door in front of my face.

My jaw clenches and I take a deep breath as I walk back to the house. Drops of water splash on my legs as Tyler jumps in the pool, swimming from one side to the other.

I step back into the kitchen and grab a pack of chips from the cabinet.

I want to avoid him as much as possible right now.

Any other person would have left at this point, but I haven't.

Is it love? Is it the money? Or is it the addictive toxicity that echoes my childhood, the kind I believe I can endure, the kind I think I can fix—because I don't know what healthy love really feels like?

Everything I believed in, every hope I held on to, lies broken around me. The truth stares back at me from the ruins of my life.

My cheeks are soaking wet, my nose runs like a baby's first cry. I don't know what I did to deserve this. *Or perhaps I do.*

Karma is chasing me like a stalker.

With a sigh, I get up and head to the bathroom. The mirror reflects back a worn-out version of myself: eyes red and puffy from crying, frizzy hair, dark circles underneath my eyes, dry lips. I splash some cold water on my face, hoping to wash away the bad and the ugly. All the things that make me the person I don't want to be.

I'm so happy that Charlie is out having a sleepover at her friend's house. She doesn't deserve to see any more of this. I don't want her to see the same things I saw when I was a child. The anger of parents who should have loved each other, cherished each other, been a family. A normal family.

From the bathroom window, I notice Sadie's figure disappearing down the sidewalk, her red hair flies all around her face. I glance towards the guesthouse. A cold shiver crawls up my spine. I have a nagging feeling that won't go away—a sense that she's hiding something.

Something inside our guesthouse. The lights are all turned off, the gray curtains are drawn as usual. There should be a key underneath the back door doormat. We've always kept it there. I wonder if Sadie removed it.

I walk back out, my eyes scanning around to make sure Tyler is not here. It'll be easier to cover my tracks than risk him hearing me use the interior connecting door. I bend over in front of the guesthouse door and pull the doormat up. The silver key shines under the small lamp next to the door. Holding it between my fingers, I place it into the door gap, but before I turn it I feel a pressure just behind my neck.

Like someone is staring.

I clench my jaw and don't dare blink; I hold the key tightly —it's the only sharp object I could defend myself with out here. *Is Sadie behind me? What is she going to do if she finds me here after telling me to stay away from her space? What if it's Liam? What if he's here to get his revenge?*

"It's me," I hear a familiar female voice say. A hand grips the top of my shoulder and I turn quickly, relieved and confused at the same time.

"Rose?" I search her eyes. She never shows up unannounced like this. It almost freaked me out.

She moves her hair over her shoulder, raising her arms to the sky. "Sorry," she says as she lowers her hands. "I didn't hear from you for days. I was worried."

I sigh. Rose is right. So much has happened that I completely forgot to answer her messages.

A sudden rustle in the bushes sends shivers down my spine. I press a finger to my lips. "Sadie is out. I need to get in," I whisper.

"Why?" Rose frowns.

"She's hiding something, I'm sure of it."

"Oh," Rose raises her eyebrows, "what makes you think that?"

"She's been so protective of her space lately. She didn't want me to take one single step in here, which is weird, considering everything. Don't you think?"

Rose nods. "Do it."

I press my lips together and insert the key, turning it until the door clicks open. Darkness envelops us as we step inside, walking on tiptoe. The air reeks of lavender—the scent is so strong it's giving me a headache.

All the curtains are shut, but there's enough light from the lanterns near the pool to see without turning the lights on.

Some things inside aren't the way I left them. The furniture has been moved around, even the bed. It looks like Sadie has rearranged everything so that if someone were to peek in, she wouldn't be facing the windows, no matter where she's sitting.

Two empty glasses of wine have been left on the dark-green kitchen island, next to two pizza boxes. Two blankets are draped across the two sofas, a half-read book has been left open.

"What exactly are we looking for?" Rose asks, her eyes roaming around.

"Something," I whisper back, "anything."

I step into the small office right beside the bedroom. The shelves are full of dust, a guitar lies beside them. Clothes and two empty wine bottles are on the floor, making me stop right before the carpet.

Sadie had had someone over. Someone else had slept here.

But although Sadie can do whatever she wants in her free time, I'd never seen her hanging out with anyone around here before.

My gaze is immediately drawn to the desk. A big whiteboard is mounted against the wall just above it.

My breath catches in my throat.

My pictures are pinned to it—pictures I'd forgotten I even had—each one connected by threads, linking locations.

Linking the men I've slept with since I've been married to Tyler.

A kitchen knife with dried blood stained on the blade is attached with silver tape on to the board.

It looks like Sadie is yet to decide whether to kill me or fuck up my life.

I know what's hidden behind her eyes. I've seen the way she watches me sometimes, like she knows I'm watching her too.

But Sadie has no idea what I'm capable of. And unfortunately for her, I know exactly where to find her—*right now*.

TWENTY-SEVEN
SADIE

June 25, 3:30PM

My torso twists as if my spine were made of rubber.

The yoga instructor glances towards me, nodding in approval as she extends one leg after the other, arms pointing at the ceiling.

I've been working out regularly since I started my job with the Johnsons. It only takes me ten minutes to get here by bike and I usually spend some time afterwards browsing at the shops on Fifth Avenue or biking in circles around the lake in Central Park. It feels good to get away from the Johnsons' property. Sometimes I feel like I have so many eyes on me, which is why I keep shutting the curtains.

Madeline always seems to have too much time on her hands while claiming to be a therapist.

The exercise studio has large windows overlooking a side street crammed with street parking. I can't help but keep looking outside to see whether any creeps stop to stare at women in tops and leggings. As I lie on the mat, Amanda, the yoga instructor, whispers for us to close our eyes and focus on the present moment.

I do as I've been told, but it's hard to focus on the present when my mind keeps drifting back to Charlie's birthday. That day will haunt me forever, no matter that I was just trying to protect myself. If the police ever find that tape Madeline claims to have, it will be over for me. They will never believe my version of events.

My eyes open as everyone returns to a seated position and starts to clap before getting up and rolling up the mats. The class is over and I don't feel relaxed at all. But I guess the workout went fine, since my skin is glistening with sweat. I roll my mat and carry it under my arm, a large yoga ball under my other arm. Amanda told us to bring home all of our equipment today as they're about to renovate the studio and it has to be empty. I'm not sure how I'm going to take a yoga ball and mat home with me on my bike, but I'll figure it out.

I glance outside again. A chill runs down my spine as I see her red BMW parked there.

What is she doing here?

Madeline's eyes are covered by sunglasses, her fingers drum on the steering wheel. She seems to be staring at me, waiting for me to get out.

But why?

I saw the way she looked at me when I said that I didn't want her to go inside the guesthouse. I could see her burning inside. She can't take "no" for an answer from her husband—so imagine how she is with me, her maid.

I swallow as I grab my tote bag from the corner of the room, smiling at Amanda as I leave the studio.

I'm not sure what Madeline wants from me, but this can't be good. She's never followed me before, or at least not that I realized.

Sometimes I wonder who she really is. I've seen so many sides of her: the calm mask she wears around her daughter; the version with heart-shaped eyes on days when she isn't arguing with her husband; and her complete transformed personality when she fights intensely with Tyler. *But which side of her is the real deal?*

Who is Madeline, really?

I leave the yoga studio and I can immediately hear Madeline's cheap heels pressing against the cement as she steps out of the car, rushing in my direction. I swallow and walk towards my bike which is locked around a lamppost next to Madeline's car.

But when Madeline sees me, her brows arch with surprise as if she hadn't intentionally followed me here. "Sadie? What are you doing here?"

I press my lips together as I process her question.

Is she being serious? Are we really going to play this game?

This can't be a coincidence. I've got a gut feeling that I can't shake off. *Madeline Johnson is here for a reason.*

I swallow, tearing up a smile. I really want to confront her, but what's the point? She will lie like she always does. I could call the police and tell them everything I saw. But the Johnsons have money and I have nothing, no one, and *I* will be the one who ends up in jail. That's not happening.

"I had yoga class," I respond, tilting my head to the side as I unlock my bike.

"Oh, I came here to buy new shoes at the store across the road," she says as if I'd asked. She points to the yoga ball which is almost half the size of my body. "Had a nice class?"

"I did, thanks."

"Do you want a ride home?" Madeline gestures to her car a few feet behind me. "You're not going to roll the yoga ball beside you while you cycle back, are you?"

I hesitate for a moment, wondering whether I should get a cab instead to avoid whatever conversation she wants to have in the car. But Madeline has a point and if she wants to talk to me about something, so be it. I live next to her anyway, it's not like I can avoid her.

I nod, biting the inside of my lips and following her to the car. Hopefully the ride home won't be awkward. It will only take three minutes anyway.

"I'll get that for you." Madeline takes the yoga ball out of my hands and walks to the back of the car. I get into the passenger seat at the front, glance at my phone, and wonder if I should wear my headphones for the entire ride.

I look in the rearview mirror. Madeline seems to be struggling to fit the yoga ball in the trunk; she moves things around until a slow hiss slices through the silence and then she closes the trunk, stepping to the driver's seat.

The slow hiss turns into a squealing rasp. *Did she just deflate my yoga ball?* Madeline's fingers brush the steering wheel, she turns the engine on and pulls away from the curb.

My brows furrow. "Did you just—"

She cuts me off. "I just realized I'm almost out of gas. We're going to make a quick stop at the gas station before heading home if you don't mind."

Turns out the ride home won't be three minutes long after all. And actually I do mind. I don't want to spend such a long time stuck alone with her in her car.

Thankfully, Madeline pulls into the nearest gas station quicker than I expected. As she goes to the pump, my eyes follow her movements. From the look on her face, she's thinking about something. Perhaps she wants to have a real conversation with me, one where I can't escape any question. *Maybe she found out about how I feel for Tyler? Maybe he told her that sometimes I get too close to him?*

I bite my tongue as I follow Madeline's movements through the rearview mirror. She moves to the back of the car and opens the trunk again.

What is she doing?

A metallic click startles me. *What does she have in the back of her trunk?*

I see the edge of my yoga ball appear again and Madeline closes the trunk. *That's strange. I really thought I heard a hiss back there, but perhaps it wasn't my yoga ball being deflated? I mean, there's enough space for a yoga ball in Madeline's car.*

It's only the two of us in this car—right?

Madeline closes the trunk once again and rushes towards the pump, finally filling the car with gas.

On the drive back she doesn't say a thing to me. Nothing.

I really thought she wanted to talk and that was why she had followed me to the yoga studio. But perhaps it really was a coincidence she was there.

I stare out of the window, my elbow resting on the door. I don't know what Madeline is thinking, and when I see the Johnsons' front stoop I won't care anymore. I'll be home and if she starts talking to me then, I can just rush back inside the guesthouse.

Madeline gets out first, and before I open the car door, I check my social media; notifications fill my phone.

She opens the trunk, seemingly reaching for the yoga ball, but instead of taking it out, she seems to move her hands around it before closing the trunk.

The hissing sound appears again out of nowhere and then I hear the car locking. Madeline walks towards the back door of her house.

I frown as I try the handle of the passenger seat, but it doesn't open.

She's locked me in.

I try again and again, then unplug my seatbelt and pull with all my energy, but it doesn't work. I'm stuck here.

"Madeline, Madeline! You locked me in!" I shout. My hand bumps against the window, but Madeline doesn't seem to hear me, or she pretends not to.

I knew there was something on her mind, but I would never have guessed that she would lock me in the car.

What point is she trying to make anyway? I'll get out of here sooner or later.

Unless...

The hiss becomes louder and I turn my body to the source, which seems to be in the back of the trunk. I squeeze through the seats, panic starting to curl inside my chest. My hands grasp at the worn upholstery, pushing myself into the cramped space between the front and the back. There I see it. My yoga ball. It's deflating.

That's where the hissing sound was coming from. I stare at it for a second, trying to make sense of what Madeline did. But then my eyes move, drawn by something else.

Three canisters inside a trash bag along the trunk's edge. I blink hard and read the label—*LIQUEFIED PETROLEUM GAS.*

My heart skips. My breath catches. The pieces click together with a sickening clarity.

It's not air escaping the yoga ball.

The car suddenly feels smaller, the air thinner, its weight presses against my chest.

I want to scream, but I have no breath left to scream with. I force my eyes to stay wide, to see every detail. To understand how much time I have left.

The hiss grows louder and I move back to the front passenger seat; I'm on the verge of a panic attack.

If I die in this car, the police will never know what really happened on Charlie's birthday.

They will never know that I moved the body to stop them from framing me.

TWENTY-EIGHT
MADELINE

June 25, 4:30PM

I wonder if she felt it when the air became too thick to breathe.

Probably not. People are so naive and ignorant. Sadie probably didn't even realize she was suffocating until it was too late. Sneaky human beings like her think they're so smart, but they're as fragile as a balloon in a room full of needles.

I dip the nail of my thumb into the skin of my hand, feeling the faint pulse in my fingertips.

Sadie was useful—well, for a time. But people like her don't matter, no one notices when they're gone, just like what happened with me.

I was fifteen years old when I ran away from home for the first time.

I didn't have a plan, I just needed to leave. Home was a place I couldn't stand anymore.

When my real father died and my mother met him, everything changed. She stopped working, just like my stepfather, as if the world could bend around their laziness. They didn't care about anything. Their only concern was what they could take, what they could avoid. They were selfish. *The government will take care of us*, they used to say. *We're not working for anyone else's pocket.*

My mother never noticed what was really happening. She never saw how my stepfather was trying to rip our family apart. She was so in love with him that she would do anything to keep him.

I hated them both. But I couldn't hate her as much as I hated him. He was the one who ruled our life for a while, who sold all my toys, who let us freeze in our home, and made us eat whatever he wanted us to. He would get angry at us for the smallest things and then, as a punishment, he would lock me in the attic without water or heating for hours. Once, he forgot I was there and he didn't let me out until the day after; that was when I started searching *how to kill someone* or *how to get away with murder* on the internet. I never killed him, I just wanted to feel safe knowing what I had to do if needed.

He was an unreliable piece of shit and my mother didn't care. She let it happen. She only cared about how he felt and she would never *ever* disappoint him. I was treated like a mistake.

As the years passed, I learned to survive by becoming invisible and staying out of that house as much as possible. I watched them both grow into something less human with every passing day. My mother was drifting further away into whatever delusions she sustained to stay in that toxic relationship.

I grew to understand that while I was under their roof nothing mattered except what my stepfather wanted, and when he was out getting drunk, my mother barely existed.

I was never really a child. Not in the way other kids were. I didn't have the luxury of childhood. I learned to read people, to anticipate their movements, to manipulate my world because no one was going to do it for me. I realized I didn't need to be loved —I just needed to feel in control. I had to learn how to be cold, detached. I realized I didn't have to *feel* anymore. Until, at the age of nineteen, I met Tyler and moved in with him right away, leaving the past behind. I never reconnected with them. Sometimes, I check my mother's social media to see if she's still alive, but that is all.

Tyler saved me, until the point that the numbness disappeared and all I felt was love. For him, and for my daughter.

When I got pregnant, I made a promise that I would never let anyone make me feel small and powerless like I had in the past, and that I would shield Charlie from anything, even if I got hurt instead. I would rather pretend to be fine, as I was practiced in doing, to be able to survive through tough times.

Realistically, I should feel guilty about Sadie, but I can't. She was trying to trick me into becoming the villain of a story *she* started. If anything, I feel calmer now knowing that Sadie won't be able to speak to the police because that would've caused a fucking mess.

Everything is just the way it was meant to be.

As I reach the counter of my favorite coffee shop and grab my iced latte, I turn to leave but collide with someone. My coffee spills all over the man's shirt and I gasp in horror.

Especially when I see who he is.

Liam.

"Oh my God. I'm so sorry." I look at the stains on his white shirt and I can't help but blush. Liam's blue eyes twinkle with amusement despite the mess I've made.

I'm not sure if he's acting or not right now; he seems to be interested in my family in a way I can't understand yet. But I will.

"Wow, you really made a painting on my shirt. It's alright though," he says, winking. "Accidents happen. Besides, this is a good excuse to show up late to work—if anyone will ever believe me that my therapist bumped into me and spilled coffee all over my favorite shirt."

"Let me help you clean up. I feel terrible." *I don't.* Even though I feel like turning on my heels and leaving, I grab a handful of napkins from the counter and start dabbing at his shirt. I can't let this man become angrier than he already is with Tyler for firing him. He already broke into my house once, I'm not sure what he's capable of doing. *Good thing he doesn't know the real me, not at all.*

He chuckles, taking the napkins. "Really, it's fine. No harm done."

As Liam tries to wipe away the coffee, he tosses the napkins in the nearest trash can, his lips curving into a smile as he shakes his shoulders. "How about you join me for a coffee? My work can wait. I haven't been able to book any of your sessions on the app and it would be nice to chat with you."

"Um, yeah, I had to shut down the booking system for a while due to family issues." I hesitate for a moment, glancing at my watch. I want to know what he's thinking, what he wants, but not now. Not when the police will be pulling in front of my house anytime soon. "I appreciate the offer, Liam, but I really need to go."

He nods. "No problem. Your husband is a very lucky man." Liam points quickly at the ring on my finger.

His words catch me off guard and I force a smile, but all I want to do is punch him in the face.

The audacity.

He has never said anything like that before. "Thanks," I manage to say.

"See you very soon." He waves at me as I step out of the coffee shop.

Hopefully I won't, I think.

His words replay in my mind: *"Your husband is a very lucky man."* I wonder if Tyler thinks so.

TWENTY-NINE
DETECTIVE RYNN

June 25, 5:30PM

Sadie's head is laid against Madeline's car window, her eyes are shut.

The ambulance just pulled up and they're taking out a gurney.

But when they reach Sadie, there's no pulse.

How did she die this way? Locked in Madeline's car? Where's Madeline?

I see Madeline's daughter looking down from the upstairs window, but she turns away as soon as she sees me. I wonder what she thinks of her messed-up family. The weird thing is, Tyler Johnson made the call. He said he tried to knock on the glass, but she seemed unconscious, and he didn't think to break the window to let her out. "It's an expensive car," he said.

His words are a strange detail to fixate on in the middle of a potential murder scene. Tyler Johnson must think he's some kind of hero, the way he talks. Like he's the one who has done his part—called the police. But he didn't break the damn window.

I take a slow walk around the car, eyeing every inch of it. No signs of forced entry. No sign of struggle, either. It's as if Sadie just fell asleep in the passenger seat and never woke up. But that's not the story I'm buying.

I glance towards the house, but there's no sign of Madeline. If she's home, she's hiding. If she's not... well, I don't think she's gone far. *She's involved.* I can feel it in my gut.

Tyler Johnson's voice cuts through my thoughts. "Detective, I told you what happened. I don't know what else to say. I just—"

"Just what?" I cut him off, my eyes narrow. "If you knew she was unconscious, why didn't you do more?"

He shifts uncomfortably on his feet, glancing back at the car. "I didn't know if she was really unconscious. And the car's, you know... it's a nice one. I didn't want to make a mess. I thought maybe she'd wake up. I thought maybe she was just passed out or something. I was just trying to be careful, okay?"

I give him a hard look, but he doesn't meet my gaze.

"Anthony," I say, turning to my coworker, "call the evidence department to take the car into custody. I'll wait here until Madeline comes back."

Anthony nods without comment, already pulling his phone out of his pocket.

Madeline's a hard one to read. She always keeps a tight lid on whatever secrets she's hiding. It's like she has this instinct to shield herself, to shut everyone out—except when she lets someone in, they get sucked into her mess. Like Sadie. I bet she didn't expect it to end like this.

But why lock Sadie in the car? What the hell happened between the two of them?

THIRTY
MADELINE

June 25, 7:00PM

If I knew that fear could kill, I wouldn't have let it guide me.

But it's too late now.

A mirror on the wall catches my attention, but I force myself not to look, I know they're watching me from the other side.

When I got home earlier, I thought I had been pulled into a nightmare.

Two police cars were parked outside, their sirens still flashing. They surrounded the entire guesthouse with yellow tape, two officers carried out some evidence I've seen before. The board where Sadie was planning something to make me disappear, her phone, and the blood-stained knife.

It's useless to keep spinning around the same question when the answer is easy. Daniel's blood is on that sharp blade and his wounds will match its dimensions.

But whose DNA will be found on the murder weapon? Who are they going to blame? Who is to blame?

Sadie's body was taken away before I got there, as well as my car.

I wonder what they're thinking about me.

My legs shake beneath the metallic table while I wait for someone to show up. The ticking of the clock on the wall seems to become louder each second, counting down to the time when I'll no longer be a victim of a series of unfortunate events, but a criminal.

No. It won't go that way. I won't let it.

It's all just a terrible misunderstanding.

My palms feel clammy as they grip the metal legs of my plastic chair.

When the officers brought me in, they didn't say much. Just asked me to come to the station for a few questions while they interrogated Tyler separately at home. Then they asked me to wait here. In this isolated room. The pressure is building up.

They want me to crack. To break. To show them something they can use against me. To make their job easier, to close this case once and for all.

Detective Rynn makes her way into the room. She sits on the other side of the table and flicks through some papers she's holding. Then she fires a look at me. "Where have you been this afternoon, around four o'clock?"

I sit back in my chair, trying to steady my nerves. "I was out doing some shopping."

She raises an eyebrow. "Out on Fifth Avenue? Is that where you met Sadie?"

I nod, keeping my gaze steady. "Yes."

She consults her notes for a moment and then looks back up at me. "Did you know she was at a yoga class right in front of where you parked your car?"

I don't flinch. "No."

"Are you sure, Madeline?"

"Yes."

The detective taps her pen on the table. "We've seen footage of you and Sadie in your car, on your way home. Do you usually go out together outside her working hours?"

"No," I say quickly. "I bumped into Sadie outside her yoga class and offered her a ride back."

She leans back in her chair, steepling her fingers. "Interesting. So, you two weren't... particularly close?"

I bite my lip. "Sadie never really liked me. No, I wouldn't say we were close. She was just our maid."

"We found a deflated yoga ball in the back of your car. That's a bit unusual, don't you think? Mind explaining it?"

My throat suddenly feels tighter. Flashbacks of me filling the ball and tossing the cans of liquefied petroleum gas in a black trash bag in the trunk appear in my mind. Months ago, Tyler, Charlie, and I went camping, and I left some spares in the trunk of my car. I remember thinking how destructive these cans could be to a person if used correctly. So, I kept them in case of emergencies. Like Sadie.

"It was Sadie's, but there wasn't enough space in the car trunk for it, so I deflated it."

"Right... Did Sadie get upset by that?"

"No, she didn't even notice."

"How come?" Detective Rynn presses.

"She was listening to music the entire drive back," I reply, my hands clenched in my lap. "She never even looked at me."

"Your husband said he saw you going into the guesthouse yesterday while Sadie was out. Is that when you've seen the board with your photos on it–and realized Sadie found out something you did, and decided it was best to get rid of her?"

"I didn't see the board."

The detective pauses, her gaze cold. "Interesting. So why did you follow Sadie Kelsey to her yoga class?"

"I didn't follow her, it was a coincidence," I say, forcing the words out. "Like I said, I was shopping."

"If you say so." Detective Rynn raises an eyebrow. "We found a knife in Sadie's home and we believe it's connected to the murder of Daniel Johnson. I'm just speculating here..." She leans in closer, her gaze hardening. "Your maid has been keeping an eye on you for a while—she pinned your pictures to a board, connecting locations with red threads, and taped a blood-stained knife on the wall next to it. The question is, why? Did she know things? Did she know the truth about what happened to Daniel?"

"I don't know." I lower the tone of my voice. "If I knew what Sadie was planning, I would have told you."

"Before or after you killed her?" she asks.

I jerk back. "I didn't kill her. I didn't even lay a finger on her."

The detective doesn't look convinced. She looks at me like I'm already guilty. "We're aware that Sadie had no visible wounds when we found her," she says. "But we are going to do an autopsy, and we'll know soon enough what happened to her." She pauses, leaning in. "What I find strange is that Sadie was found in your locked car. How do you explain that? You just walked away, without realizing she was stuck inside?"

I take a deep breath.

This is all Sadie's fault, not mine. She couldn't mind her own business, couldn't keep her gaze away from my family.

Karma hits everyone at some point in their life.

Now I just need to work out when it's going to be my turn to hide from it.

"I parked my car right in front of the guesthouse. I said goodbye to Sadie and walked back to my home," I say. "I thought she was okay."

"You were the last person to see her alive, Madeline." Detective Rynn leans to one side. "That makes you the prime suspect."

THIRTY-ONE
CHARLIE'S JOURNAL

June 25, 11:00PM

Another death.

I should have seen it coming.

Being at home right now only fuels a fire within me. My heart races as if it's trying to outrun my thoughts, but no matter how fast it beats, a sense of dread keeps catching up. Every creak of the floorboards, every distant sound—it's all amplified. I jolt at every single little thing, like someone is going to come and kidnap me or worse, kill me.

I don't want to be here anymore. A bomb is ticking underneath this house and sooner or later, it's going to explode.

There are too many secrets that will never come to light. My dad, for example. He hasn't been the voice of the truth in this mess, quite the opposite. He lied and lied until it was too late.

When Mom got back from the police interrogation about Sadie's death, I heard Detective Rynn talking to my parents. Mom was ordered not to leave the country until the autopsy on Sadie's body is complete and they have tracked the DNA from the knife found in the guesthouse.

The police have an eye on us, all because of him. Because of his mistakes, now I'm no longer able to do anything without feeling observed at all times.

It's all his fault we're in this mess.

All I want to do is run away. But even though I pulled out my pink suitcase from underneath my bed and started throwing clothes in it, I stopped halfway, looking at myself in the mirror.

There's nowhere for me to go.

It hit me when Mom opened my bedroom door all of a sudden, surprised. "What's going on?" she asked, kneeling on the floor beside me.

I tried not to sob, but as soon as I opened my mouth, I burst into tears. "I want to leave. I can't do this anymore. I—I can't keep living in a horror movie. I hate this house. What happened to Sadie, Mom? What happened?"

Her forehead creased and her eyes glowed. She pulled me into a hug, caressing my hair. "Oh baby, I understand. You can't imagine how sorry I am that you have to go through this. But whenever you feel like this, I want you to talk to me. Never hide like this in your bedroom, please." She released me from our hug and held my shoulders, gazing into my eyes. "There's nothing in this world that matters more to me than your happiness. Do you understand that?"

I cleaned away the tears on my cheeks, nodding. "How did Sadie die in your car?"

Mom shook her head like it wasn't a big deal. But of course it is.

"I don't know," she replied.

My tears threatened to spill over. "You don't know?"

"Detective Rynn said they're going to run an autopsy. She might've been ill."

"I don't think she was sick."

"Charlie, you don't have anything to do with this. Stay out of it." Mom's voice became more serious.

"I know I don't, Mom. But how can you expect me to do that? My friends are already avoiding me because they think that Dad killed that man."

"Your real friends will always stay, no matter how hard things become. But you must try not to let this situation break you. I don't want to see you hurting."

"I don't—I don't know how to do that. I'm not you. You seem... almost unbothered." My voice trembled.

Mom's jaw clenched. "I have to be strong for our family. Your dad keeps getting angry, you have every right to be upset, and I *have to hold it all together even if I don't feel like it. Please, stay out of this."*

"I saw you, Mom. From the window."

Mom paused, then swallowed and just said: "It's late, you should go to bed."

I did what my mother told me, but just before I hid my journal inside the pillowcase, I glanced out the window—my bedroom window, looking down at the pool and the guesthouse where Sadie used to live.

But she's not with us anymore, and so the curtains are wide open.

THIRTY-TWO

MADELINE

July 1, 12:30PM

"Sorry, darling, I have a lot on my mind. Am I pulling your hair too hard?" Charlie's silky hair slides through my fingers.

"No, it's okay. What are you thinking?"

I shake my head and seal Charlie's braid with a scrunchie. "Don't worry about it."

"Is it Sadie? Dad?" She turns towards me.

"It's not your job to worry about me, Charlie. I'm okay," I say, lying to her and ultimately myself by forcing my mind to stay positive and trying to steer the conversation in a different direction.

I didn't like seeing her like that last night. Sobbing for my mistakes, her suitcase open on the floor. I hated how much she reminded me of me when I was her age and I'm willing to do anything for that not to be repeated.

If she ever wants to run away, I will run away with her. But I won't lose my daughter. *I won't.*

Charlie nods and rises in front of the vanity, but I can tell she's not so sure of my answer. She's perceptive like me, always attentive to people's body language. As much as I try to protect her from the investigation and my complicated relationship with Tyler, teenagers like her have a way of sensing when things aren't quite right.

"Do you miss school?" I try to deviate the conversation somewhere else.

"A little bit. I miss coming home and doing my homework without having the police around. I miss... normality," Charlie replies while she checks her lip gloss in the mirror. She turns, biting her lower lip.

"I know you do. But hey, at least you'll see your grandparents and your auntie today. Let's not think about this, okay?"

She shakes her shoulders. "Okay."

It's moments like these that remind me of how much I want to protect her. She's repressing everything inside her because she knows there's no other choice than this. Otherwise, it would cause more chaos. Especially if she really had left home yesterday.

I'm so glad she didn't. So glad I got to talk to her.

"Let's go downstairs." I place a hand on her shoulder. "They should be here soon."

Charlie's gaze gets lost for a moment, then she nods. "Yes."

The doorbell's chime cuts through our conversation. Charlie walks towards the staircase and I follow.

"Guess that's them," she mumbles. She doesn't seem very excited about this lunch with Tyler's family.

I'm not either, I would rather open up some slots at work and see if Liam shows up instead of having to deal with my in-laws, especially when I know they're Tyler's accomplices—they didn't think twice about paying the judge.

As I reach the front door, I hear faint murmurs filtering through it.

There they are. The happy family.

I pause briefly, pulling out my widest smile before Tyler

turns the knob and opens the door. He's wearing a fancy shirt and trousers today, as if he's meeting with a big client. He always looks spotless for his devoted family. But that ankle bracelet doesn't really match the outfit, does it?

His mother walks in, pristine as always, her sharp eyes skim over me with a hint of judgment she probably doesn't intend to hide. Pam's curls are tied up in a bun with every strand in place; red lipstick and sparkly eyeshadow distract from her aging skin.

Dave stands beside her, his posture rigid, arms crossed like he's already pissed about something nobody is aware of, or at least I'm not. His blue suit is a bit much for a dinner altogether on an average Sunday.

"Hello, dear." Pam places her hand on my arm and leans in to brush a quick kiss against my cheek. "We didn't keep you waiting, did we?" she finally asks, glancing at the gold watch on her wrist.

"No, not at all." A giggle escapes my lips involuntarily, more like a reflex than anything genuine.

Charlie steps forward and hugs both her grandparents with a forced smile; she passes them and welcomes her aunt Laura, who is dressed more simply than her parents. High-rise jeans and a white top.

When Tyler brought me home to meet his family fourteen years ago, I initially thought he and Pam shared similar manners, but their looks couldn't be more different. Back then, his dad Dave had chocolate-brown hair like Tyler does.

His sister, on the other hand, is almost a carbon copy of their mother. She has the same hair and eye color, and she's even the same height; they're both short and petite.

Pam has always been Tyler's inspiration—hardworking and devoted to her family.

"Mom, Dad, good to see you." Tyler steps forward and wraps his arms around Pam first, then gives Dave a firm handshake, exchanging a slight nod.

"Please, have a seat in the dining room. I'm just finishing preparing the starter, so it won't be long now." Tyler gestures towards the dining room adjacent to the living room; he plays the perfect host despite the mess that's been going on lately.

Do they even know that our maid is dead? Or are we playing pretend until someone dares to speak first?

The chandelier in the rarely used dining room hangs at the center of the long, polished table. High-backed, burgundy velvet chairs surround the table. Gold-framed paintings line the peach-painted wall. This room has always felt more like a stage set than a place for family meals. It's only used on special occasions such as Christmas, birthdays, or Sunday dinners like today. If today can be considered special.

Pam and Dave settle into plush chairs next to each other as Charlie bounces towards the kitchen, making small talk with Laura about how she's looking forward to visiting the Hamptons. Tyler leans in, brushing his hand against my upper back as he passes by and sits at the head of the table, right next to me and his parents.

As I take a sip of water from the crystal glass beside the plate and cutlery, Charlie's question lingers in my mind: *what am I thinking?*

Memories of who I used to be before Tyler came into my shitty past life flow in front of my eyes. I used to love painting, traveling, learning new things—anything creative or adventurous. But over time, those passions faded into the background, almost forgotten, as if I left a part of me in that train station where I met my husband.

Or perhaps this is part of growing up?

Deep down, I know it's not too late to pursue my passions again, to find a balance between responsibilities and personal fulfillment. But I need inspiration, and inspiration comes with happiness.

When will I truly be able to say: gosh, I never felt so happy in all my life?

Charlie and Laura glide into the dining room and take the only empty seats at the table.

Tyler follows, carrying an elegant silver tray filled with shrimp cocktails, bruschetta, and stuffed mushrooms. The aroma spreads through the air. He sets down the dishes in the center of the table next to an empty candelabra.

I keep my eyes from rolling and push out my frustration by inhaling and exhaling deeply as Pam casts a critical eye over the food. "Tyler, this looks delightful, though I must say, it's rather light for dinner."

"Don't worry, Pam, this is just the starter," I say before taking a bruschetta with tomatoes and olive oil and placing it on my plate.

"Eating light is the key to keeping a slim figure anyway, isn't it?" Tyler adds, chuckling softly, as if he didn't realize he'd just shared an inappropriate joke. He grabs a shrimp and eats it, his eyebrows lifting to indicate his approval.

"Absolutely," Pam replies, her gaze turning to me. "What about you, Madeline? Do you like to eat light and healthy?"

A slight flush creeps up my cheeks. "I guess it depends on my mood."

Dave clears his throat, leaning forward slightly as he interjects, "How's the company doing, Tyler? I heard the investors are getting a bit restless."

Tyler's smile stiffens for a moment. "Mom seems to be managing things well. I'm only supervising from a distance."

"I've read that the market's been volatile lately," Dave presses. "Have you considered diversifying? You don't want to put all your eggs in one basket, after all."

"Yeah. We're always looking to expand." Tyler waves a dismissive hand as if to brush away the concern. "I have a few exciting projects in mind that I think the investors will love once I'm able to leave the house."

I squint. *What is he doing? Who cares about this?*

I can't believe my ears. I get that Tyler's family are trying to talk about something else, but they don't seem like they're even the slightest bit worried that their son will end up in jail.

The way Tyler nods and talks as though everything is under control is scary. *Nothing is under control.* But the worst part is— he's not pretending. He truly believes that nothing will happen to him, even though there's proof that he went to Daniel's house on the day of the murder. It's surreal watching him play this role so effortlessly, so convincingly. I can't help but wonder how many times I've lost in his game of manipulation. For his parents, Tyler is an angel fallen from the sky. He never does anything wrong.

That's probably the reason why they're all so comfortable with him wearing an ankle monitor, because they're convinced he's innocent, they're sure that their youngest child would never kill a bee.

But even if he did, they would rather blame the wife than admit their son is a fucking liar.

Everything could change in just one week. At trial. My mind still spins when I think back on it. I was hoping for more time, but the higher profile the case, the greater the pressure to resolve it quickly.

Pam dabs a napkin on her lips. "That's good to hear. We're so proud of you."

"Thanks, Mom." Tyler grabs another shrimp and I can't help but notice the lump in his throat as he swallows, almost unable to keep up with this bullshit.

"Don't you like shrimp, Madeline?" Laura asks as she bites a stuffed mushroom.

I blush and force a smile in response. "I'm just not a fan of seafood." Laura knows this already, they all do. *Why do I have to feel embarrassed about my eating preferences every time?*

"Oh, come on." She tilts her head slightly and places her knife on her plate. "You have to try one. It's not like it's going to kill you." Her laugh is airy, but it grates my nerves.

I glance at Tyler, searching for some sign of support, but he's too engrossed in his performance, his smile glued in place.

"Don't worry, Laura," Tyler finally chimes in, waving a dismissive hand. "Madeline's just a little fussy about her food. We all have our flaws."

Is it a quirk to want to enjoy what I eat?

Laura's eyes narrow slightly, but she simply nods and shrugs her shoulders as if it's not her problem after all. Newsflash, it wasn't earlier either.

Tyler gets up to clear the plates. The clinking of cutlery against porcelain punctuates the awkward silence before Laura finally moves her attention towards Charlie. "Are you excited to head back to high school? Junior years were the most amazing times for me."

Charlie straightens in her seat. "I guess. I mean, it's just school."

"Oh, but you have to make the most of it!" Pam says, leaning forward, her eyes sparkling as she tries to micromanage my daughter's life. "This year will be critical for college applications. You'll want to impress them with your grades and extracurriculars."

"Yes, I know," Charlie mutters, subtly rolling her eyes.

"Well, Tyler, we must find a way to get that ankle monitor off before your fifteenth anniversary. Exciting times ahead." Laura's voice is bright with enthusiasm as she leans backwards to let Tyler serve her a plate of smoked salmon with potatoes.

I arch my eyebrows. It takes me ten seconds to realize what she's talking about; it's something I've put in a hidden shelf in my head but it's still there. I was only waiting for the perfect moment to bring it up.

And here it is.

Laura is talking about the inheritance Tyler will receive on our fifteenth wedding anniversary.

Tyler clears his throat and glances between me and his sister quickly. He looks down at his main course. "We're not really thinking about celebrations right now."

It's funny how Tyler never remembered our anniversary date until money was involved.

The energy in the room shifts as soon as I open my mouth. "Oh, aren't we, darling? I mean, with all that money we can even rent a castle to celebrate."

Everyone seems to freeze for an instant except Charlie, who frowns at me with confusion.

I don't play pretend unless I have no other choice.

Tyler opens his mouth, but waits a few seconds before he speaks. "How do you know about that?"

I place a hand on my chest. "Oh, me? I just know. Is that a problem? Was it a secret?"

Pam holds her fork in the air, glancing between the both of us.

My lying husband clears his throat again. "N—no, I just didn't know you knew."

I shrug my shoulders, smiling. "I also happen to know that you asked your lawyer, Laura, what would happen to the money if you filed for divorce beforehand."

Tyler's cheeks are on fire. "It's not what it seems, Madeline. Let's eat and talk about it later."

"Why can't we talk about it now?" I press sarcastically. "I mean, every other member of your family knew before me, so let's talk about celebrations. Laura, what do you think?"

Laura does everything she can to avoid my gaze. Charlie's fork hovers above her plate. Tyler's gaze darts between me and his mother; panic flares in his eyes for a split second before he masks it with a forced grin. "Enjoy your meals, everyone," he says hastily. His voice betrays a tremor I can't ignore.

Charlie shifts uncomfortably, flashing a look at her dad.

Pam's perfectly manicured fingers tighten around her napkin. "Yeah, let's focus on dinner."

My heart races as Tyler's family exchange confused glances as if they're all silently communicating—except me and Charlie.

I always thought the only place I'd ever feel like an outsider was my childhood home, but that feeling just came rushing back.

THIRTY-THREE

MADELINE

July 1, 4:00PM

Everything he does goes against me.

Tyler's family left a few hours ago, and I tried my best to keep the anger buried within me, but I'm not sure how much longer I can ignore what he did.

Was he going to divorce me if it wasn't for the clause in his grandmother's Will?

I step down into the basement where Tyler has a gym. He's running on the treadmill, but as soon as he sees me, he presses a button on the machine and slows it down until it stops.

Tyler steps down, pressing a small towel against his face. He starts gesturing around as if trying to find the right words not to piss me off even further. "I know what you're going to say. But what you know isn't—"

"I opened one of your letters, Tyler." I step closer, arms crossed over my chest. "It was from Laura. I read everything, so you can't say that what I know isn't the truth."

His jaw clenches and he takes a step closer. "Madeline—"

I place a hand in front of me to keep him at bay. "Don't try to manipulate my feelings with sweet words. You use your lies to confuse, destroy, and disarm all the time," I say. "I try to be on your side, but every day I discover something about you, and I don't know what to do anymore."

For the first time ever, I'm saying what I feel out loud without thinking about his reaction. He can't think that the longer he keeps secrets from me the longer I'll stay. It doesn't work like that.

"Please, come here." Tyler takes my hand, but I pull away.

"Don't touch me," I snap. "Just admit it. Admit that you're only with me because you want the inheritance."

"Please, don't think like that." Tyler sighs. "A few weeks ago, just before we got caught up in all this, I thought about leaving you. We're always fighting, Madeline. It's not healthy." He pauses, looking away. "That's why I asked Laura about the inheritance. But you have to believe me—I don't want to separate. I was just angry. The more I thought about leaving, the more I realized that I can't live without you."

Tyler's hands slide on to my hips and a chill prickles my skin. I told him not to touch me, but he always does whatever he wants without considering how I feel. *This has to stop.*

Tears sting my eyes as I look at him. The pain in Tyler's eyes seems to be genuine, but how can I believe him?

Everything is so fucked up.

The trust is broken and the wounds run deep. Two dead bodies have been found just outside our house in a space of a few weeks. I can't bear this.

As much as my heart aches, I know I can't ignore the truth anymore. "Charlie is hurting, Tyler... all of this shit is hurting her."

"I know, I'm so sorry." Tyler reaches out to kiss my forehead. His tears mingle with mine, tracing a path down my cheek. "All of this will be over in just a few days, I promise. The trial will change everything."

His words tug at my heart. "I can't think straight," I whisper. "I need time to process—"

"Please, Madeline," his voice cracks, "I love you. I'll do anything to make things right."

I shake my head and stare out the small window at the top of the basement, but Tyler gently turns my face towards him. His brown eyes are red and filled with tears.

"Don't look at me like that," I say, trying to steady my voice. "You're trying to make me feel sorry for you. But you're not fooling me anymore."

"I can't look at you any other way," he whispers. "You're the person I love."

Tyler leans in to kiss me, but I move away.

His tone shifts. "What do I have to do for you to forgive me? I... I told you—I was just angry, I didn't mean it."

"I don't know what to believe, it feels like I don't know you." I clench my fists, overwhelmed by conflicting emotions, and Tyler pulls me into a tight hug, sobbing. For a moment, I don't move, unsure of how to react. But gradually, I feel my arms moving, wrapping around him, our hearts beating in unison.

"Just promise me"—I pull back from the hug, forcing myself to meet his eyes—"promise me there will be no more secrets between us from now on, and that you won't end up in jail. I can't lose you like that. Charlie needs you."

Tyler shakes his head slightly. "I won't. I didn't do anything. You have to believe me."

"We have to find a way to fix this," I insist.

"I know." Tyler caresses my cheeks, our foreheads meeting. "But you must trust me."

I slowly move my head back and gaze into his eyes.

Tyler never mentioned Sadie. I can't help but wonder—does he know and is he deliberately avoiding the conversation? Or maybe, just maybe, he understands what it feels like to take someone's life and he's trying to protect me from carrying that same burden...

A sudden thud comes from the floor above, followed by the sound of footsteps rushing across the hardwood floor and then a crash—like glass has shattered on the living room floor.

"Where's Charlie?" Tyler asks, glancing up the stairs.

"She's hanging out with the neighbor. Who—"

"Stay here," Tyler orders me as he runs upstairs. Ignoring his warning, I race after him, my heart pounds harder with every step.

What's going on? Who's up there?

A tight grip forms around my chest as I see her. It was too good to be true to think that she would have left us alone after all of her threats. I wonder if she was peeking through the windows while Tyler's dad was here, making a plan of how to get rid of Pam.

Victoria Parker stands in the middle of the living room, her fingers curved into her palms. She's wearing a tight black dress that reaches her ankles. It's clear from the way she stares at us that she's angry.

"How the hell did you get in?" Tyler approaches her closely, but she doesn't move an inch.

"What did you do to her?" Victoria snaps, her eyes shifting between Tyler and me. She looks like she's ready to explode.

"Get out, Victoria," Tyler responds. "You need to leave now before I call the police."

Victoria's eyes narrow and then she points a shaking finger at me. "Sadie hated you." She steps forward, leaning her head to one side. "She said you were the fakest person she's ever met. And now she's gone. Dead in your car."

Did Sadie say that? What did she mean by it? I never did anything to make her believe I was being fake.

"Enough, Victoria," Tyler growls. He grips her arm and gently pushes her towards the front door.

Victoria jerks her arm out of his hold. "You should be ashamed of yourself." Her eyes move from Tyler's head to his ankle monitor. "Look at you. Caged in your own home."

Tyler's teeth grind together. "I want you gone. *Now.*"

But Victoria refuses to move. "I have proof that your family paid the judge." She turns to me, "and I know everything about you, *Evelyn.*"

Tyler's face pales as he glances at me.

My legs feel wobbly and I have to place my hand on the rail to steady myself; I'm terrified that I might collapse. Nobody has called me Evelyn since I moved away from my hometown with Tyler. Not since I severed all ties with the woman who I used to call my mother. My husband is the only one who knows my real name, but he never mentions it. It's probably the only secret we share.

I try to swallow the rising panic in my throat, but it's like swallowing glass.

When I turned eighteen, my mother said she needed me to take care of her, to be her primary caregiver. She used to say that my stepfather couldn't do it the same way I did.

And I believed her. At first.

But the longer it went on, the clearer it became. My mother wasn't sick. She just didn't want to work, the same as him. She didn't want to pay the bills, didn't want to lift a finger. She and my stepfather had become so skilled at playing the system that they had managed to convince a judge that I was the only one capable of looking after her.

One day, I heard my mother and stepfather talking and found out the worst possible thing about my mother—she had killed my real father.

I couldn't stay there. I couldn't. I had no life outside of that house and legally I couldn't leave. I was bound to her. Bound by the judge's order that I was her primary caregiver, bound by the financial burdens that she and my stepfather had managed to shift on to me. I didn't have the freedom to walk away, not without facing the consequences. I was their prisoner in every sense of the word and they knew it.

Evelyn died the moment I packed my things and left. The moment I chose to take back my life, even if it meant erasing every part of it and ensuring that my mother and stepfather wouldn't ever have the power to find me again.

If Victoria knows about my past, there's a chance I will find them knocking at my door. "What do you want from us?" I ask.

Victoria tilts her head, amused. She chuckles again. "So, you want to buy my silence, huh?"

"Just tell me what you want."

Victoria's lips curl into a cruel smile. "You're right. Too many deaths around here. Too much blood. But what do I want? Let me think..." She pauses, pressing her finger against her chin. "How about one hundred thousand dollars? You promised me, remember?"

I freeze. I remember that day in the office, but I didn't think Victoria would push for the money, I didn't think she was going to blackmail me this way. I thought her words were just words, but this woman is dangerous.

Tyler narrows his eyes; his jaw is clenched tight. I wonder if he's more furious with me or with her. Without another word, he walks over and opens a kitchen drawer, grabbing a checkbook from inside. He rips a check out and scribbles on it quickly, his hand shaking as he writes. "Here." He hands the check out to Victoria, his body tense. "But if you *ever* get close to this house again, I'm going to make sure you end up in jail."

Victoria looks at the check, then back at Tyler. A grin curls on her lips. She steps forward and snatches it from his hand.

"Pleasure doing business with you." Her gaze moves to me briefly. "I'll be watching you, *Evelyn*. I'll make sure you two end up the same way Sadie did."

I swallow hard as I watch Victoria walk out. Tyler's chest rises and falls faster than usual.

The past is no longer a shadow; it's a storm, and it's here.

THIRTY-FOUR

ROSE

July 4, 2:00AM

The room is so filled with smoke that I can barely see anything.

I'm in Madeline's office. Blood drips down the wallpaper. My heart pounds in my chest. I'm stuck behind her desk, the familiar surroundings distorted.

The wooden door creaks open. Detective Rynn steps inside, her judgy eyes looking for something. Or someone.

Tears bleed from her eyes like ink, spreading, swirling, transforming the color of her face into a shade of gray.

"What's happening?" I ask in a trembling voice. She doesn't respond. Instead, she inches closer, her eyes locked on to mine. The color spreads further, consuming her entire irises, turning her gaze into a void.

I try to stand, but my legs are rooted to the chair. Detective Rynn's face contorts into a twisted smile. "I will find out everything."

A cold, invisible force wraps around me, squeezing the breath from my lungs. The four walls surrounding me start to move closer. I struggle, gasping for air, my vision blurs as a bright light from the ceiling blinds me.

"Help!" I scream, but nobody hears me.

Where's Madeline?

The detective's face looms closer. "You can't escape this."

With a jolt, I sit up in bed, drenched in sweat, my heart racing in the darkness. My fingers brush my face and move to my pounding heart. I close my eyes and try to steady my breathing, to return to reality.

It was just a nightmare. A nightmare that screamed more truths than I ever did.

I glance around my bedroom; the only light source is the lamppost in front of my apartment. I can't shake the image of Detective Rynn's eyes, her words. Her voice felt so real.

"What's wrong?" The woman I met a few hours ago at the club rolls on to my side of the bed; her eyes narrow as she pulls a blanket against her chest.

"Just a nightmare." I don't turn to face her, I keep staring in front of me. I can feel the way she's looking at me without having to look at her.

I hear her sighing. "You need to chill."

I nod, turning to face her. "Yeah, maybe you're right. You should go."

The mattress curves to her side while she rolls out of the bed. "I'll make my way out then."

I wave to the woman as she puts on her clothes and leaves. I lie back down. *It felt so real, too real.* I know I won't be able to fall sleep again, but I have to try. I slip back under the covers, my mind still racing, but I force myself to close my eyes. The detective's words circle around my head. I need to shake them off and focus on something different.

It's the middle of the night. I wonder if Madeline is awake. I grab my phone and dial her number.

"Rose? What's going on?" she whispers, likely trying not to disturb her asshole of a husband.

"Hey... I was thinking, would you be up for a girls' trip? You should bring Charlie, too. We could leave in the morning."

"Tomorrow?"

"Yeah, you know, to my place in the Hamptons for the weekend. Charlie would love it and you could use a break before the trial."

There's a long pause, followed by a quiet yawn. "I guess that's fine. I don't think Tyler will mind."

Tyler can't go anywhere anyway, and that's a relief.

"Great. I'll pick you up tomorrow.",

We hang up at the same time and I pull the blanket over my head, letting the darkness swallow me as I try to fall back asleep. With every attempt to quiet my mind, I try to visualize the sound of ocean waves, the warm sand, and the sun-soaked weekend.

But even as I roll to the other side of the bed, the ghost of Daniel keeps holding my hand.

THIRTY-FIVE

CHARLIE'S JOURNAL

July 4

My mom announced that we're going on a weekend getaway with Rose. I couldn't be happier to take a break from this house.

As soon as she told me, I rushed to my wardrobe and pulled on a light summer dress and comfortable sandals, then quickly tied my hair back into a ponytail. Mom loves the beach, the ocean, the sun. It'll be good for her. Her mood changes a lot depending on the season, so maybe this will help.

"Charlie, let's go before Rose annoys the entire neighborhood with that honking," my mom called from the bottom of the stairs. I ran down quickly, finding my dad sprawled out on the couch, looking way too comfortable. He kissed me on the cheek and opened the front door for us like he always did.

"Are you sure you're going to be okay?" Mom asked him, glancing at his ankle.

He gave a lazy nod, a small smile curling his lips. "Yeah. You guys have fun."

"Call me if you need anything. And if the police show up... or if..." Her voice trailed off.

"Got it," Dad said, cutting her off a little too quickly. "Don't worry about me."

Outside, Mom and I placed our bags in Rose's truck, while she leaned against her red car, arms crossed. As soon as Dad caught Rose's eye, she raised an eyebrow and straightened up, grinning.

"Aren't you coming for a ride, Tyler?" Rose teased, her smile growing wider.

Dad rolled his eyes and exhaled sharply. "Very funny, Rose."

I've never understood why Rose hates Dad so much. She's always been defensive when it comes to Mom, like she's looking for any reason to tear him down. Maybe I don't need to understand. Some things are better left unknown.

If there's one thing Rose can't hide, it's how she feels. I can tell she's got something on her mind, something she's dying to say.

Rose kept her eyes locked on Dad as she slid into the car. "So, what's he doing while we're gone?"

I slid into the back seat and closed the door, glancing at Mom as she answered. "What do you mean? He can't go anywhere."

Rose's hate for Dad seems to grow every day, even when nothing happens. I get it, she's protective of Mom and me, but sometimes *her words cut too deep. It's like she's just waiting for our family to fall apart.*

Rose started the engine, tapping her fingers against the steering wheel in time with the radio, her eyes focused on the road ahead. "Yeah, but people can still visit him."

Mom bit her lip, her eyes flickering towards the window. "Well, I guess he could have people over."

Rose let out an exaggerated sigh. "Do you trust him?"

Her words hit me like a punch to the stomach. I wanted to tell her to mind her own business, but I couldn't. Rose is basically part of the family now—she's Mom's best friend, the only friend she has.

"Yes, Rose," Mom answered sharply. "That's not what I'm thinking about right now."

Rose raised an eyebrow. "Oh right, with Sadie, Daniel, and all the mess."

*My stomach twisted at the mention of their names.
Sadie... Daniel... I still can't forget the things that happened in our house, the blood that stained the floors. It feels like it happened yesterday. But Rose talks about it like it's no big deal.*

I pressed my lips together. Rose is on Mom's side—she always has been. She never thought for a second that Mom might be to blame. In fact, I get the feeling she has her eyes set on Dad for a reason.

Rose thinks he did it. But where's her proof? Is it just a gut feeling or does she know something else?

"You say that like it's nothing," Mom finally responded, reading my thoughts.

"Two people died in your house, Madeline," Rose snapped, her voice sharp. "Of course it's something. I'm just looking out for you."

I couldn't take it anymore. I stared out the window, watching a row of colorful houses pass by as we left the city behind.

"I know you don't trust him, Rose," Mom said quietly, almost to herself. "I'm struggling with him, too. But this whole thing... it's a mess. I just want it to be over."

Rose nodded, but I could tell she wasn't satisfied with Mom's answer. She never was. "So, what do you think will happen at the trial?"

My throat tightened. I didn't want to think about the trial.

"I think they'll call me to the stand," Mom answered after a beat.

Rose glanced at me in the rearview mirror, then focused back on the road. "What are you going to say?"

Mom hesitated. "The truth."

Rose's eyes narrowed. "Define truth."

"You know what I mean," Mom replied quickly, her voice tight.

My heart skipped a beat. I wished I knew what she meant.

Rose waved her hand dismissively. "You know how rich families are. Everything's about money, power, and protecting themselves. Daniel was a half-blood, so he didn't get all the benefits. And Sadie probably discovered something she wasn't supposed to. The Johnsons will pay for this."

I fidgeted in my seat. If Rose ever decided to become a detective, she'd probably be hired on the spot.

"We'll see what happens," Mom said finally.

"You're right," Rose agreed, extending her arm towards Mom and placing her hand on top of Mom's leg. "I'm just trying to protect you."

It might be my imagination playing tricks on me, but I swear that every time Rose looks at Mom, there's this softness in her eyes. It's hard to ignore.

THIRTY-SIX

MADELINE

July 5, 5:00PM

"I keep dreaming about him," Charlie says, her eyes fixed on the horizon.

I swallow, squeezing her hand. "Dad?"

She nods. "Yeah. I'm... I'm scared."

"Things will be over soon, I promise." I try to cheer her up. "I just want you to be okay."

"I'm okay," she replies. "But I never expected the police to arrest him."

I hate that there's nothing that I can do to change what's happening in our lives. We're stuck in a circle of secrets and lies, waiting for someone else to dictate who's going to end up in jail. Even if Charlie doesn't get along with her father particularly well, she's still hurt. I bet she's wondering why we're not like her friends' families, why we have to drive an hour away from home to find some peace.

Somehow my past is repeating itself, and she's feeling what I used to feel when I was younger.

I have to find a remedy for this.

"There you are." Rose cuts off our conversation, a cocktail glass in hand.

"Where were you?" I smile, glancing up.

Since we got here yesterday, Rose has been wandering around the house, searching through drawers, shelves, and the wardrobe for something. I don't think she even knows what. I'm not entirely sure why she's acting so mysterious. But she seems... distant in a way.

It's hard to read her. She's different, distracted.

"I went for a swim." Rose points at the ocean, her bikini drips water over the balcony tiles.

"Charlie, do you mind if your mom and I have some alone time?" Rose asks, laying on the balustrade.

"Okay. I was going to go check out a party on the beach anyway." Charlie gets up quickly, passing fingers through her hair.

"A party?" I frown. *What kind of party?*

"Oh, she'll be fine, Madeline. It's just at the house next to us." Rose smiles.

"Be careful," I yell towards the bedroom. The door clicks shut behind her. Charlie has already disappeared around a corner of the house. Rose sits on the swing chair where Charlie was just a few seconds before.

"She'll be fine. Let her have some fun," Rose exclaims, raising her glass and taking a sip.

"I know. I have to trust her. It's so hard though, she's growing up too quickly."

Rose shifts on the swing chair, placing her empty glass on the floor. "You know, I've noticed something about you. You're changing."

There's something in her eyes that confuses me. I try to brush off this feeling, but her words make my heart race. And the longer I don't respond, the longer I look suspicious. "What do you mean?" I clench my jaw.

She doesn't answer right away. Her fingers trail along the armrest of the swing. "You've always been... so loyal to Tyler." Rose pauses, almost as if she has to think twice before saying more. "But I think you know, deep down, that you don't want to be married to him anymore."

I swallow hard, biting the inside of my cheeks. "I—I don't think I understand where you're going with this."

Rose chuckles, scratching her scalp nervously. "Why don't you want to face the truth?"

I'm not sure what she knows, what she's thinking. It's like she's being indirect on purpose, like she's tempting me to dig into her mind until I find out what she wants to tell me. But I've never liked mind games.

"What are you trying to say?" A knot forms in my chest as I ask that question. *I'm not sure if I want to know the answer.*

"You're not fooling anyone," she leans closer, her eyebrows arching, "I know what you're really afraid of, Madeline." Rose's knee touches mine as she slides closer, her head tilting to one side. "You're afraid of what I could give you."

I freeze. "What are you talking about?"

She lets out a slow breath. "I would do anything just to make you see me the way I see you."

What the hell is she saying? She's my best friend.

This can't be real. She can't be saying these things.

My chest tightens and I pull my legs away from hers instinctively. My heart is racing. I can't handle this. I can't even begin to process it. I've never *ever* looked at her in a different way. I can see Rose swallowing, her eyes wandering around until she meets mine again.

"Rose, I..." I don't want to hurt her, but she has to know the truth. "I don't... I don't feel that way about you."

Her lips twitch into a small smile for a moment.

And then I realize. *The protective best friend. The one who always had my back. But all along, she's been falling for me. My* stomach churns. I don't want to hurt Rose, but I can't help but question everything I thought I knew about her. I look at her and see the vulnerability in her eyes. I see the way she's holding herself together, but I know she's breaking on the inside. I draw in a shaky breath. "I'm sorry," I whisper.

Rose rolls her eyes to the sky and her reaction makes me tilt my head back. "No, you're not."

Something inside me snaps, a cold rush of panic floods my veins. I don't understand why she's angry. I understand that rejection hurts, but what did she expect from me? She knows that I love Tyler; I would never break that bond or ruin our friendship the way she wants to.

"I don't want to hurt you. I never wanted to hurt you. You're my best friend and this will never change."

"I've always been there for you and you never once appreciated it. No one else would've done the things I've done for you —*no one*." She points a finger to her chest.

Why is she reacting this way? I never asked her to do anything, and it was always a two-way thing. Rose has been there for me, and I've been there for her too. This situation is making me anxious, too anxious. For the first time, I look at Rose and I see someone else. *Someone who could have got rid of anyone standing between us: Sadie. Daniel. Even Tyler. She hates Tyler.*

My mind races. I need space. I stand up abruptly, almost knocking over the small table in front of us. "I... I need to go," my voice shakes. "I need some time on my own." I don't wait for her response. I don't even look at her. I just head for the door and rush downstairs, my bare feet sinking in the sand.

I don't even know what I'm running from anymore. Or who.

The salty sea breeze does little to ease my nerves as I scan the shoreline. My heart skips a beat when I spot Charlie standing near a group of older boys on the porch of the house next to Rose's beach house.

"Charlie!" I call. She shifts from one foot to the other. Slowly, she turns towards me, her lips parting, her eyes blinking in disbelief—as if she's just seen an alien. The guys are holding up red plastic cups, but she isn't. Although there is one on top of the bench she is holding on to.

"Mom, what are you doing here?"

I reach her quickly, ignoring the curious gazes of the boys surrounding her.

"Are you drinking?" I ask, shooting a look at the older guys.

Charlie rolls her eyes and pushes a strand of sandy hair away from her face. "No... this is soda," she says, pointing at the cup on the bench.

I sigh. "It's late, let's go back home."

Charlie hesitates. "But..." She glances at the boys. As I tilt my head to the side and raise my eyebrows, she sighs and nods, walking back beside me. "You're so annoying sometimes!" She speeds up, quickly moving in front of me, her fists clenched.

I roll my eyes. Maybe I'm not perfect, maybe I stumble and fall along the way, but that doesn't make me a bad mother. *I will always protect her.*

And I don't care what Rose, Tyler, or his family think about me. I'd rather be a bad friend or a bad wife a thousand times over than be a bad mother, even once.

My phone buzzes in my pocket, and a message from Rose pops up:

You can't run away from the truth.

THIRTY-SEVEN

MADELINE

July 6, 8:00AM

Blinking away memories of a sleepless night, I stretch, feeling the tension in my muscles before pulling myself out of bed.

It was hard to switch off my brain last night when I knew that Rose was in the room next to Charlie and me.

Her behavior creeped me out and that message couldn't have been clearer. She would do anything to have me all to herself.

If it were just me, I wouldn't feel this weight on my shoulders. But Tyler is bound to an ankle monitor and I keep wondering what Rose said to Detective Rynn. *Is she the reason that my husband is now under house arrest?*

I never knew she liked women. I always knew that she hated Tyler, but I would never have imagined she had feelings for me in that way.

I step on to the balcony, I inhale deeply and the salty morning air fills my lungs, almost soothing me... until my phone rings on the desk right next to the window. I grab it quickly and close the balcony window before me, not wanting to wake Charlie.

Detective Rynn is calling.

This can't be good. "Hello?"

"Good morning, Madeline. We've received the DNA results from the knife recovered at the guesthouse and the full autopsy report of Sadie. We need to speak with you at the station as soon as possible."

My breath catches in my throat. "Um, okay. I'm in the Hamptons, but I will be there as soon as I can."

I hang up and stand there paralyzed for a moment.

What are they going to say? Am I in trouble?

I glance back into the bedroom. Charlie is still asleep. I don't want to wake her, I don't want to drag her into whatever this is. *But we have to go.*

My stomach churns like I'm about to throw up and my mind races.

What if this is the moment they find something on Tyler and there's no way back?

What if Rose framed him?

The knife.

The guesthouse.

Sadie and Daniel's deaths.

Why would they call me now, at this point in the investigation when the trial date is approaching? Has something new come to light? Or worse, are they blaming me for what happened to Sadie?

No, no. That can't be it.

In the pool, Rose glides through the water on a yellow float, her hands slicing the surface of the water. Watching her from afar, I already feel nostalgic about our friendship. I don't know if things will ever be the same after what she told me.

I rush downstairs to the edge of the pool, my arms crossed to my chest. Rose notices me and places her hands on her lap, smiling.

"Charlie and I are leaving now."

Her eyebrows rise and she tilts her head back gently. "Leaving? Where?"

"We're going back home. Detective Rynn called, I have to go to the station."

Rose scoffs, pushing herself to the edge of the pool. She gets out and water drips from her wet hair. "What did the detective say to make you decide to leave so urgently?"

"Rose, it's important for me to show up for anything at a detective's request."

Her jaw tightens. "So, you're just running away from me—"

"I'm not running away." My voice rises. "I have to go," I finally say, turning back into the house.

She sighs and turns away with a dismissive wave of her hand. "Fine."

I ignore Rose's manner and continue wondering what Detective Rynn wants from me. The more my mind spins with thoughts, the more the sea within me starts to get stormy, violently crashing my insides.

I wake Charlie gently; her tousled hair is spread across the pillow. "Charlie," I say, brushing a strand of hair away from her face. She stirs slightly, frowning with confusion.

"What's up?" she growls.

"We need to leave," I respond. My voice trembles even though I promised myself that I would be stronger for her. *But how can I?*

I can't control where this situation is going.

She sits up slowly. "Why?"

Tears well up in my eyes as I take a deep breath, struggling to find the right words. I don't want to scare her. "Detective Rynn called and I have to go to the station."

Her eyes widen in disbelief. "Did something happen to Dad?"

I sit beside her on the bed, gathering her hands in mine. "No. They want to ask me some questions."

Her brows rise. "But you didn't do anything wrong, did you?"

I shake my head gently, my heart breaking. I can't keep doing this for long. "Neither has your dad. They just need some more information from me before the trial, that's all."

Charlie nods slowly, her lower lip quivers as she processes the news. "I don't want Dad or you to go to jail—"

"We'll be fine. Please don't think like that."

She nods again and her gaze drops to her lap. I wrap my arms around her, holding her close.

I can't lose my daughter.

I won't let them take me away from her.

"C'mon, pack your stuff. We need to go," I push.

Charlie nods. She moves quickly towards the bathroom and stands in front of the mirror to brush her teeth and hair. I feel so guilty knowing that this isn't what she expected from this getaway, from her family. Everything she knew has been destroyed since Rose and I found Daniel's body right outside our home.

I wish I could go back. I wish I had never found his body.

"Are you ready?" Charlie asks, grabbing her bag.

"Yes."

She nods. I know it isn't easy for her to go back to reality. A reality she doesn't belong to. She should live peacefully and be able to hang out with her friends without having to hear them asking questions about her father. But it's hard when people like Tyler get in trouble. Powerful people who also own a business that's about to fail. It's all over the news these days: drama after drama about the Johnson family.

"Is Rose staying here?" Charlie asks, glancing at the window. Rose is sunbathing by the side of the pool, seemingly unconcerned about the circumstances.

"Yes."

"I'll go to say goodbye—"

"No," I cut her off, shaking my head. I don't want Charlie to speak to her right now.

Charlie looks at me with a puzzled expression.

"Sorry, there's no time." As we make our way to the main street, my fingers tremble as I dial Tyler's number. The line rings once, twice, before going to voicemail. I swallow the lump in my throat.

"We're coming back home. I have to go to the police station to speak with Detective Rynn. Just thought I would let you know."

I immediately call a taxi. When it arrives, the yellow car stops and the trunk opens automatically. I place our bags inside and get into the passenger seat.

As the car moves away, Charlie glances out the window, looking back at Rose's beach house. I wonder what she's thinking; I wonder if she's angry at me, but she's keeping it all inside.

And I don't blame her.

THIRTY-EIGHT
DETECTIVE RYNN

July 6, 11:00AM

I flip through the case file and remove a photo of the knife—the murder weapon. I slide it across the metallic table.

Madeline glances at the picture, then at me, confused.

"We found your DNA on the kitchen knife. Along with your husband's and Sadie's. So, I need to ask—how did your DNA end up on that knife?"

For a moment, she stares at the blood-stained knife in the picture and then she slides it back to me. "I have nothing to do with this, but I used to visit the guesthouse before we hired Sadie. I must've touched it then."

I raise an eyebrow instinctively. "Before you hired her? That was like what, three and a half months ago? You didn't use that knife recently?"

"I don't remember, Detective. That knife could have been used to slice the cake at Charlie's birthday, I don't know which one it was. What I mean is that the guesthouse belongs to my family, so you will find fingerprints everywhere there."

"Let's talk about Sadie." I slide another photo across the

table—it's an image of Sadie's head pressed against the window of Madeline's car, her eyes closed. "The autopsy report says she died from inhaling liquefied petroleum gas while she was in your car. The weird thing is, it wasn't from a gas leak or anything ordinary. It came from the yoga ball found in the passenger seat. That ball was deflated when we found it."

Madeline's brow furrows. "The yoga ball? That's... that's insane."

I lean forward, trying my best to search for the truth in her eyes. "The ball was used to hold a lethal amount of liquefied petroleum gas. You see, Sadie must've been exposed to it for a long time—long enough for her to inhale enough gas to cause her to pass out from suffocation. When we examined the ball, we found traces of something strange inside it. The ball was supposed to be inflated with regular air, but someone inflated it with gas canisters. When that ball was deflated, it released the gas that killed her. Mind explaining why you did it?"

Madeline places a hand to her chest, shaking her head as if she would never, *ever*, do something like that. "This sound awful. I... I don't know why you think I did it. It could've easily been someone from her yoga class. Why would I do that to Sadie?"

"So, now you're suggesting that someone else inflated the yoga ball with gas? You told me previously that you were the one who deflated it."

Madeline clears her throat.

I'm not sure what game she's playing at, but Madeline Johnson is a hell of a liar.

"Yes, it could have been someone from Sadie's yoga class. Besides, if the gas was coming from the ball, wouldn't I be dead now too?" She tries to deflect, her voice growing in confidence as she focuses on a possible loophole in my theory. "If I was in the car with Sadie, then why didn't I suffocate? Why didn't I die too?"

I nod slowly, twisting my lips. She has a point. But I'm positive that the gas was released *after* Madeline left the car. Thing is, it's not possible to prove that. "When we took your car, we noticed it was filled with gas. Did you stop at any gas stations on the way back home?"

Madeline blinks once. Twice. *Is she going to lie?*

"No, I refilled my car the day before."

"Do you have any evidence to prove that? Someone who saw you fill up your tank the day before perhaps?"

I'm not going to give up until you confess, Madeline.

"No. I did self-service. I was there by myself." She responds quickly, almost as if it really did happen.

But I'm one step ahead. Always.

I lean back on the metallic chair, folding my arms. "So, you're telling me, after all this—the gas, the yoga ball, the DNA on the knife—you've got no alibi, no witnesses, no one who saw you refill your car. And yet, here you are, saying you have no idea what happened to Sadie *and* Daniel. I find it hard to believe that you didn't commit either of these crimes, Madeline. Very hard."

Madeline shifts in her chair, shrugging her shoulders as she leans back. "I won't say another word without my lawyer present."

I almost laugh. "Oh, how convenient. Who is this lawyer again? Your husband's sister? You really think she's going to defend you over her own brother?"

"Tyler and I are in this together."

"No, Madeline. You're not. It's either you or him who will go behind bars. Or both of you. That's how I see it. You can leave now." I stand, scraping my chair back, but Madeline remains seated.

"I know who did it."

My eyebrows arch and I sit down again. If she hasn't done talking, I'm all ears. "What are you saying?"

"Victoria Parker."

I cock my head back. "Why would Victoria Parker kill her own son and Sadie?"

Madeline hesitates for a moment and glances at the floor before meeting my eyes. "Victoria came to my office and my home to threaten me. Tyler had to give her money or else she would have done something stupid. Perhaps she got rid of Sadie to send us a message."

Nothing Madeline says makes sense. It looks like she's trying to buy time by distracting us. I fold my arms again. "And how does Daniel fit into this?"

Her lips curl into a thin line, her gaze is steady. "Can I tell you something off the record?"

"I can't promise that anything stays off the record, Madeline."

Madeline looks away, then back at me. "Victoria hired a private investigator to look into me and my family, and I don't want anything about my past to come out in a way that could be misinterpreted as incriminating. It was a stupid mistake..."

My eyes narrow. "What is it?"

"I slept with him." Madeline blushes as if it's the first time she has ever said this out loud.

My arms drop to the side of the chair and I have to compose myself before asking the next question.

"You slept with Daniel Johnson?" I repeat, raising my eyebrows.

Madeline nods.

I rub my temples as I process this new, unexpected information. "So now we're supposed to believe that Victoria Parker went from being slightly possessive over her son and your family to becoming a full-blown murderer?"

She nods again. "Yes. That woman is crazy. She's mentally unstable."

My lips twitch. "What part do you play in this little twisted love triangle? You really think that admitting you slept with Daniel is going to clear your name, just because you came forward instead of us finding out?"

Madeline shakes her head. "I just told you this because I didn't want it to come out at trial."

"So Tyler doesn't know then, does he?" I sigh. "I'm not going to be the one who spills out your little secret, but this is unlikely to stay only between us."

She leans forward. "I didn't do anything wrong."

I slowly stand, pushing my chair back. "You keep saying that, but I'm not sure you believe it yourself."

Madeline gets up. "What's going to happen now?"

"Tyler's trial is tomorrow." I open the door and flash a warning look towards her. "You will either play the role of key witness, or you will sit next to your husband at the next hearing." I tilt my head towards the exit. "It's up to you which side you want to pick."

She grabs her bag and heads out, her gaze fixed in front of her.

Madeline knew Daniel. They had an affair. I don't know to what extent, how long it carried on, but she knew him.

The truth is buried somewhere beneath her practiced calm, but am I getting to it? It's going to take more than simply asking a few questions.

THIRTY-NINE
MADELINE

July 6, 3:30PM

Every corner of my mind whispers doubts and unanswered questions until the weight of it all makes me so restless that I can't sit still.

I stand and grab my glass of wine, my fourth or fifth of the afternoon, and take a long, burning sip; the liquid fuels the fire of my anger and despair.

In an uncontrollable rage, I scream and throw the glass against the living room wall, watching it shatter into a thousand tiny pieces. The red liquid stains the walls he painted.

It's all Tyler's fault.

Because of him, now Detective Rynn is on to me.

Because of how kind I've been to him, now my family is being investigated by the police.

And my daughter, my baby, is suffering.

Tears stream down my face as I start tearing my home apart. I take down every framed photo from the walls and shelves; every picture that once told the story of our love now feels like a fucking lie, and perhaps it is.

It's not about assumptions anymore, I know what he's doing. I don't want to be part of his sick game. I don't want to be part of his family.

I've been such an idiot. And it hurts, deeply.

Each small gift he ever gave me, each token of fake affection, ends up where it belongs, the trash can. The house soon becomes a mess of broken glass, torn photographs, and discarded memories.

My breathing is ragged, my heart pounds, and my vision blurs as I struggle to walk in a straight line. I collapse on the carpet, my back on the couch, my body trembling with sobs.

Why?

"I just want to know why," I say to myself, sobbing, my hand holding my forehead, my knees hugged close to my chest. "Why do you keep all these secrets from me? What have you done?"

The front door opens and I rise quickly, maybe *too* quickly, tasting my own tears.

Everything is spinning as Tyler steps into the living room, his clothes stick to his skin, drenched in sweat. He was probably working out in the backyard. He didn't hear me coming in, even though he knew I'd been interrogated by the police the whole morning.

He doesn't care about me.

My heart starts beating faster and faster. Each of his steps feel like a threat and I can't help but be scared of him.

Scared of the person who used to make me feel the safest.

His eyes widen in shock at the sight of the shattered glass, torn photos, and discarded gifts. Tyler rushes to my side, his eyes filled with worry.

"What happened?"

Fuck. You. Motherfucker.

"Stay away from me." I cover my eyes with my hands. I just want to be left alone.

I can't bear to look at him.

I don't want to see him, I can't.

I can't let his begging to stay get to me.

He doesn't give a shit about me.

He just wants the money and to save his fucked company.

Tyler pauses. "Madeline, talk to me. What's going on?"

"Don't come any closer," I repeat.

"Madeline, you're drunk. Let me take you to bed."

"I don't want you near me. Don't you get it?" I scream, still covering my face with my hands.

Tyler gently tries to pull my hands away from my eyes.

"Fuck you. Move," I say, jerking away from Tyler, focusing on keeping my eyes anywhere but on him.

I stumble, trying to walk upstairs without falling back, but a piece of glass stings the underside of my right foot. My expression betrays the sudden pain.

"Did you hurt yourself?" Tyler's voice is filled with concern as he sees me stop and rushes over. I can feel his breath on my shoulder, his damn perfume invades my senses as he places his fingers around my arm.

"This is nothing compared to the hell you've put me through." I push his hand away and slowly continue up the stairs, the pain from the glass shard intensifies with each step.

"Madeline, what the fuck are you saying? Do you still believe I had something to do with Daniel? What did the police tell you?"

"It's not for that, asshole. I wish you were in jail already."

"You're incredibly rude when you drink."

That comment ignites a fire within me.

I turn, descending the three stairs I've managed to climb, and lock eyes with the devil.

My eyebrows furrow, the corners of my lips quiver. Every part of my body is pushing me to cry, but I can't.

I can't.

"I want you to..." I start, struggling to push away my fake

feelings for him, "go away," I finish. I feel a huge pang of remorse in my stomach.

The curse's demons make me feel so guilty, and the mix of alcohol and raw emotion make me feel like I'm going to throw up or faint at any moment.

I clutch the railing, trying to steady myself, fighting against the overwhelming urge to collapse under the weight of my own despair.

Tyler takes a step back. "Madeline, I don't understand. What happened?"

"What happened?" I echo, my voice breaking. "You happened, Tyler. In my life. You and your lies. Your manipulation. I won't be your puppet anymore. Tomorrow you will be sent to jail and I won't need to see you anymore."

His eyes widen. "Is this what the police told you?"

"All of this," I say, pointing at the broken framed photos on the floor, "it can go up in flames for all I care." I clench my teeth as I look at him, my rage barely contained.

"Please, Madeline. You're drunk. Let me help you get upstairs, clean up your foot, and put you to bed."

"I'm more sober than I've ever been," I say, hiding my shaking hands behind my back. The conflicting emotions I'm feeling are tearing me apart.

Tyler snorts and raises his hands.

"You know what? Do whatever you want, Madeline. At the end of the day, we both know that your words are just words," he says, giving up and sitting on the sofa, his eyes filled with a dark, threatening certainty. He thinks I can't leave.

But this time I will, because I know. I know that these feelings pulling me closer are just made to break me, to forget forever the person that I am. That I used to be.

Maybe I can use the fact that he doesn't know I know to my advantage. But how can I do that when every fiber of my being wants to forgive him, to kiss him, to fall to my knees and beg for him to never leave me?

The thought of losing him feels like losing my skill to breathe properly. A slow walk towards death.

What if I have to work through this feeling to finally get rid of him?

I take a deep breath, fighting against the tidal wave of emotions. "You think you have me figured out. But you don't know me. You have no idea who I am."

He raises an eyebrow. "Is that so?"

"Yes."

I turn away from him, heading more purposefully up the stairs. Each step embeds the glass in my foot more deeply into my skin, but I push through the pain. *I will not let him control me any longer.*

Reaching the top of the stairs, I pause, looking down at my soon-to-be ex-husband. "You'll see."

He doesn't respond, just watches me with infuriating indifference.

I retreat to our bedroom, closing the door behind me.

My heart pounds, my mind races—I can really feel the glass in my foot right now.

I sit on the en-suite bathroom floor, carefully removing the glass and cleaning the wound. The pain shoots through me, but it's not enough to make me cry. Nothing will ever cause me pain like he did.

As soon as I finish cleaning the blood around my wound, I twist my body and throw up in the toilet. Tears stream down my face and I wipe them away.

I lean against the wall, my body and my mind are exhausted.

All I wanted in my life was to be truly loved. But instead, he lied to me, like my parents did.

I slowly get up and splash some water on my face. I haven't

seen myself in this drunken state since my early twenties, and boy, I don't look good. At all.

Fuck him.

I will push myself to get rid of the stupid feelings that have trapped me for years and I will show him how strong I truly am.

And after that, with a graceful royal bow, I will shout at the top of my lungs for him to fuck off.

FORTY

MADELINE

July 6, 7:00PM

I wake up three hours later with a pounding headache and I can't help but moan even before I open my eyes.

The room is spinning, my mouth is dry, and I don't have the energy to lift a finger.

As soon as the bedside table stops shaking, I see a hand-written note on a glass of water.

Drink me :) I love you and I'm sorry.

My eyes roll in frustration—his obsession is evident: Tyler really wants the inheritance and he won't let me go, no matter how many scenes I cause.

One good thing about me is that I remember every single thing I do while I'm drunk, and unlike the times where I have regrets, I don't regret a single thing.

As soon as I get up and head downstairs, I see Tyler standing in front of the main door, holding red roses and heart-shaped balloons.

It feels like a punch in my stomach, and I can't figure out if it's butterflies or remorse. A part of me feels like I should apologize for earlier, but I resist the urge.

I can't pretend that everything is fine anymore. But I have to play dumb in his twisted game until I figure what to do.

"Thanks," I manage to say, forcing a smile. "I appreciate it."

He steps closer, trying to read my expression. "About this afternoon... I know things got heated, but I want us to work through it. You're so important to me and I can't afford to lose you. Are we okay?"

I take the roses from his hands. "We are," I lie.

"I ordered Chinese takeout," he continues, his eyes searching mine. "I want to make it up to you."

I nod, knowing I must play along for now. "Alright. Sounds nice."

Tyler's face brightens. "Great. I was craving it."

I place the roses in a vase and fill it with water from the sink. Detective Rynn's words echo in my head: *You will either play the role of a key witness or you will sit next to your husband at the next hearing. It's up to you which side you want to pick.*

I won't sit next to my husband in jail. I won't let them take Charlie away from me. I have to make a plan.

I will play the part of the loving wife, no matter how much it tears me apart inside, and I will remind myself that every sweet thing he says to me is a lie. *For money.* That's all he cares about.

Tyler glances at me placing the flowers in the middle of the coffee table in the living room. "We need to talk about your drinking."

"What about it?"

He sighs. "You were completely out of control. You know I don't like it when you drink that much. It's not good for you, and it's certainly not good for us. What if Charlie saw you? Thank God she was out."

My lips press into a thin line. *How dare he talk about Charlie when he barely remembers when her birthday is?* "I just needed to unwind, Tyler. Things have been stressful lately. As you know."

He shakes his head. "That's not an excuse. You need to find healthier ways to deal with stress. Drinking like that isn't going to solve anything."

I nod. "You're right. I'll try to be more mindful in the future."

Tyler reaches over and squeezes my hand. "I just want what's best for you. I care about you and I want us to be happy."

I look at our intertwined hands and fight the urge to pull away. "We can't pretend to be the perfect family, Tyler. Your trial starts tomorrow."

Our conversation is interrupted by the doorbell. *Thankfully.* I was almost going to explode.

He's touching my nerves a bit too much.

Tyler grabs the two Tupperware containers and places them on the coffee table next to the flowers. He sets two pillows on the floor in front of the table. I step closer, sitting next to him. "I ordered you duck noodles, your favorite," he points out, pushing my portion towards me. "We should order sushi sometimes, just for a change."

I suppress an eye roll and offer a polite smile. He knows I don't like it. "Yeah, maybe one day."

He sighs, shaking his head. "Besides, how can you say you're a foodie if you always stick to the same thing?"

"I don't say I'm a foodie. I just have my preferences."

Tyler continues to lecture me about the virtues of sushi, but I let his words wash over me.

I don't care.

"Also," he takes out the chopsticks from the delivery bag, placing them on the side of my plate, "you should learn how to use chopsticks. It's embarrassing that you don't know how to use them at your age."

I have to bite my inner cheeks to keep my face neutral. "I prefer using a fork. I'm more comfortable with it."

He sighs. "Let me show you how to use them."

He picks up my chopsticks and begins demonstrating like I'm a five-year-old kid. "You hold them like this," he says, positioning my fingers on the chopsticks. "It's not that hard, Madeline. You just need to practice."

I force a smile. "Thanks."

As he watches, I awkwardly attempt to use the chopsticks, struggling to grasp the noodles. He continues his commentary, oblivious to my growing frustration. "See? It's not so difficult. Just a bit of practice and you'll get it."

I manage a few bites with the chopsticks before giving up and discreetly switching back to my fork when he's not looking.

Tyler notices right away. "Are you kidding? Hiding like a child to be lazy and not learn how to eat properly?"

"I don't enjoy having to eat slowly because you want me to use chopsticks. It shouldn't be that big of an issue."

"Whatever, it sounds like you're always right. Keep going, being so perfect like you think you are. I don't care. It's just embarrassing for me."

I can't play this part anymore. I get up. "That's it, I've had enough," I say, grabbing my plate and going to sit at the counter in the kitchen.

"What the hell is wrong with you now? I don't get it. We're supposed to be having a nice dinner. You're not supposed to be throwing tantrums over chopsticks."

"You know what, Tyler? Since the day of our anniversary is approaching, get this, you have two options: you either remain married to me and refuse to get the inheritance from your grandmother, or we divorce and you get all your precious money."

His jaw drops. "Wh... what? This is ridiculous. It would be our money, not just mine."

I shrug my shoulders. "I don't care. Think about it, the anniversary is in just over a month. I want a marriage that is built on real love, not around cash."

Tyler's face pales.

It's clear he's struggling with not being fully in control anymore.

And that realization seems to be eating him alive.

FORTY-ONE

MADELINE

July 7, 9:00AM

Victoria Parker grips the railing of the staircase in the courthouse.

It's like she's putting all her weight on it, like she can't stand on her own two feet anymore. Black circles surround her eyes—partly makeup, partly the result of stress and sleepless nights.

I keep wondering whether the police will think that she might have had something to do with her son's murder. Like I said to Detective Rynn, maybe Daniel reminded Victoria of Tyler's family, of Dave, the man who rejected her, who kept her and Daniel hidden in shame.

She's dressed in a turquoise suit; high, pointy heels make her appear slimmer and taller than she is. The prosecutor is standing next to her, holding a file that might contain information about my husband. Information that could send him to jail.

I spin my heels around, glancing around to check if someone has seen me, but Tyler's parents haven't arrived yet.

The courtroom door is open, the sound of my heels bounces

from wall to wall; I feel like the eyes of all the ghosts in this room are focused on me.

Rose is sitting all the way at the back wearing sunglasses. She waves a hand in my direction, but I sit behind Tyler and Laura's table and ignore her. We haven't spoken since she shared her feelings for me, and I can't handle her right now. I have too many things in my mind already.

I shouldn't be worried though, this trial isn't about Sadie, it's about Daniel. I will be fine even if they call me to the stand.

Tyler's family finally walk in. Pam and Dave sit together next to me, their bodies tense for the first time.

"Where's Charlie?" Pam asks, glancing around the room.

"Home. I don't want her to see whatever is going to happen," I respond. Pam raises her eyebrows like she can't believe her ears, but she doesn't say anything.

Nothing good ever comes from a courtroom. I don't want Charlie to attend a trial where there could be more lies told than truths. I want her to live a normal life for as long as possible. Even though defining our lives as "normal" is a challenge at the moment.

Victoria and her lawyer enter the courtroom, followed by Laura and Tyler, who sit in front of us. Tyler turns to squeeze my hand for an instant, before a cold look from Laura makes him shrink back. She then turns her gaze towards me for a few seconds. Not blinking, just staring.

She thinks I have something to do with it.

Of course—she is defending her brother.

Too bad she won't find anything on me.

Everyone stands and sits in unison as the judge makes his entrance into the courtroom. "We are here today to begin the trial of Tyler Johnson, charged with the murder of his half-brother, Daniel Johnson. Prosecution, you may present your opening statement."

The prosecutor stands, straightening her tie. "Ladies and

gentlemen of the jury, the case before you is one of betrayal, greed, and cold-blooded murder. On May 5, Daniel Johnson was found killed in front of the defendant's home with a head wound and a stab wound to the stomach. We identified the murder weapon, a knife found inside the previous accommodation of the Johnsons' maid, Sadie Kelsey, before she was killed, too. And there's more."

She pauses, studying Tyler and my eyes for a moment. "Tyler was seen outside Daniel's building on the same morning; he changed into a new suit at lunchtime, but his DNA was found on Daniel's shirt. This would be enough to put him behind bars, but I'm not done here."

The prosecutor walks over to the evidence table and picks up *the* letter. "This is a letter from Tyler Johnson's lawyer about an inheritance from his late grandmother—an inheritance that would be delivered on the fifteenth anniversary of his marriage to Madeline Johnson."

I look at Tyler. He turns towards me, his face flushing red. He glances over at my fidgeting hands.

He can't even look me in the eyes. He probably thinks I handed the letter to the prosecutor.

And I did.

I was feeling angry, betrayed. He'd been thinking about divorcing me for a while, and he almost went through with it. But I forgave him. So, I don't see why he wouldn't forgive me if I handed that letter to the prosecutor. *An eye for an eye, right?*

"Five million dollars," the prosecutor continues, "who would want to split that?" She gestures to the public gallery, arching her eyebrows.

"Objection, Your Honor." Laura stands, shooting a look at the prosecutor.

"I'm done here," the prosecutor says, sitting back on to her chair.

Laura takes a deep breath. "Tyler Johnson is not the man

the prosecution would have you believe. And the idea that he killed his brother for money? It's a theory based on nothing but assumptions. In fact, it's not even the most pressing question here. Someone else died within Tyler and Madeline's household: Sadie, the maid. She died in Madeline's car... and the cause of death? Liquefied petroleum gas poisoning. The strange thing? She was killed by a yoga ball. It's... unorthodox to say the least."

I frown. *What's going on? Why is Laura talking about Sadie?*

This trial is about Daniel's death; it's not about Sadie.

She takes a step towards the jury box. "Sadie was not a random victim, and her death was not an accident. I believe that someone wanted her to stay silent—someone who was hiding their own secrets. Secrets that were far more dangerous than Tyler's alleged inheritance."

Laura gestures towards me and I feel lightheaded, dizzy. The crowd turns in my direction. I swallow, moving my eyes around, trying to process what's happening.

At least Charlie is not here to witness this.

"Those secrets belonged to Madeline Johnson. Tyler Johnson is innocent. The truth will come to light."

My face tightens, but I don't react. I don't blink.

I'm not afraid of her. They're trying to pull me into a storm, but they have nothing. That's the truth.

The old me, Evelyn, might have been terrified at those words. But Madeline Johnson isn't like Evelyn.

Madeline Johnson is not afraid of anyone.

FORTY-TWO

DETECTIVE RYNN

July 7, 10:00AM

Someone chuckles from the right side of the courtroom, where the prosecutor stands.

I don't care to see who it is, but then it carries on a bit longer than expected.

I crane my neck only to catch a glimpse of Victoria Parker, her hand pressed to her mouth, trying to stifle her amusement. I roll my eyes and turn back to face the judge, trying to ignore the ridiculousness of it all.

Madeline had told me they paid Victoria to stop, but whatever money they gave her clearly wasn't enough.

What's it gonna take? Probably the only thing that would give her relief would be to see the Johnsons in a cell.

The prosecutor finally breaks the silence, cutting through the heightened tension in the room. "Your Honor, the prosecution would like to call its first witness—Madeline Johnson."

My pulse quickens. *Here we go.*

I wonder which side Madeline decided to pick. *Is she going to tell the truth, or is she going to keep being a coward?*

All eyes turn to her as she steps forward behind the stand. I didn't expect Tyler's family to try to tear her down this way. But I guess that's what happens when you're not a blood relation of the Johnsons. Tyler would rather be against his wife than his family.

I bet that Madeline won't give up so easily. Somehow, I think these games only make her stronger.

The prosecutor clears her throat. "Tell me, Madeline, what was your husband doing on the morning of May 5, before he left home?"

"Tyler woke up around six, as he usually does. He was smoking in the living room before he left home."

The prosecutor steps right in front of her. "Smoking what specifically?"

"Weed."

"Are you sure, Mrs. Johnson? You're absolutely sure that Tyler was smoking weed?"

Madeline hesitates for an instant. "I... I think so."

"Did Tyler ever smoke anything else? Anything that might have affected his judgment? Made him, perhaps, forget what he was doing?"

My stomach tightens. The truth is, we have no idea how scopolamine made its way into Tyler's system that day if he didn't take it himself. But the way he behaved during the interrogation... it wasn't just nerves. There was something off, something forced about his denial. I can't shake the feeling that he's lying about never using drugs.

"I'm not sure."

Tyler shoots Madeline a look. He would probably yell at her right now if he could. Tyler Johnson is a man with no patience at all.

"Let's talk about your relationship with Tyler. You've been married to him for how long, Mrs. Johnson?"

"Almost fifteen years."

I wonder if Madeline is excited about reaching that milestone, considering the inheritance and all...

"In that time, did you ever feel scared of your husband?"

The temperature of the room rises.

"Yes," she almost whispers.

I clench my jaw. I didn't expect the prosecution to ask such probing questions.

Tyler's lawyer, Laura, shakes her head in disapproval.

"Can you tell us about those times?"

Madeline fidgets. "Sometimes... Tyler overreacts to the smallest things. He broke furniture. Threw things. Insulted me."

The prosecutor raises her eyebrows. It looks like she didn't expect this answer. "Did he ever hit you?"

"No."

"How did his reactions affect your relationship with him?"

"It made me feel... trapped. Like I couldn't escape. Like I had no say. But I always believed—I always believed he would change. That it was just a phase. So, I stayed."

"I'm done with my questions, Your Honor." The prosecutor nods and sits back behind her table, writing down some notes.

Laura steps closer, leaning her head to one side, smiling like this is a joke. Like Madeline's feelings about Tyler's behavior are a joke. But if everything that Madeline says is true, which it could be based on the way her lips are trembling, then *that* is abuse. "Madeline, you've just told us that you stayed with Tyler because you loved him. But tell me, did you love him as a person —or did you love the life he could give you? The money? The expensive townhouse on the Upper East Side?"

I know where this is heading. Laura is trying to undermine Madeline's credibility, to paint her as someone who cares more about money than her husband. But Madeline doesn't strike me as that type of person. I can tell from the way she's dressed, from her relaxed hairstyle, that she is not a spoilt woman.

"I never cared about money. Tyler knows that better than anyone else."

Laura tilts her head back. "Then why stay with someone who treats you that way, Madeline? Why stay with someone who—by your own admission—scared you? Someone who broke furniture, insulted you? Why stay with someone who treats you so poorly, if not for the luxury, the lifestyle?"

"Because I love him. I stayed because I love him, despite everything."

"Right, right. Let's talk about love, then. Your former maid, Sadie, wasn't she... fond of Tyler? Perhaps a little more than she should have been?"

I shrug my shoulders. "Yes. She was."

"And did it bother you that your maid, the woman who was supposed to be taking care of your house, seemed overly interested in your husband?"

"No, it didn't bother me. Because I knew Tyler wasn't interested."

"Interesting. Well, let's move on then. The police found something rather telling in your guesthouse, where Sadie used to live. A board with photos of you on it. Why did Sadie have a photo board with pictures of you? What did she know about you, Madeline? And what about the fact that Sadie died in your car the same day you sneaked into the guesthouse? Should we call that a coincidence?"

As I listen to Laura Johnson describe the evidence in the guesthouse, my palms sweat and my legs tense. Something big is about to emerge from this investigation.

"I'm sorry—am I being questioned here? Why are you asking me about Sadie? This trial is about Daniel's murder, not Sadie's death," Madeline snaps.

"But you have to admit the coincidences are stacking up. Even the police believe there might be a connection. So I'm just confirming how far love can take us. Do you have any problems with that?" Laura raises her eyebrows and her lips curve into a smile.

Laura thinks she's winning, but Madeline looks at her like she wants to leap out of her seat and strangle her right here in front of everyone.

FORTY-THREE

MADELINE

July 7, 10:30AM

My head spins. Laura's words are like a noose tightening around my neck.

Laura grabs a photo from her table and shows it to everyone in the room. She then lays it over the stand for me to see. My eyes widen over that wrinkly photo.

A young Madeline, Evelyn at the time, smiling and laughing, with Daniel Johnson carrying her over his shoulders at a beach party.

What does Laura Johnson know?

"We found this picture of you and Daniel, taken at a beach party sixteen years ago. You never mentioned knowing Daniel before his death. Care to explain this?"

I exhale sharply. "I wouldn't say I knew him. He was just part of the group of people I hung out with back then."

"Well, in this picture you two seem pretty close."

I clench my jaw. "I was probably drunk."

Laura raises an eyebrow. "Weren't you underage back then?"

"Yes, underage. Christ, everyone drinks when they're minors. What are you implying?" I grit my teeth, my patience running thin.

"So, you didn't know that Daniel was Tyler's half-brother until his funeral, then?"

"I didn't know until the funeral. Yes. Your family did a great job keeping it secret."

Laura steps closer. "Did you keep in touch with Daniel after that beach party?"

I shake my head. "No. Like I said, he was just part of the group of friends I was hanging out with. People change. Not everyone keeps in touch with their college friends forever."

"However you're still close to a college friend, your best friend Rose."

I nod.

"So, your relationship with Daniel was nothing more than a brief, drunken encounter at a party years ago?"

"Correct."

Laura turns towards the judge. "Your Honor, we've heard testimony today about Madeline's proximity to both Daniel's death and the suspicious circumstances surrounding Sadie's. I believe the evidence at hand makes it clear that Madeline Johnson is a far more significant person of interest than Tyler Johnson. After all, she's the one whose behavior is most suspect. And as we can all see, she had the opportunity to manipulate the narrative to her advantage."

I bite the inside of my cheeks. This bitch wants to take me down.

The judge's gaze moves towards me and Tyler. He clears his throat. "Given the circumstances surrounding the two deaths, it's not out of the question to reconsider the terms of Tyler Johnson's house arrest. I will review all relevant evidence before making any decisions."

I wish I could tear down these walls, burn what's left, and disappear into the night.

But I can't.

I get up, my legs tremble as I walk out of the courtroom before everyone else. I push through the courthouse doors, my heels clicking against the stone steps.

I fix my gaze on my steps. I don't want to face anyone.

I keep my head down, but I can hear the reporters yelling and trying to stop me, I can see the cameras flashing, trying to blind my vision.

"Madeline Johnson, is your husband going to jail?"

"What happened to Sadie?"

"What do you know?"

I don't answer. My fingers tighten around the strap of my purse and I wrap my jacket around me as I push through the gathering crowd.

I grit my teeth as I run into a narrow alley and hide behind the fire stairs of an old brown building.

The reporters' voices seem to be going in a different direction.

The air suddenly thickens and my breathing accelerates; the protective walls I've built around me are slowly collapsing, squeezing the air from my lungs. A relentless drumbeat pounds in my ears. My vision blurs.

My body slides down the wall of the building. I can't feel my legs anymore.

Shadows stretch out, twisting and curling around me, colors melt into one another. I glance up, but the sky looks different.

I clutch my chest, struggling to breathe. I can't think straight, can't hear anything over the frantic pulse in my head.

"Madeline!" Rose calls my name. Her voice doesn't sound too distant, but I can't respond.

I can't find my words, can't find my breath.

There's nothing I can do to stop this.

There's nowhere I can hide long enough.

There's no way I can disappear.

I don't want to go home to face Tyler and his family.

They believe I did it, they believe I should go to jail, not him.

I always thought I had everything under control, that nothing would ever happen to me if I believed I was innocent myself.

But what if I was wrong?

FORTY-FOUR

DETECTIVE RYNN

July 9, 8:00AM

Two days since the trial and still no verdict. Extended deliberation is never a good sign. I don't believe in coincidences. The timing of everything is too clean. The jury's been given more evidence to sift through than I ever thought possible. The more suspects, the more potential angles, the more they have to question.

Interestingly enough, today there's a conference at Vertex Capital.

I'm certain Tyler Johnson, now that he's no longer on house arrest, will be there.

And so will I.

I don't believe he's completely innocent. After everything that came out in the media, he shouldn't be allowed to come back to work. He scammed people. But hey, he's a millionaire—there are plenty of people covering his ass.

I slip into the luxurious fabric of a red, sleeveless jumpsuit, feeling its silky texture against my skin. It accentuates my figure in all the right places. I'll be there undercover, just to keep an eye on things. Watching him, watching the crowd, making sure nothing slips through the cracks. But, of course, there's a good chance Tyler will recognize me. At least I'll try to find out if he's playing clean now, or if he still thinks he's untouchable despite his mistakes.

Stepping out the door of my new apartment, I glimpse Anthony's smile at the bottom of the stairs. He's wearing a suit. "You look stunning, Detective."

My partner has been very supportive over the past few weeks and eventually we got close. He invited me out for dinner once and we had a nice time.

I needed someone like him to get through this. Since the Johnsons' case began, I've been feeling like a failure. But then again, this family is fucked up. Everyone, literally everyone, has something to hide. It's going to be hard to find the sinner.

I smile at Anthony. "Thank you."

We catch a cab and get in. "Vertex Capital please," Anthony says to the driver before turning to me. "What do you think Tyler Johnson is going to say?"

"Nothing that will make him look bad. He'll put up a nice presentation to brainwash his followers. You'll see."

"How will we get in?"

I pull out two fake IDs. "With these." I hold them up for him to see.

"Great, they should do the trick," Anthony nods. "I bet they have a guest list."

We arrive at Vertex Capital, a towering building with sleek glass walls that gleam under the city lights.

"Ready?" Anthony asks, his eyes meeting mine.

"Always." I take a deep breath.

We step out of the taxi and make our way to the entrance, blending in with the crowd. Anthony and I take the lift to the fifth floor. The conference atmosphere is formal, with rows of chairs facing a stage where a large screen displays the Vertex Capital logo.

We shuffle through the crowd, careful not to bump into anyone. The people here are all suited up, they're mostly greedy men. They murmur in hushed tones about numbers, projections, and the next big move in cryptocurrency. I can't help but roll my eyes internally. Cryptocurrency is the new playground for the rich. A world where the rules are blurry, the risks high, and the rewards even higher. It's a game of smoke and mirrors where you don't need to understand the technology, you just need to have enough money to throw at it. I will never understand what all the excitement is about.

The men around me exchange business cards as if they've already figured out the secret to success.

Anthony and I take our seats; I can't help glancing towards the side of the backstage area. Blonde hair sways just beyond the curtains and, for a moment, I swear I see Tyler Johnson's wife. *But surely she wouldn't be at Tyler's conference?* I doubt she'd show her face, not after everything that went down at the trial. I bet the two of them aren't exactly doing great these days.

Soon enough, people start clapping and cheering.

The event has begun.

Tyler Johnson's silhouette is outlined against the bright lights. He stands confidently at the podium displaying a charming smile that was made to enchant people.

To make them believe him while he fills their ears with lies.

Will it work this time?

The stage lights illuminate his brushed-back hair. "Thanks everyone for being here. Today marks a significant milestone at Vertex Capital with the launch of our app."

He gestures around like he knows exactly what he's doing, like he's absolutely certain that everyone in this room is going to fall for it. "We look forward to a future where you will be able to have full control of your money." Tyler's gaze sweeps across the audience. "A revolution in the way we think about value and trust."

He pauses and points at the presentation behind him. "This app, it's going to be your weapon. It gives you the power to track your investments, manage your portfolio, and make real-time decisions that can alter the course of your financial future. And of course, it's backed by our cutting-edge technology that keeps your assets secure and your transactions transparent."

Suddenly, Tyler's face freezes as he glances to the side of the stage.

Someone just stepped out. A woman strides on to his stage, ruining his speech.

Madeline.

What is she doing?

Her movements are unsteady, like she's fighting to stay grounded, but her feet can't quite find the way. Her shoulders are slightly slumped, her head is tilted just enough to show that she's having trouble focusing but is trying to look composed. Her smile is wide—too wide.

Is she okay?

Madeline's laughter comes a little too easily, a little too loud, as she glances around the room, clearly unaware of how much she's drawing attention to herself.

She's definitely drunk.

Tyler's face conveys instant shock when he sees her. He knows that she's not here to congratulate him on no longer wearing an ankle bracelet. "Security, we have an—"

"Intruder," Madeline finishes his sentence. "How amusing."

Tyler steps down to the side of the stage and gestures for his microphone to be turned off. He hisses something in Madeline's direction, but she brutally ignores him.

Confident, commanding Tyler is now reduced to a desperate supplicant.

"Thanks for clearing the podium for me." Madeline steps

confidently on to the center of the stage, leaving her husband speechless. "I'll start by introducing myself before security ruin all the fun. My name is Madeline Johnson and I'm Tyler's wife. I'm here to expose my lovely husband before he takes me and our daughter down with him."

I notice cameras closing in, recording her, and she smiles.

This is exactly what she wanted.

"Tyler has been scamming people, selling a fake cryptocurrency under the promise of big returns. He's been so focused on making money that he didn't care who he hurt along the way. He lured investors in with promises of wealth, all while he was lying on his couch in his townhouse on the Upper East Side, bought with *your* money. And I promise you, he's not done."

The audience gasp in unison, staring at each other wide-eyed, some of them cover their mouths. Security guys start to approach, but Madeline holds her ground. I have the feeling she's not leaving until they start looking at him like he's guilty.

"I understand you might be shocked, but I mean, what do we expect from someone like him... a boy who partnered with his sister lawyer to try and drag me down in court?" Madeline's voice rises above the murmurs. "Even when some of his victims realized what he was doing, when threats began reaching our doorstep, when someone broke in to go through his documents, he turned a blind eye. He never cared about the safety of his family. Of his daughter."

Cameras start flashing. I glance at Tyler, anger and panic mingles in his eyes.

"We had two bodies, two dead bodies found just next to our house, but it didn't matter to Tyler," Madeline continues, "because as soon as he had an opportunity to step outside his home, he went running to his company to check if anybody had started to realize what he was doing."

Tyler remains shocked into silence as he realizes the extent of the exposure.

"So, here's the truth behind Tyler Johnson's mask, he thought that the five-million-dollar inheritance from his late grandmother would save him. That he could start to pay back those who believed in him, even though he owes them much more. It's a shame that he will never see that money," she declares.

Are the Johnsons about to divorce?

Tyler's cheeks flash red.

"I want to apologize to the families and people who are struggling financially right now because of my husband's actions. If I'd known about his schemes before, I would have stopped him. I would have intervened long ago. I hope that the police now see him for who he really is and that they do something about it instead of blaming me for everything he has done. Scamming and killing innocent people."

The guards reach Tyler, grabbing him by the arms. He jerks away, his eyes wide with panic. "This isn't true! She's lying!" he screams.

Madeline shakes her head. "You are the architect of your own ruin."

"I will not be taken away like this! You don't understand! This is my company! My money! I've done nothing wrong!" Tyler yells while the guards push him towards the exit.

Madeline steps away from the podium, leaving a stunned silence behind. Tyler believed his power was unshakable. But he was wrong.

Tyler's empire of lies just crumbled beneath his wife's feet.

She got just what she wanted.

FORTY-FIVE

TYLER

July 10, 1:00PM

Every corner of that goddamn townhouse reminds me of my mistakes.

Like her.

Madeline was the biggest mistake of them all.

I should have listened to my family when they told me that a low-class, pregnant girl would bring nothing but trouble.

But she was carrying my daughter. Charlie. *How could I have said no?*

The silence of what used to be our home is almost suffocating—a constant reminder of what I've done.

I don't know if Madeline is capable of murder, I don't know if she would ever kill to silence someone. But the way Sadie's body was found... so out of the blue, is crazy.

I always thought there was something weird about some of Madeline's reactions.

There are days where she's obviously looking to fight, to argue, for me to explode, so she can point a finger and say, "See?

You're the one who has anger issues," even though she has this skill of driving me mad.

I'm the one who's trying to hold it all together right now, to bite my nails until my fingers start to bleed. She's fucking up my life second by second, but I can't do anything. My sister said that the police are looking at every move I make and if I head back home and lose control, it will be the end.

That's why I'm staying at a hotel right now—to have some peace and quiet, without living among traitors walking barefoot on the wooden floor that I paid for.

Madeline ended my career, my life. I will probably spend the rest of my life in prison even though there is no proof that I killed Daniel.

I'm only guilty of one thing that happened on Charlie's birthday—I was high as fuck. I don't remember much. I don't know the exact reason why I went to Daniel's building, I don't know what I was doing there for an hour, I don't remember anything about my drive back home.

I only remember his corpse lying on the ground in front of my porch.

What the fuck happened that morning?

My fingers trace the edge of the couch in my hotel suite. The room is furnished with a dark-wood coffee table, a large, wall-mounted flat-screen TV, and a sleek glass desk. The vibes are modern, minimalist, just the way I like it. When I moved in with Madeline, I had to adapt to her awful taste, or else it would have been a constant fight with that woman.

Nineteen-year-old Madeline and I were very different from the strangers we are to each other now. We used to take bubble baths together, and I would listen as she talked about her day, her dreams, her fears. It all seems so distant now, like memories from another life. A better one.

I hold my phone, my eyes drifting to the background picture

of Madeline and Charlie laughing together on the beach. A pang of regret twists inside me. *What have I done?*

I ruined a family. My family.

My pride and ambition brought me here. I have nobody to blame but myself for the mess I'm in. I should have been more present; I should have cared less about money. I thought I could bend fate to my will, but instead, I am left with nothing but the ashes of my failures.

All I wanted was to be revered, admired, and powerful, but all I managed to achieve was the destruction of my empire and the only person I ever truly loved in my life.

But does she still love me?

The questions in my mind have no answers. Madeline is pissed, of course she is. She shouldn't have found out about the inheritance that way, and if she really wants to divorce me, then I'm fucked big time.

I close my eyes, trying to escape the weight of the guilt that presses down on me. I try to forget the past, to pretend that things could have been different if only I had made other choices. But the memories are inescapable. And the past can't be changed.

What can I do to save myself?

As much as I want to hate myself right now, all I was trying to do was make her happy.

I didn't mean for things to spiral out of control. My company is under investigation and my wife has turned on me. Betrayed me. I only wanted what was best for us. The inheritance and the scheme were meant to bring us closer together, to ensure our financial security. I could have taken Madeline anywhere with that money; I could have spoiled her and Charlie. And eventually it could have been a great idea and helped many people, if only she could have seen the potential, the beauty in my vision.

I think of the conference—the moment she walked onto the

stage and tore everything apart. She was so eager to bring me down, to destroy the very thing I worked so hard to build. She turned the spotlight on me, not to show the world my brilliance, but to expose my vulnerabilities. It wasn't about justice for her. It was about revenge. She couldn't accept that I was the one who had the power.

My sister shouldn't have talked about Madeline in that way in court. I know she was trying to save me from going to jail, and I know that she believes that Madeline is guilty, so she didn't say all of that just to save my ass. There is evidence to suggest that she could be guilty, but that applies to me too.

Because I can't remember a fucking thing.

One thing is certain: I didn't kill Sadie. I don't know what happened. But perhaps that's a question I should ask my wife.

She can't lie to me. She's really good at lying to strangers—really good at putting on a show that she has rehearsed in her head a thousand times like a psychopath. But with me she knows that it doesn't work that way.

I've always seen through her, even though the version of her in my head is twisted now.

That bitch, how can I still have feelings for her?

I gave her everything, and in return, she left me with nothing.

I built Vertex Capital from the ground up, and now, just like that, it's all gone—reduced to ashes by the woman who was supposed to stand by my side, to support me, to cheer for me. She never told me that she was proud of me, she was too busy complaining.

How could she not see the sacrifices I made for her? I gave her everything she could have ever wished for—a life of luxury, security, and comfort. I provided her with the best of everything, and what did I get in return?

Betrayal.

Madeline should have been grateful for all I did. I gave her a beautiful home, affection, and a daughter who thankfully hasn't inherited our fucked-up personalities. Yet Madeline chose to see me as the villain instead of the generous husband who provided for her family.

Why can't she see that I was the one who made her life better?

She could have confronted me privately, she could have worked with me to fix this, but instead, she chose to grab a mic at my conference and make a speech. *I swear, she makes my blood boil.*

She should have been grateful. Who knows what loser she would have ended up with if I hadn't given her the chance to be with me.

But even though she has pissed me off big time, I want her back. I need her with me. Not only for the inheritance; I need more than just money. I feel lost without her. I need her to understand that we can work this out.

I think back to the evenings we spent together curled up on the couch, the warmth of her presence beside me. I close my eyes, trying to hold on to her. To have sex with her, to kiss her, to savor the taste of her skin. But my memories are elusive, slipping through my fingers like grains of sand.

I want to tell her I'm sorry.

I think of the countless ways I could have made things right. I could have been honest, transparent. I could have listened to her instead of using her as a pawn in my schemes. But she could have been a better wife too.

Why did she have to be so demanding, so unsupportive?

She was so quick to judge, so quick to see faults in everything I did. *What about her faults?* I wonder. *She was always too emotional, she always got upset so quickly.*

She was the one who pushed me away.

She was the one who made me feel unappreciated.

She was the one who never believed in me.

Even when I said that I didn't kill anyone.

Madeline's weakness drove us apart, I tell myself. *If only she had been stronger, if only she had been more like me.*

She was just a weak, ungrateful bitch.

Yes, I've made my mistakes and she's made hers. She's not perfect like she thinks she is.

We are both wrong here. We are both sinners. *But we can still make things right.*

I wonder if she would even listen to me; I wonder if she is capable of seeing beyond the man she thinks I became.

I want to tell her that I love her.

The words are on the tip of my tongue, but they feel hollow and meaningless now.

I want to turn back time.

But time cannot be turned back.

I love her so much, but she has ruined my life.

I grab my jacket from the coat rack by the door and close it behind me.

I need to go meet my wife at her lawyer's firm.

The streets are alive with people moving on with their lives, while mine is still stuck on the same traffic light. I hate not being in control of my own life. I am a ghost among the living, a shadow of the man I used to be. I hate myself.

I walk to the lawyer's office.

Madeline wants to take charge—she gave me an ultimatum. The inheritance from my grandmother, the one I've been counting on, hangs in the balance. According to the clause, I have three weeks to stay married to her and then it's mine. But Madeline? She doesn't want any part of it. She doesn't want to be stuck in a marriage that feels like a transaction.

She's made it clear—either I give up the inheritance and we try to fix our marriage, or we go through with the divorce. She doesn't want to be used and a part of me understands what she means. But the money... it's more than just cash.

It's security—it's our future.

But at what cost?

I refuse to sign the papers.

Her lawyer's office looms ahead, I walk through the revolving door. The receptionist glances up from her desk, her expression is detached.

"Mr. Johnson, welcome." She smiles, even though there is nothing to smile about. She knows why I'm here. "Mrs. Johnson and Mr. Davis are already waiting for you in meeting room number five."

I nod. I follow her down a long corridor. A walk of shame.

When we reach the door with the number five hanging on it, the receptionist turns to leave, and I pause, taking a deep breath. *I need to be calm, collected,* I remind myself. I need to convince her that we can fix this, that we can still be a family. I can't let my anger ruin everything—the police are giving me a break for now, and that break has to last a lifetime.

I push the door open and see Madeline sitting at the long mahogany table, her back straight. Beside her sits the lawyer, Mr. Davis, a stern man with graying hair. Laura used to be Madeline's lawyer too, but now they have obviously parted ways.

Madeline's eyes meet mine and, for a moment, all I see is sadness. *She didn't want this, I know it. She still doesn't.* Her family always pushed her away, never truly loved her, treated her in ways that she didn't deserve. All she wanted was to be loved.

And I can still do that.

"Tyler," her cold voice calls my name. A chill runs through my spine. "Thank you for coming."

"Sure," I reply, trying to keep my tone as even as hers. I take a seat at the opposite end of the table. My eyes flit nervously between Madeline and Mr. Davis. I know what's coming and it terrifies me.

Mr. Davis clears his throat; his gaze is fixed on the documents laid out in front of him. "Shall we begin?"

Madeline nods, her eyes fixed on mine. "Yes, let's get this over with."

It feels like she wants to tell me with her gaze that she's not afraid, that, for once, she's the one in charge, she's the one deciding what's best for her. But what she doesn't understand is that the way she looks at me doesn't make me feel uncomfortable. It makes me feel wanted. I know she still wants to be with me, I'm sure of it.

"Madeline, can we talk?" I finally say. "I mean, before we start with the legal stuff."

Madeline's eyes narrow. "There's nothing to say."

"Please," I press. "We've been together for too long for this to be happening."

She crosses her arms. "I know that, but—"

"It's not too late. We can fix this, inherit the money, and put our marriage back on track."

Madeline's face is a mask of indifference. "We can't. I don't want to be part of this anymore, Tyler. Not if it's just about money or keeping up appearances. You have to make a choice."

Mr. Davis interjects, "Perhaps we should proceed with the paperwork."

I turn to him, frustrated. "Don't interrupt, just do your job. You're still getting paid for your time." My fingers curl into fists; I gaze at my wife again. "I... I don't want to choose, Madeline. I can't—"

Mr. Davis clears his throat, leaning forward. "Let's make this clear, Tyler. You're being offered a choice. A very clear one. If you want the inheritance, you'll lose your marriage. If you want Madeline, well, then you'll have to forfeit the money. There's no negotiating."

"No," I say, pushing the papers away. My voice is a low growl. "I'm not signing anything."

Madeline stares at me with intensity. "Don't make things worse for you."

"No, it's not over. Not with us, and not with the money." My voice rises, betraying my sense of losing control.

Mr. Davis looks up, his brow furrowing. "Mr. Johnson, please control your voice."

"I don't care," I snap. "This is my life we're talking about." I slam my hand on the table. "You think you can just end it like this? After the show you performed at my conference?"

Madeline's eyes are cold. "Tyler, we've both made mistakes. For once, I'm trying to do something right. How can you think that this situation is unfair for you but fair for me?"

"You're trying to do the 'right thing', are you?" I laugh bitterly. "You think this is right? For who?"

"For me. For Charlie. I'm not going to stay married to someone who doesn't care about me."

She probably thinks that she would win both ways. If I lose the money, she gets to keep me close, but if she divorces me... I believe she thinks that the police will stop looking into her. But she's so wrong.

"Madeline, be realistic for a moment."

"I am being realistic."

"Are you fucking kidding me?" I yell, standing up and knocking the papers to the floor. "You're running away from your problems. You have something to do with Sadie's death and you're trying to move forward but you can't! You're not going anywhere on your own!" I look at her, my eyes blazing. "You think you're so independent, so strong? You're just as fucked up as I am. We both made mistakes, but you're the one who's going into hiding like a coward."

Madeline doesn't flinch. "Are you done?"

"No. No. I just started talking," I shout. My hands grip the edge of the table. "Answer me. Why are you doing this? We can split the money! Are you trying to part ways because you've done something and don't want to tell me? You owe me the truth, Madeline."

"I owe you nothing," she says, her voice cool and detached. "Not after all the secrets you kept to yourself."

I am out of control now—anger consumes every last bit of patience I had. "I didn't do anything. I didn't kill anyone. That's why the police released me, that's why I'm here now, talking to you. Telling you to stop and think, for once."

Mr. Davis's expression is stern. "Mr. Johnson, if you do not make a decision, we will have to go to court."

The weight of his words slams into me like a wrecking ball. *I can't go back to court. They will think I'm to blame for every-thing, I already have too many eyes on me now.*

I can't believe this. A fire is spreading within me. I hate not being in control, I hate that Madeline is in control even though she should be in handcuffs. She is free.

I can't stand the way she is looking at me like she has won.

I smash my fist down on the table, sending the glass of water flying to the floor. It breaks into pieces. Madeline gasps, her eyes widen in shock, her hand covers her mouth.

"Oh please. You're so shocked I punched a table, really?" Her acting skills are improving by the day. I've done much worse than this. She knows, I know. My rage is like a ticking bomb and she's the one who sets the timer to zero. Every. Single. Time.

Mr. Davis's eyes widen as he gestures towards the chair in front of him. "Mr. Johnson, please calm down and sit."

"Don't tell me what to do," I roar, my breath coming in ragged gasps. "This is a carefully planned setup. I should be the one who divorces you, Madeline. But I won't. I won't. Because I love you, I still love you despite everything."

Madeline stands up slowly. She stares at me like she's about to spit in my face. "You still love me?"

"Yes. I swear."

Madeline's expression doesn't waver. "It will pass."

I feel the room close in on me and I can't help but chuckle. This is a bad joke. "You like to pretend like you're the victim here."

Madeline takes a deep breath. "I'm not the victim. I don't have to be."

Mr. Davis clears his throat. "Mr. Johnson, the clock is ticking."

I clench my jaw. I'm not going to do this.

I get up and walk away, back to where I came from. Back to the hotel, where no one will complain if I smoke in the living room, if I scream too loudly, if the way I criticize is too rude.

There's a woman who's waiting for me at the hotel—a woman who doesn't complain or ask questions. I can't help but wonder if she knows something about Madeline that I don't, and I intend to find out.

Sadie.

FORTY-SIX
CHARLIE'S JOURNAL

July 15

Our home has never been so quiet.

There's no yelling, no crying. Just silence.

Now it's just me and Mom.

Dad hasn't been home since the day of the trial. Mom said he's just staying at a hotel for a while because he needs space, that everything's fine, that it's just temporary. She says it's not a big deal, that it's what he needs, and that he'll be back soon.

But I don't know. I don't feel like everything's okay. I can't remember the last time she looked at me and smiled the way she used to. She seems different—more tired, less talkative. And when she talks about Dad, it's like she's saying the words because she has to, not because she believes them.

The thing is, I don't think he's coming back anytime soon. If everything was fine, why wouldn't he come home? Why would he leave without even saying goodbye to me?

I want to ask Mom what's going on, but I'm scared she'll just tell me the same thing again—that it's fine, that it's just a phase, that he'll be back when he's ready. I don't know if I believe her anymore. I don't even know if she believes anything she says. Sometimes, I catch her staring out the window, her face all closed off, and I wonder if she's thinking the same thing I am—that maybe he won't come back at all.

It's not just the silence that's getting to me, though. It's the way things feel off between Mom and me now too. She's not angry, she's just... distant. Maybe she doesn't know how to talk about it with me, or she doesn't want to make it worse? And I get it. I don't know how to talk about it either. But I don't know what to do. I don't want to ignore it, but I also don't want to make it feel more real than it already does.

What happened in the trial? I don't know the details, but I can sense that something big happened, something that shifted every-thing. I don't even know if I want to know. Part of me wants everything to go back to how it was, but I don't think that's ever going to happen.

I don't know what's worse—the silence, or the not knowing? At least if I know what's happening, maybe I can start figuring out what to do.

But instead, I'm stuck with the feeling that something's broken and I don't know how to fix it.

FORTY-SEVEN

MADELINE

July 15, 1:30PM

I walked through a dense fog, confident, shameless, determined to defend myself.

And I almost gave up.

But my heart is a rusty door, resisting the change, begging to maintain the stability I used to hold on to so desperately.

So, I didn't.

I know what's wrong and what's right. It doesn't matter how hard Tyler and his family try to draw me down, I can still scream underwater.

There is a void within me that no one can fill, an unfillable tunnel that makes me react indifferently. I used to believe in love when I met Daniel the first time, a few months before Tyler's charm pulled me closer to him, trapping me in a toxic relationship where I couldn't see beyond his eyes.

I am still trapped. Because even though they want to kick me from their sight once and for all, Tyler will try to manipulate me to stay with him even though he believes I'm capable of murder.

He won't push me away before he gets what he wants. Before he sees the five million dollars in his bank account.

He never cared about me. He never cared about the consequences of being unloving, of being careless, of pushing away the only person that believed in him.

I was in love with the idea of him. A man who doesn't exist, or perhaps a man who isn't him. He's just a boy who likes to wear down his favorite toys until they break, and then he tries to fix them, but they will never be the same.

The woman I used to be is curled up somewhere within me, I know that. The only way of letting her out is to get rid of whoever stands in the way.

But the fear of reliving the bad moments, or worse, repeating them with someone else, gnaws at my insides. I can't let anyone treat me the same way he did.

How do I break free from this cycle?

What if I'm destined to repeat the same mistakes because I know no better?

I hate what he did to me—Tyler's smile was a mask behind which a serpent coiled, and when he struck me numerous times, his poison spread so quickly and deeply within my veins that it never mattered how wrong he was, I was still so in love.

It feels impossible to imagine falling for someone without fearing that I will lose my mind.

How do I move past this?

My phone buzzes. Tyler's mother holds a knife behind my back, texting me relentlessly, telling me what I should or shouldn't do to protect her beloved son.

You can't hide forever in the house MY SON paid for.

Tyler told me EVERYTHING.

If Tyler has gone to his parents' place, I'm sure he's

receiving plenty of sympathy—he has always been the victim in their eyes. I bet that they thought I was lying about the ways he treats me when he goes mad.

But deep down, Tyler knows that sooner or later, he will lose what he cares about the most.

Money.

I've been telling Charlie that Tyler is staying at a hotel for a little while—that it's just a break, that he'll be back soon. But I think she sees through me. I can feel her doubt when she looks at me, when she asks, "When's Dad coming home?" She wants to believe me, but she's starting to look at me the way I've been looking at myself: like I'm pretending that everything is fine, when deep down I'm scared of what might happen if it's not.

It's hard, because I don't want to make it worse for her. She's been through enough and I want to protect her from the truth. The last thing I want is for her to feel like this is her fault. But the silence is so loud between us now. I can't keep pretending that everything's the way it was, because it's not. And I think she knows that, too.

I'm trying so hard to keep it together, but I don't know how. I don't even know if I'm still holding on to the same person I married, or if I'm just holding on to the idea of him, to the life we built.

It's easier to act like it's just about him needing space, but I know it's more than that. I don't think I've been the kind of wife Tyler needed, or maybe he's just not the kind of husband I thought he was. Something changed in him after the trial, and something changed in me too. The distance between us isn't just physical anymore. It's all-encompassing.

I don't know if I can fix this.

I keep hoping I'll wake up tomorrow and it will all be normal again. That he'll come through the door and we'll pretend like nothing ever happened. But I don't think that's going to happen. And maybe that's what scares me most. The silence. The space. The feeling that maybe... maybe I'm not just losing him. Maybe I'm losing myself too.

In the quietness of being alone, my mind keeps drifting back to the way I grew up. I hate how the past still ruins my present, even if I do everything I can to ignore it.

But I know very well that if I go back to my past, all I will find is an empty town. And in the theater of lies, truth is the final curtain call. As much as Tyler thinks the police will come knocking at my door, I know it won't happen. It can't happen.

Suddenly, the doorbell rings and my heart thumps in my chest.

Is it the police?

Did they find out about the canisters?

Am I going to jail?

I should have been prepared for this moment, but no amount of planning, no amount of rationalizing could ever have prepared me to face the truth.

What if that blank canvas is about to be covered by blood?

The knock comes again, louder now and more insistent. My pulse quickens and my legs feel like stone, but I know I must answer the door.

I walk towards the living room, my palms already sweaty.

I reach for the handle to open the door.

"Surprise!" Rose stands grinning in front of me. She holds three pizza boxes in her arms.

"What... what are you doing here?" I stammer, completely taken aback.

I thought our friendship was over after what she told me and the way she reacted. I'm not sure what I need right now. I'm not sure if I need time or space, or to just forget it ever happened. Part of me wants to pretend like nothing changed, like our friendship is just the same as before. But I can't pretend forever. And I can't help but wonder if the way I see her now will always be different. I'm scared of it. I don't want to lose her, but I don't know if I can ever go back to the way we were.

I'm still thinking about everything that Rose said at her beach house. I wish I knew how to feel about it, or what I should do.

"I thought you could use some cheering up." Rose steps inside, giving me a one-armed hug while she holds the pizza boxes. My arms hang on my hips. "And pizza," she concludes, breaking our hug and smiling.

Has Rose forgotten the things she said to me and the message she sent after two dead bodies were found outside the place I used to call home? *I would kill for you.* A chill runs down my spine.

I will never forget that text, whatever the meaning behind it.

"What are you doing here, Rose? I thought you and I weren't talking anymore." I fold my arms across my chest. "I'm not sure how to feel about you being here."

"I miss you," she replies. "I know I messed up, but I don't want to leave you on your own... not with everything I know."

I take a deep breath, trying to steady my racing heart. "You're really going to pretend like nothing happened? You told me you were in love with me, Rose. I know you can't help how you feel, but I didn't expect this."

Rose lowers her eyes. "I know. I know it was wrong. And I can't take it back. I understand why you pushed me away. I just... I just want us to go back to being best friends, like we used to be. Before everything went so wrong. Forget I said that, please."

I sigh. "How can I be your best friend when I know that you have feelings for me?"

"I... I don't want to make things complicated," she says, her voice a little shaky. "Just forget I ever said that. I won't bring it up ever again. I think I just had too much to drink that day."

My shoulders drop and I pass my hand over my face. She's not lying and she's not drunk now, I can tell. I guess it would be nice to reunite with a friend—especially a friend who knows everything that I've done both right and wrong. *Extremely wrong.*

"Fine," I say reluctantly. "But it's going to take me a while to fully trust you again."

Rose smiles and places the pizza boxes on the coffee table in the living room. "You know you can trust me, I've never spilled your biggest secret, have I?"

I shake my head. "You haven't."

"And I never thought that you were capable of all the things Tyler's sister said. You know I trust you. Fully."

She opens a bottle of champagne in the kitchen and takes two glasses from the cabinet. She fills our glasses up and we clink them together.

"To new beginnings," Rose says, raising her glass. She comes closer and whispers, "Stay out of jail."

A chill runs through my entire body. I know she's joking, but it's true.

I have to protect my lies.

"Charlie, there's pizza down here!" Rose yells, glancing upstairs.

"Coming!" Charlie responds.

I smile. "Thanks for the pizza."

"No problem. And um, I saw the show you put on at the conference. You were such a bad girl, I loved it."

"Oh, that... well, I had too much to drink that day admittedly. But I've seen the videos online now and I have to say I don't regret a thing. Tyler got what he deserved. Somebody had to say something."

Rose heads to the small stereo in the living room and turns the dial to a radio station that plays pop songs. Charlie runs downstairs and smiles; she heads to the pizza boxes and opens one—the comforting smell of cheese invades the space.

Luckily, the living room and the kitchen are the only parts of the home that remained tidy after Sadie died. My bedroom and Charlie's room are still a bit messy, but I'll tidy up at some point. There's also a bucket of paint in the bathroom, and I need to finish the walls.

Rose sits on the couch, placing her half-empty glass on the coffee table. "So, Charlie, how are you?"

I sink into the couch cushions next to Rose, Charlie sits on the floor beside the coffee table.

She hasn't talked to me about how she's feeling lately. Not about Tyler anyway.

"I'm okay, I just... I just have a bad feeling about Dad," she responds, mumbling between mouthfuls of pizza.

"Oh, your dad is fine! You'll see," Rose lies, smiling like she did when she walked through the door. She's trying too hard to convince Charlie. "Sometimes grown-ups just need a little time to figure things out, but it doesn't mean it's the end of anything. He'll be back soon, you'll see. Everything will be fine."

A knock interrupts Rose and Charlie's chat.

I move towards the door, thinking it might be either the police or Tyler, but I'm greeted by an unexpected visitor.

Liam Wilson stands on the doorstep, his hands hidden in the pockets of his jeans.

"Hello, Madeline."

FORTY-EIGHT
MADELINE

July 15, 2:00PM

"Can we talk somewhere private?"

Liam stands in front of me, tall and broad-shouldered; his presence fills the space. He's wearing a gray T-shirt and jeans that hang perfectly on his frame, his golden hair catches the last bit of sunlight lingering on the edge of the porch. His gaze is steady like he's been thinking about this moment for a long time.

I have to pretend I don't know what he's up to for the sake of my family.

I hesitate, then nod. *God, this feels wrong.* "Sure." I close the door behind me and step out on to the porch. I cross my arms. "Are you okay? Is there something you need?"

He takes a step forward, close enough that I can smell alcohol on his breath. "I'm fine. I just needed to see you."

"Oh." My stomach twists. *Why?* The question almost slips out, but I catch it just in time.

He doesn't seem to notice my hesitation. Instead, he glances around, looking over my shoulder like he's making sure no one's watching. "How have you been? Is Tyler around?"

"If you came here to talk about getting your job back, you won't be able to. Tyler isn't here." I hope that I sound dismissive enough to put an end to this conversation and make him go away.

Liam shrugs. "Chill. I didn't come for him." He chuckles, although there's nothing funny about what he's saying. "I just needed to see you."

I straighten up, fighting the rush of unease that floods through me. *Why am I so uncomfortable right now in my own home?* I try not to shift on my feet much, but it's hard when his eyes never leave mine.

"Okay." I clear my throat. "What is it that you want, exactly?"

Liam tilts his head. "I don't need anything. Not really." His lips curl into a small smile. "I just want to talk."

I keep my posture upright, trying to convey a sense of control. "We're talking now."

There's something intimidating about the way he looks at me, it's as though he knows more than he should. "I see things differently now. I'm starting to understand... why you did what you had to do."

I swallow. "What are you talking about?"

His smile widens and his eyebrows arch. It's chilling. "I'm talking about Sadie... I saw you filling up the yoga ball at the gas station."

I freeze. *He can't know. He can't.* But the way he says it, the certainty in his tone—it makes my blood run cold. "Were you following me?"

Liam shakes his head. "I'm not a stalker. I just happened to be there."

He's lying. He is a stalker. I bet he's the one who broke into my house, he spied on us multiple times. But if I told him that I know, how would he react? I'm afraid of what he can do, he's unstable.

My pulse quickens, but I force my shoulders to stay relaxed even though every muscle in my body is screaming for me to step back, to get away from him. "I don't know what you think you know, but you're wrong." I try to sound calm, controlled.

Don't show weakness. Don't show fear.

He shakes his shoulders as if he doesn't believe me. I find myself asking the question that might change everything: "What do you want from me?"

Liam smirks. "I'm glad you finally asked. I would like to take you on a date."

I blink, thrown off guard for a moment by the absurdity of his suggestion. "A date?"

He chuckles. "Well... your husband isn't here, is he? I followed him. He checked into a hotel. So, I guess you're divorced now? Or at least separated?"

I stare at Liam, trying to process his words. *He's been drinking way too much.* "Tyler and I aren't divorced."

Liam shrugs, as if my denial means nothing. "Still, he's not here. So..." He lets his words hang in the air.

"So, nothing," I cut in, stepping back. "I want you to leave. Now."

His grin widens, but it's almost goofy. "Should I go to the police station? I can do that, you know." He pauses, watching me with a new intensity. "Maybe I should tell them to check the footage at the gas station and..."

My stomach lurches. *The gas station?*

He saw?

I push down the panic rising in my chest, and I force my voice to stay even. "Why are you doing this, Liam? I don't get it."

He leans in just a little too close. "You really wanna know?" His voice drops low as if he's sharing a dark secret. "Your husband ruined my life. He left me without a job, just like that, from one day to the next." Liam snaps his fingers. "And when I saw your family being investigated for murder, I thought, *perfect*. I thought I just wanted to watch Tyler sink. But then... well, then I saw you." His gaze flickers, there is something twisted in the way he looks at me. "I realized that nothing would piss Tyler off more than seeing me with his wife."

I feel a cold shiver run through me. *Is this really happening?*

"You're pursuing me to take revenge on Tyler? What are you, fourteen?" I ask in a state of disbelief.

Liam chuckles again. "I'm not fourteen, but your daughter is, right?"

My breath catches. "Don't you dare talk about my daughter," I snap, stepping forward, my heart hammering in my chest.

His smile doesn't fade, it only grows. Something in Liam's eyes makes me shiver.

"Oh, Madeline, Madeline... You have no choice, you know. You have to hang out with me. Or else I'll reveal a lot more than you orchestrating a murder at the gas station." He leans closer to my ear. "I know much more than that."

His breath warms my skin. "I know about Charlie."

I try to shake off my rising sense of panic, but it's useless.

He's not just drunk. He's dangerous.

His threats aren't idle. He knows too much—far too much.

I inhale a shaky breath and run my fingers through my hair. *What do I do?*

Liam is right. I'm trapped. The moment he mentioned Charlie, everything changed. I thought I could handle this.

I can't risk him going to the police. I can't risk him digging further into what we've buried—what I've buried. *The footage at the gas station, the secrets I've kept. The lies I've told.*

If Liam tells the police everything he thinks he knows, if he pushes the right buttons, if he convinces the wrong people, my whole world will shatter. Everything I've worked for, everything I've tried to protect—it will all unravel in an instant.

And if he really knows about Charlie... *If he really knows about the things I thought we left behind?* There's no going back from that.

I have no other choice.

I have no other choice than to go on a date with him. Or else...

My breath catches in my throat.

Or else everything will fall apart.

FORTY-NINE

SADIE

July 16, 8:00AM

When I found out that Tyler had been released from house arrest and that he was having issues with his marriage and no longer living in their big townhouse, I couldn't believe it.

She was right.

This was the perfect opportunity for us to be together, on our own, without Madeline ruining our connection. So, I kept checking the media until a news story came out showing Tyler walking out of a hotel. That's when I found him. He was shocked to see me at first; he couldn't say a thing, it's like he was seeing a ghost.

I mean, I get it. I was supposed to be dead. But I wasn't.

When the ambulance arrived and took me away, my senses returned, but I kept my eyes closed, almost pretending to be in a coma, until I heard a familiar voice.

I opened my eyes, the oxygen mask covered half my face. Victoria Parker was standing next to me in a nurse's uniform, flipping through my file. When she turned and saw me awake, she smiled. "I'm so happy that you're alive, Sadie."

I was confused, with a pounding headache. "What... what happened?"

Victoria glanced around as if to check that no one was coming in. "Madeline tried to kill you, Sadie."

The heart monitor beeped faster. "What?" I asked in shock.

Victoria placed a finger on her lips. "Don't yell. I have a plan."

She lifted the oxygen mask from my mouth a little and I coughed, then she tucked a strand of hair behind her ear. "Listen to me. I have a friend who works in the autopsy department. We're going to fake your death."

I thought she was going mental. I thought she was joking maybe, but her expression was serious.

"Are you insane?" I asked.

"Think about it," she responded. "You want Madeline to face justice, right? Once they find out that you're alive, she'll be free from suspicion." Victoria shook her head. "You and I, Sadie, we want the same thing. We want the Johnsons to suffer."

"I don't want him to—"

"I know you like Tyler, Sadie. But how would you feel if you could sneak to see him without Madeline being there? I'm sure they won't stay together much longer."

"Do you really believe that?"

"Yes, I do," she replied. "Now listen to me. I'm going to help you get a new ID. I'll give you some money that Tyler gave me so that you can find an apartment wherever you want to live. You won't need to work for a couple of months or so. In exchange, I want you to agree to fake your death, so that the Johnsons go down. I don't care which one of them takes the blame; it will be like a domino effect from that point onwards. They have to pay for what they did to my son. Once the Johnsons get what they deserve, then you won't have to see me or hear from me again."

It took me a few minutes to consider Victoria's proposition, but she waited patiently until I finally said, "Yes."

I had never seen her face light up like that before.

From that moment, everything worked out in our favor.

Victoria is gradually getting her revenge while I lie curled up, naked, in an expensive hotel suite with the man I love.

It sure beats being dead.

FIFTY

TYLER

July 16, 10:00AM

The sound of someone knocking at my door wakes me up.

I know I should probably answer it, but I'm naked, peacefully stuck beneath Sadie's perfect curves. I'm not in the mood to deal with whoever is disturbing my time in heaven.

I still don't fully understand how Sadie can be here. When I asked her how she was even alive, she said that it didn't matter, and then she started to kiss me, to touch me, to whisper dirty things, and I couldn't keep my hands to myself.

But I still want her to talk. I still need to know what she knows about my wife. If she saw something, anything.

I'm not the type of man who cheats. In fact, I usually find cheaters disgusting. But I don't even know if Madeline and I are still a thing at this stage, and I need to unload all the feelings I have for my wife for a moment. To unwind. To be able not to think.

Since she started working for us, Sadie has always been at the top of my list when it comes to fantasizing about someone. I missed seeing her in her maid's uniform, cleaning my house and looking at me with hunger. She has always been a great listener, and sometimes I couldn't help myself but stare at her legs. She's a great shape even if she's also a bit crazy. *I know that. I mean, she faked her death, after all. Who does that?*

But anyway, it doesn't matter how crazy she really is, it's not like I'm going to fall in love and marry this girl. I just needed a good time and to uncover some information about my wife's sketchy dealings. Manipulating someone like Sadie comes easily to me—getting inside her head, making her weak. Sadie has fallen for me, I knew it for a long time, but I always tried to avoid her. Mainly because I knew that she would want me more and more and it makes me feel so good to be wanted, so powerful.

Sadie moans at the persistent banging coming from the door. My eyelids close again.

Maybe if I ignore whoever wants to talk to me, they will go away.

"Mr. Johnson. Open up." A female voice echoes through the walls. *Detective Rynn.*

Fuck. What is it now?

There's no escape now. Sadie pulls herself up quickly, wraps the white blanket around her, and rushes to the walk-in wardrobe, closing herself in. I hope she stays quiet, I could get in trouble for knowing she's still alive and I have too much on my plate already.

With a groan, I slip out of bed, pulling on a pair of pants and a shirt. *I'm not ready for another trial, I'm not ready to be handcuffed again for something that I didn't do. But how do I explain the fact that I can't remember a thing from that morning?*

It's strange, though. I smoke all the time, almost every day. Weed has never affected me in that way before.

I open the door to find Detective Rynn standing there, her eyes already telling me something's wrong. She's not here to tell me that I'm in the clear, that I'm no longer the prime suspect. No, she's here to slap me in the face and call me an idiot.

Because I don't know what I did on the morning of Charlie's birthday.

I don't know if I killed my half-brother. And the more I try to think about what happened, the less I know, the more I feel guilty.

What if I did it?

"What's up?" I casually ask, clenching my jaw. Detective Rynn is holding on to a piece of paper. She hands it to me, crossing her arms over her chest. "We have a restraining order here from Liam Wilson."

"Who?"

"Liam Wilson, your previous employee."

My eyebrows rise in shock. *Why would Liam Wilson get a restraining order against me? Of all people, me?*

I stare at the detective, blinking as I process her message. It doesn't make sense.

Detective Rynn narrows her eyes and glances over my shoulder; she's clearly trying to decode who I really am.

But she's not going to find anything in here—except a woman who was supposed to be dead hiding in a walk-in wardrobe.

I don't even know who I am.

"You must maintain a distance of at least one hundred feet from Liam Wilson at all times," she explains. "Any violation will result in immediate arrest."

I feel a strong urge to rip the document apart. My brows furrow. "Are you serious? I haven't done anything to that guy. I haven't seen him in months. He's painting me as a criminal, he—"

Detective Rynn's partner, standing beside her, takes charge of the conversation. "Mr. Johnson, just follow the rules, okay?"

My lips part, but I pause for a moment. I'm not sure what

he means. This is too strange, too random. "I think this guy is up to something, you should look into him."

"What are you accusing Liam Wilson of?" Detective Rynn's partner—I believe his name is Anthony—asks.

"I'm not accusing anyone, I just—"

Detective Rynn steps forward. "Then stay away from him. If you keep overreacting every time someone accuses or rejects you, you'll only create problems for yourself. Understood?"

I nod.

"Good. Have a nice day." She turns abruptly on her heel, followed by her partner.

I slam the door shut and lean against it.

My phone vibrates on the desk. I reach to pick it up, my face is on fire.

It's him. Liam Wilson has just sent me a text.

> Just checking in to make sure you won't come between your wife and I on our date.

I stare at the screen, blinking as I process his message. It doesn't make sense. I reread it,

> Just checking in to make sure you won't come between your wife and I on our date.

What the fuck? How does Madeline know Liam? And why would she go on a date with him?

No, something bad is happening. I try to call him, but it looks as though he has blocked my number.

Sadie emerges from the wardrobe, her hair ruffled. "All clear?"

I nod. I can't stop thinking about Madeline and Liam together. Or about what Sadie told me Madeline did to her, or tried to.

She could have been jealous of Sadie being obsessed with me and decided to let her fall asleep forever without even touching her. But who, in their right mind, would think of killing someone by inflating a yoga ball with gas?

Only a master killer would. And surely Madeline isn't that.

She can't be.

My thoughts return to the present moment. *Liam Wilson isn't well and I must find out what his intentions are.*

I walk back to the bedroom; Sadie's blue eyes track my movements.

I throw the restraining order document into the trash and sit on the edge of the bed, running a hand through my hair. I try to shake off my frustration, but it lingers, gnawing at me. I can't believe that he's trying to keep me away from her just because I fired him. He didn't give me any other choice—he found out about the scheme. If I hadn't stopped him in time, he was going to turn everyone in the company against me and make me look like a monster.

Thank God I have my family. My family will never believe anyone else: my wife, Sadie, asshole Liam... even if I lied about everything, they would still help me to get rid of the skeletons hidden in my basement. They will always support me. And the police? Well, Detective Rynn seems to love her job, but if she tries to put me in a cell and throw away the key one day, I bet that a few thousand dollars might help to change her mind.

As I step into the bathroom, the cold tiles soothe my bare feet. I make my way to the shower and turn the warm water up to a steamy, hot temperature that will transform the bathroom into a sauna.

"Join me," I call to Sadie. I drop my clothes to the floor and let the water hit my skin.

She doesn't have to be asked twice. Sadie pads into the bathroom, her eyes sparkling as she sees me undressed. She slips under the shower spray first, letting out a soft moan as the hot water splashes against her slim face. I watch as the water slicks down her body, following every curve.

I step closer, pressing my hard muscle against Sadie's back as she leans her body back against gray tiles, her eyes closing in pleasure. With one hand, I reach around and cup her full breast, feeling her nipple pebble in my palm. She leans back into me, her ass pressing against me. With my other hand, I trace the outline of her neck, my fingers slide slowly down to her chest. She bites her lip, her eyes flashing with desire.

I don't want to waste any more time.

I turn Sadie to face me, my mouth meeting hers in a hungry kiss. She tastes of strawberries and sin, and I groan as her tongue dances with mine. My hands move lower, squeezing her curvy ass, pulling her against me. Her hips start moving in slow circles, her needs are clear—*she wants me, she desires me.*

Sadie starts kissing and licking her way down my chest, her hands reach around my back, pulling me against her. She doesn't wait another second to sink to her knees. My eyes roll back as her tongue does its magic, her soft lips wrap tightly around my skin.

I'm in heaven, but I want more.

I pull her up, her eyes sparkling with desire.

"I want to feel you," I whisper in her ears.

But as she steps out of the shower and lies in my bed waiting to serve me, I feel a sense of emptiness.

Everything around me turns hollow, and all I can visualize is Madeline.

The way her blonde hair flows down her lower back. The way her long, natural lashes flutter, giving me butterflies. Our chemistry—a connection I know I'll never have with anyone else.

I shared a bed with Madeline for years. We made love thousands of times.

I close my eyes and, for a moment, I can almost feel her beside me, her warmth, her scent, the way her body fits perfectly against mine. But when I open them, it's just Sadie. *A maid who I will probably never see again.*

What's the point of this?

"Don't make me wait, Tyler." Sadie's voice is playful. She rolls on the bed, her tone of voice hitting my nerves.

I force a smile, pushing my thoughts of Madeline away. "Yeah, just a moment."

I glance at the restraining order in the trash bin.

I hate Madeline when she acts like this. I should have known about Liam. If he was trying to blackmail her, she should have told me. But I can't blame her for keeping a secret when I've told her so many lies during the past few months.

But I can't keep my mind off her.

It would have been easier if I had been poisoned, if there was a way to switch off my feelings with some sort of antidote. But this feeling is natural, real.

How do I escape this feeling? Is it guilt for the way I treated Madeline at times? Is it love?

I sit on the edge of the bed, staring at the ceiling. Sadie sighs. *I don't care what she's thinking about me. She's here, yet she's not. I've never felt more alone.* Madeline's face keeps appearing in my mind, her smile, her laugh, even the moments of anger. It's all too vivid, too close. A wound that's too fresh.

Is this my punishment? To be haunted by the very person I tried to keep close? To never receive the inheritance from my grandmother because of a stupid clause? To feel a gnawing sense of emptiness that no casual flings or parties can fill? I clench my fists, trying to push these negative thoughts away, but they keep coming back, unforgiving.

"Don't be boring, Tyler. We can make whatever is going on in your mind go away in one second." Sadie's finger traces invisible patterns on my back, until her lips reach the corner between my neck and shoulder.

I press my lips together.

There's nothing that would make me feel better. But maybe I can get some pleasure out of this.

"You're right."

Sadie giggles and then steps in front of me and pulls me down beside her. Her hands caress my body. I try to lose myself in the sensation, in the escape it offers.

But it's no use.

Every touch, every whispered dirty word, only reminds me that I can't feel what I felt with Madeline. There's no chemistry, no connection, no fire. Those flames I felt when she would tease me until I exploded... I'm not sure if I'll ever feel so heated with anyone else. Sadie is hot but she's giving me goosebumps of remorse and guilt. My muscles should be relaxed, but I'm so tense. I never thought I'd feel like this in this situation.

Sadie's lips find my neck and I close my eyes, trying to focus. But all I can see is Madeline's body. She knew what I liked, she knew how to give me pleasure in a way this woman will never be able to.

I can't help but think about how I felt when she was on top of me. Her facial expression, her messy hair. So sexy, so provocative. The memory is so vivid—it's like she's right here. She was mine and now she's not. I suddenly feel like I've been punched.

I push Sadie away gently and sit up. "I'm sorry. I just... I can't do this right now."

Sadie tilts her head to one side. "What's wrong? I thought you wanted this."

"I did." I run a hand through my hair. "I do. But I need to clear my head."

I get up and walk to the bathroom, closing the door behind me. I lean against the sink and stare at my reflection in the mirror.

Who have I become?

This isn't me.

This isn't who I wanted to be.

I want to go back to my bedroom, and have sober sex with this wonderful-looking girl. But I can't.

I take a deep breath and splash cold water on my face, trying to wash away my thoughts. But they cling to me, stubborn.

I can't escape this.

I can't run away from Madeline.

I turn off the tap and dry my face with a towel, looking at myself one last time.

"Damn it," I yell, throwing the face towel on to the floor.

I open the bathroom door and walk back into the bedroom. Sadie is still on the bed, hoping that I would change my mind. Hoping that whatever's going on inside my mind will pass in a few minutes.

But it won't.

"You need to leave," I order.

Sadie sits up and raises her eyebrows. "Are you serious?"

"Yes, I'm serious. Go." I gesture to the door. "I'll call you later," I lie so that she doesn't make a scene.

Sadie sighs and starts gathering their clothes. "Whatever, Tyler. Call me when you get your head straight."

The silence that follows after she slams the door of the suite is almost deafening.

I walk over to the trash can, remove the crumpled restraining order, and smooth it out on the table.

The words stare back at me.

ORDER OF PROTECTION

Effective immediately, Tyler Johnson must stay at least one hundred feet away from Liam Wilson.

The paper shakes in my hands. I sit down heavily on the edge of the bed and clutch it.

I love Madeline, although I've hurt her more than I can ever compensate her for. But I don't want her to fall into Liam's trap. That man isn't hanging out with my wife coincidentally.

I pull out my phone and stare at her number, my thumb hovers over the call button. I need to hear her voice. I need to try and make her understand. But what can I possibly say that will make a difference? She doesn't believe anything I say. She doesn't want me.

Instead of calling her, I type out a message; my fingers fly over the keys as I text everything that comes into my mind.

> Madeline, why are you going on a date with Liam Wilson?

> I know I've hurt you, but you can't go out with him. He's mentally unstable.

> Also, how is that fair? I've done nothing but try to provide for you and our daughter. I gave you everything you could ever want. And now this? We're still married!

> This whole thing is just… it's insane. I love you, Madeline. I always have. Why can't we just talk this out like adults? Why does it have to come to lawyers? For Charlie's sake, can't we at least try to communicate?

> I want to make things right. I want to fix this, even if you don't believe me. But I need you to meet me halfway. I need you to stop acting like I'm some kind of monster and remember who I am. And who you are.

> Please, let's talk. For Charlie's sake, if nothing else.

I hit send and drop my phone on to the bed; my heart pounds in my chest.

The ball is in Madeline's court now.

FIFTY-ONE

TYLER

July 16, 3:00PM

In the afternoon, I pace in the living room of our townhouse, glancing at the clock every few minutes.

Madeline agreed to meet. She and Charlie are coming back from a walk in Central Park, and I can't help but feel anxious. Something is squeezing my heart and lungs out. I need to find the right words to tell her I still care, and to explain that I'm not only here for the money, or Liam.

When the door finally opens, my heart leaps into my throat. I take a deep breath and step closer to the entrance. Madeline and Charlie come in. Charlie looks just like her mother—they're both so beautiful.

Charlie rushes inside clutching her small bag, her shoes echo up the stairs as she makes her way to her bedroom. She doesn't even look at me in the eyes. She must be so upset that I left like that. I don't blame her. *I'm a terrible father.*

I wonder what Madeline has said to her about me, but I know that she won't try to derail Charlie's relationship with me.

She's not like that, she cares deeply about our daughter's well-being—even more than her own.

Madeline lingers by the door, her arms crossed.

"Thank you for agreeing to meet up."

"I'm doing this for Charlie. Hopefully you two can reconnect."

"I hope so, too. But Madeline, you have to tell me about Liam. What's going on with him?"

Madeline's gaze falls to the floor, then back at me. "I'm not cheating on you, Tyler. I just..."

I step closer, trying to read her eyes, but she seems so lost. I caress her arms and her lips tremble slightly. "You can tell me anything. I swear, I won't judge."

"I... I can't, Tyler. Not now, but I'll explain. One day."

I nod. Madeline has always been smart and very loyal to me. If she says she's not cheating, then she isn't. But something is worrying her, and I can't stay away from my family any longer. "Okay, but I'll stay here now. With you and Charlie. If you need your space, then take all the space you want, but I want to be able to protect you."

Madeline's eyes glow underneath the LED lights. "Thanks."

"I know that everything is fucked up right now. I just think we should stick together. We need each other. I can protect you." I hug her and she hugs me back; I can feel her shaking a tiny bit.

"Don't ever leave again," she whispers, "no matter for how long."

I shake my head, placing it next to hers. "I won't."

"I don't want you to believe that I'm a monster." Madeline's voice is so quiet that I can barely hear her.

"I never said I believed you killed someone." That's something I've never said before that she *has to* believe. Her past needs to remain in the past, and she needs to be able to live with it and write her own story—a different story from her childhood family. "You're not like your mother."

FIFTY-TWO
DETECTIVE RYNN

July 16, 6:00PM

"Package from anonymous." Anthony drops a square-shaped envelope on to my desk with a thud; there's a glint of curiosity in his eyes.

I glance at him, then at the package. The paper is worn at the edges, like it's been through a few hands before landing here. Slowly, I open it, carefully peeling back the edges. Anthony leans forward, resting his palms on the desk.

Inside is a journal. One of those teenage journals that you can lock with a key, but it's not locked—it's easily accessible. It's not signed, but the handwriting seems childish.

Anthony tilts his head, as if waiting for me to make sense of it. "It's not signed or anything, I'm not sure who this belongs to..."

I flip through the pages, each one is a blurry mess of letters, but it slowly starts to make sense. A knot tightens in my stomach as I read the first few sentences. It's unmistakable. "Oh," I mutter under my breath. "It looks like it's Charlie Johnson's journal."

Anthony's eyebrows furrow. "Charlie Johnson? You mean Madeline and Tyler's daughter?"

I nod, my fingers tightening on the journal.

"Do you think she sent it to us?" Anthony asks.

I hesitate, glancing back down at the pages. "I'm not sure," I murmur. "But it might help with the investigation. Thanks, Anthony."

Anthony's face softens as he gives me one of his sweet looks only meant for me. "Sure thing. Anything I can do to help."

I watch him leave, his smile lingering. Anthony is the perfect work partner and boyfriend, I couldn't ask for more than that.

Shaking off my thoughts about him, I turn my attention back to the journal and start reading.

May 5

Mom says I'm not allowed to ask where Dad is anymore.

I know he's gone, though. I don't understand why she doesn't just tell me the truth.

I bet if I asked Sadie, she'd tell me, but Sadie never talks much anyway. She just moves around the house, dusting and cleaning, glancing over at Tyler as if he's going to randomly fall in love with her just like that.

I know I'm not supposed to call him by his name, so I'll keep calling him "Dad" like I always have until today.

I spend a good hour reading Charlie's journal, and I've never been more disappointed in myself in my whole life.

I know who killed Daniel Johnson. Charlie couldn't keep her promise, and she had to write it down to free herself from it.

How could I have missed this?
How could I have gotten this investigation so wrong?

FIFTY-THREE

MADELINE

July 17, 10:00AM

There's a part of me that still clings to the feeling of the good times I had with Daniel—the moments when keeping a secret was exciting, sexy, wild, soul-consuming. And then there's the guilt, the fear of getting caught, the flames that heated my body with shame—with the anxiety that slowly killed me inside until I was nothing more than ashes.

But then I would rebuild myself, over and over. My confidence grew the more I understood the world, the more I knew how it worked—how I could blackmail someone, silence them to keep them from talking more than they should.

My secrets.

It's crazy how the body can yearn for the past, even when the mind knows it's not what's best. I wonder if it's some kind of primal instinct, a longing for the comfort of the familiar, even when that familiarity is laced with hurt. With blood.

Or maybe it's just that the heart is more forgiving than the mind. The heart holds on to hope, on to dreams of what could have been, even when reality is so harsh. It's hard to believe I pushed the truth away so many times. Sometimes, I forget what I've been through. What I've done.

I take a deep breath, letting the poisonous air of New York fill my lungs and letting the venom spread in my head. *I don't want to remember anything. Madeline is not who I want to be.*

Maybe I should have drugged myself too that morning, hours before the party started—right before someone moved Daniel's body to the front of the townhouse. Then I wouldn't need to keep fighting off these persistent memories.

Tyler should thank me. I did him a favor. He doesn't recall a thing. But he's such a good liar—God, he really is. Nobody wondered if he could have committed murder without remembering. They just dismissed the idea, thinking that some weed couldn't possibly make someone forget or not realize what they were doing. And it's true, weed is not that strong. *Weed is for dummies.* But a couple of drops of scopolamine in someone's coffee is enough to cloud their mind for some time.

Just saying.

Tyler still hasn't made his choice, but he will.

I know he will choose me.

The rays of sunshine warm my skin from inside the coffee shop. I settle into my chair and the barista sets down my iced mocha and cake, but as soon as I focus my gaze on the warm mug in front of me, a male voice almost makes me jump out of my seat.

It's Liam Wilson. That asshole.

"Is this seat taken?" I look up to see him standing beside me, holding a cup of coffee.

I try my best not to roll my eyes. He has to stop following me, he has no idea what I'm capable of. *But what else can I do?* This guy won't stop until I give him what he wants—a date, or who knows, even more?

How can I stop him from talking?

"No, it's free." I gesture to the chair across from me.

He sits down and I can't help but sigh. At least we're in a public space, so I don't feel frightened.

Liam's hair fall in curls around his face. "It's been a while," he says. He takes a sip of his coffee and sets it down on the table. "How are you? You still haven't said yes to our date."

"I'm good. Enjoying a peaceful moment while it lasts," I respond sarcastically.

He nods. "Is your husband still away?"

"No." I clear my throat. "He's back home."

Liam seems to hesitate for a moment. "Well, we're still hanging out, aren't we?"

"Yes," I say through gritted teeth.

He leans in slightly, a smile plays on his lips. "Well, I can't say I'm not happy to hear this."

Psycho.

"Don't you have anything better to do?" I wonder aloud.

He chuckles softly. "Nah. There's something about you, Madeline... I don't know how to explain it."

I force a smile and nod. "Don't bother trying. I don't want to know."

Maybe it's better that he doesn't see my dark side. Let him keep his rose-tinted view of me—blurry, softened, distorted. Because once someone hands him the right pair of glasses, it's over. He'll see what I really am. And he'll be terrified, like a lost puppy cornered by a predator it never saw coming.

"How is Tyler?" he asks. "I sent him a message, you know? To make sure he doesn't come between us."

I bite my tongue. *So that's how Tyler knows about Liam and me.* Liam thinks he's being smart, but he's so stupid. Tyler will find out that Liam is threatening me to do this.

"Tyler's fine."

He nods, raising his eyebrows. "Not for long, I bet. I can visualize Detective Rynn knocking on your front door already, looking for him."

I swallow. "Whatever you say, Liam."

"I'll let you carry on with your day now. I'll text you the details for our date for this evening."

I stare fiercely at Liam as he waves and leaves the coffee shop; his figure gradually fades into the sunny street and disappears around the corner.

My vision goes blurry for a second. I close my eyes, trying to block out reality.

There's another thing stopping me from going on that date. Something hiding within me, something deeper, darker...

The fear of making the same mistakes again.

FIFTY-FOUR

MADELINE

July 17, 7:00PM

My leg starts shaking, my heart and stomach heat up.

As much as my gut is telling me that I don't want to be here, *I have to be.*

Liam Wilson has been looking at my family for a long time, and I have to adhere to his rules until he's no longer able to ruin my life.

Liam opens the car door for me, and I slip into the passenger seat, clenching my jaw. The car is a sleek black sedan, the scent of fresh leather gives me a slight headache, but at least the seat is comfortable.

He starts the engine and the doors automatically lock as soon as the car starts moving. My eyes roam around, my pulse quickens. I've got pepper spray in my bag in case things go very wrong. I squeeze my bag on my lap, feeling the two small glass vials inside.

"So, tell me something about you I don't know," Liam asks, glancing at the rearview mirror before returning his focus to the road.

He really shouldn't want to know.

"Well, I... I was born in a small town near the border of New Jersey."

"Was that where you went to school with Daniel Johnson?"

I swallow, blushing. He's making me furious. I would spray the pepper spray into his eyes now if I could. "Yes."

"I see. Does Tyler know about your past with Daniel?"

"Is this a police interrogation? I thought we were going on a date. Dates are supposed to be nice."

He glances over at me with a grin. Liam seems to love challenging my patience. "Well, if you want to know about me—"

"I don't, but you give me no choice."

He chuckles. "I'm originally from Chicago, but I moved to New York for work a few years back. I have a dog, Max. He's a rescue, a bit of a handful, but I adore him."

"Interesting."

"Oh, Madeline, the world is unfair in many ways."

My brows furrow. "What do you mean by that?"

He shakes his shoulders. "Well... let's just say that people get away with everything these days."

I don't have to think too deeply to know that he's referring to Tyler.

Liam parks in front of a downtown bar, and I can hear the noise of Latin music through the car windows. As he switches off the engine, he turns to me and places a hand on top of my leg. "Did I already say that you look stunning in that dress?"

I tilt my leg to the side. *I find this man repulsive. But I have to stay strong.*

For Charlie.

My face feels like it's on fire, but I try my best to pull out a smile. "Thanks."

I shouldn't be here. This is wrong.

Liam is dressed in dark jeans and a crisp white shirt that

highlights his tan; the sleeves are rolled up just enough to show off his toned forearms.

I open the car door, wanting to avoid any chance of a pre-date kiss. I clench my jaw as I follow each of his movements, trying to study him. Trying to understand what his next move will be.

Liam smiles as he takes my hand and guides me towards the entrance. A chill runs down my spine as I hold it. I don't want to think about how he'll react if I snap my hand away. Hs fingers curl around mine and all I want to do is throw up. He seems relaxed, as if he knows this date is going to be great.

What kind of lunatic can feel this way?

He seemed okay during the first half an hour of our first session—but this guy? I don't know who he is, and I still don't know what he wants. *How long do I have to pretend that I want to be here?* If it wasn't for him mentioning Charlie and threatening to go to the police and tell them to check the footage at the gas station, I wouldn't be here right now.

"Actually." He stops in front of the bar, tilting his head to one side. "Let's go this way."

He takes my hand and pulls me towards the back of the building. I shiver with fear.

Where is he bringing me?

I follow him up the fire stairs that lead all the way to the top of the building.

Outside, I gasp in surprise at the view. The tall buildings of New York City stretch out before us, their lights twinkling like stars. But then his arm brushes against mine and an electric pulse makes my heart go quicker.

Is he going to push me off the roof?

"This is incredible." I try to sound casual. To use reverse psychology on him. To brush off my feelings and avoid goosebumps. I don't know what to feel. But my gut is never wrong.

Something tells me that I must protect myself as much as possible.

Liam smiles. "I thought you'd like it. Sometimes it's nice to get away from the crowd and just... be alone. On top of the world."

I nod slowly and cross my arms for comfort.

Liam points to two camping chairs in a corner of the empty rooftop, and we sit down next to each other. The chairs creak under our weight.

"Do you ever think about erasing everything from your life and just starting from scratch?" he asks, gazing towards the horizon.

I bite the inside of my cheeks. My nails pinch the palms of my hands. I swallow once. Twice.

What kind of question is that?

"No," I respond, curving my lips and turning my head towards him. "I wouldn't change a thing. Now, if you'll excuse me, I have to go to the restroom. I'll be right back."

I stand quickly, my legs unsteady, as if the strange energy emanating from Liam is pressing down on me. I force a smile, push the rooftop door, and make my way towards the stairs, not daring to look back.

There's only one time in my life that I felt this feeling before. This deep, sudden rush of fear.

And that was with my stepfather.

The downstairs bathroom is at the end of a narrow hallway, far from the crowd and the music. I lock the door behind me, but the sense of danger still crawls under my skin.

I pull out my phone, the screen is cold against my fingers. I think about calling Rose or Tyler to explain what's going on, to seek help. But I don't know if that might make things worse. Instead, I do a little research to try and find out more about Liam—*I should have done this before.*

I type his full name into the search bar and wait as the

results load. I need to know who he really is before I go back outside. If he's not as smart as I am, his real identity will show up on social media. Some people post every single thought they have on there. Literally everything.

His social media profile pops up almost immediately. It's mostly photos of him traveling, posing with friends, looking charming and kind. But something about the way he looks in each one feels off. Like he's playing a role that doesn't quite fit.

Then I see a post. *The post.* The proof that my gut was right.

The case of the Johnsons will take a deadly turn. I can feel it. The wife is the one to blame.

The words burn my eyes. My heart drops into my stomach.

I stare at the post for what feels like a lifetime, the words repeat in my mind—each syllable grows louder, more suffocating.

What does he know? What are his intentions tonight?

A soft thud on the other side of the door jolts me from my thoughts. I freeze, my pulse pounds in my ears.

Did I lock it?

I slowly turn towards the door, my fingers tremble as I grip the edge of the sink.

Of course I did, I'm sure of it.

But then I hear it again—the soft shuffle of footsteps on the other side of the door, followed by a gentle knock. "Are you alright in there?" Liam's voice is calm, too calm. Too measured.

I swallow hard, my throat is dry. I don't respond. Instead, I take a step back, glancing around the small bathroom for something—anything—I could use as a weapon. But there's nothing. No sharp objects. Just two abandoned shot glasses with what smells like vodka in them.

My eyes widen.

I place my phone back into my bag, take out a tiny vial next to the pepper spray, and unscrew it. Three drops of scopolamine fall into one of the shot glasses and I watch the two liquids mix together.

I open the door, forcing a smile as I hold out the drink. "Hey, I brought this for you from the bar."

Liam looks up from where he's been standing by the window. "Oh, um, did you bring it to the restroom with you?" he asks, confused.

I gaze at him, half smiling. "Yeah, like I said, I had to go to the restroom. What's the issue? Don't you want to have fun on our date?"

He steps closer. "No, no. I didn't mean that."

Liam reaches out and grabs the drink from my hand, lifting it above his head. "To new beginnings."

I smile, feeling my stomach tighten as he stares at me. "To exciting ones," I reply, raising my shot to the air and clicking it to his.

"Aren't you going to drink it?" Liam asks and raises an eyebrow. He's waiting for me to take a sip.

He thinks he's smart, but he's so stupid. *I know everything.* Sometimes I wonder what would have happened to me if he saw me on the day he broke into my house.

I shrug my shoulders and giggle, sipping the vodka down in one second. The liquid burns as it slides down my throat, warming me from the inside out.

Liam watches me, and for just a second, I wonder if I've just made the worst mistake of my life.

Until he winks at me and drinks his shot too.

All of it.

We walk back to the rooftop. Liam reaches for the low railing at the edge, his fingers brush it slowly. He stumbles, shifting from one foot to the other. The drug's clock is ticking, each of its hands point at different symptoms of scopolamine fucking up Liam's senses.

No one plays with me without getting hurt.

Liam starts laughing out loud as he points at a corner of the rooftop, then to another one, then to me. He stares, leaning his head to one side, then to the other. "You're not even here, are you?" he asks between breaths before stepping too close to me. *Way too close.* "Everyone knows who you really are."

He keeps looking at me, then his lips press into a thin line.

My teeth grind together as I push him to the rail of the edge of the rooftop, my fists clenched. Liam chuckles, raising his hands to the air, but then propelled by adrenaline I push him away from the railing.

Off the building.

His scream fades between the skyscrapers.

Like my real father used to say: "If a man stares at you for too long, he either wants to kiss you or kill you. Promise me you will always kill first."

I always keep my promises.

FIFTY-FIVE

TYLER

July 17, 8:00PM

My heart collapses as I see them walk into that dingy bar, the one I used to visit to drown the words I threw at her in anger.

Every step I take feels like walking on the edge of a razor. If Liam sees me, he will call the police. I can already visualize Detective Rynn shaking her head in disapproval, mouthing the words, "I told you to stay away from trouble."

I run up the stairs after them, my breath hitching, the music fading away with every floor.

Where is he taking her?

When I reach the rooftop, the wind almost slams my body to the edge. Madeline is acting strange. She's sitting on a plastic chair next to him, but her body is tense, her eyes are looking away from him.

She's afraid.

Madeline stands up, a strained smile on her face. She says something and then turns towards the door leading downstairs. I bend down. I don't want her to see me. I'm only a few feet away. The door slams behind her.

"What a bitch," Liam murmurs.

I furrow my brow. He's acting strange.

Is she in danger?

The idea of Liam hanging out with Madeline slams into me like a fist to the stomach. His vibe is off. Something is off. He's shaking his head. It's like he's being forced to play a part he doesn't want to play.

But why?

If only I hadn't been so selfish, I could be here with Madeline. If only I'd been the man she needed instead of the man I wanted to be. My regrets settle heavily in my chest.

Madeline deserves better than me. Maybe I'm just overthinking. Maybe Liam isn't dangerous. Maybe I'm just annoyed by the idea that she's found what I couldn't give her.

I'm choking on the bitter taste of jealousy.

What if I've lost her?

FIFTY-SIX

TYLER

July 17, 9:00PM

I stumble through the door of the townhouse, my head and my legs feeling heavy as I gaze at Charlie hanging out with her friend in our neighbors' backyard.

Will she ever forgive me?

I need to drown this feeling of guilt. To feel lighter. To forget everything for just a little while.

The amber liquid glints under the overhead light as I pour it into a crystal glass. I knock it back, the burn of the alcohol stings my insides. I pour another glass, and then another, the whiskey flows within me like a river of regret.

I'm fucked up. I'm a mess.

A loser.

The loud music I blast from the speakers does nothing to drown out my guilt.

The police didn't find out, Detective Rynn is still investigating. But I know, I'm certain.

I killed my half-brother.

It must have been me. I don't know how, I don't know when, but I did it. All the evidence points to me.

On that morning, I was in front of his building, what was I doing?

Why can't I remember a thing?

Daniel and I had a plan. He wanted to partner up with me, to invest in my project. *Why would I kill someone who wanted to help me?*

There's something missing inside of me. A lost piece of puzzle that I can't find anywhere. But someone must have it, someone must know the truth.

Perhaps a security camera recorded me dragging Daniel's unconscious body down the street and cleaning up his blood? No, that can't be. New York is too crowded for that to go unnoticed. Perhaps Sadie saw something and told Madeline, and that's the reason she decided to hang out with Liam? Or perhaps nobody knows what happened, and I'm just here overthinking about the endless possibilities?

Daniel was innocent. He wasn't a mistake like my family thought.

But now he's gone.

He didn't choose this.

I crank up the volume of the speaker until the bass reverberates through the floor and walls. I pull out a gun from the kitchen drawer and place it in the back pocket of my jeans. I always keep it there in case of emergencies.

I want to get lost—to vanish in the storm I've created. The walls of this mansion are a prison of my failures.

The sound of an electric guitar fills the room. I slam my glass on to the table, the liquid disperses over the marble counter. My hands ruffle through my hair and I pull until it hurts too much.

I throw myself on the leather sofa, sprawling out as I stare at the ceiling. I think back to the rooftop, to the way Madeline looked at Liam. *Was it the start of a new love story?*

I take another swig from the bottle on the floor. The room starts spinning and I let myself sink deeper into the pillows of the couch.

I pick up the remote and flick through the channels, but the images on the screen are a blur. I turn the TV off and throw the remote into the corner.

Why did I let this happen?

How did I screw up everything so badly?

I stumble to the window. People wander down the sidewalk, moving on with their lives while I'm left here, wallowing in my own mistakes.

Alone.

I raise my glass in a shaky salute to the city; to the life I lost; to my daughter who doesn't care about me; to my family who love me for their idea of me rather than the reality; to Vertex Capital, whose name will soon be forgotten; and to the woman who made my life miserable, but who also made me understand what a fuckup I am. "Here's to you, Madeline," I mutter into the empty room. "You deserve better than what I gave you."

I let the alcohol consume me, numb the pain. I don't want to think about my soon-to-be ex-wife's words, or the sight of her with that weirdo, or the future that's been stolen from me. I just want to forget it all, if only for a few hours.

But as the night wears on and the alcohol takes its toll, a nagging thought refuses to leave me. I'll wake up tomorrow to find that nothing has changed. Madeline will still be gone. That guy will probably still be in her life. And I'll be left with nothing.

My hands are stained by Daniel's blood.

I'm a killer.

A murderer.

"You played yourself, Tyler," I say aloud, my words echoing

in the empty room. "You thought you could have it all. You thought you could fix it all."

I throw the empty bottle across the room, watching as it shatters against the wall. The sound of the glass breaking is almost satisfying—like it healed something inside me for a split second.

I collapse back on to the sofa. I'm alone, surrounded by meaningless wealth and luxury. *Why didn't I realize this before?*

I guess this is what I deserve for trying to manipulate people.

This is what happens when you only think about money.

You lose sight, you lose your freaking mind.

My half-brother...

I'm stuck in this mess, and I have no one to blame but myself.

My hand brushes over the lighter sitting on the coffee table. I pick it up, turning it over in my fingers. I flick the switch and the flame springs to life, casting a warm, flickering glow in the dim room. The only source of warmth in the coolness of this house. A house full of lies, of useless secrets, of hate, of twisted mind games.

I look at the extravagant furnishings, the intricate artwork, the elegant, expensive wallpaper, the ten-thousand-dollar marble counter. *What's the point of all of this?* I wonder.

My eyes settle on the gold-fringed curtains that hang across the tall living room windows. Madeline picked them, she once said that they shimmer when the sun sets. I reach for the curtains, my fingers brush against the fabric one last time. I can almost see her there, the way she used to be.

I move the flame closer to the fabric—it catches rapidly on the curtains. Reducing them to nothing in a blink of an eye.

The fire starts to spread, the hungry flames devour everything they touch. The scent of burning fills the house. Flames dance shamelessly, like ghosts from the past.

A beautiful display of destruction.

The smoke grows heavier. It clings to my clothes, my skin.

I don't care.

I don't want to be here anymore.

The front door bursts open. Madeline's eyes dart around the room as she registers the fire that's consuming everything from the curtains to the shelves. She looks at me, her mouth open, a frown slowly forming. "Oh my God! Are you okay?" Her voice is frantic, her eyes wide with alarm. She covers her nose with her arm, coughing.

I open my mouth to speak, but the words won't come. It's like my throat's been clogged with guilt, with everything I've done, and now she's here and I don't know how to explain it. I can't even explain it to myself.

"Madeline," I say, my voice cracking, "is your date over?"

"Charlie called, she said she saw flames," Madeline replies. She steps closer, raising her voice. "We have to get out of here now."

I swallow hard, my mouth is dry. I should say something. I should tell her the truth. I should tell her that it was me—that I did it. I should tell her that I killed Daniel. But the words get stuck somewhere inside me.

"I did it," I finally manage to whisper, my voice thick with shame. "It was me."

A bigger flame explodes in the corner; Madeline reaches her hand out to me. "Please. Please let's go outside. Now. We can talk outside."

I take her hand and move towards the door of the backyard, the fire is eliminating everything.

We reach the end of the pool. My gaze is low, I stare at the reflection of the flames in the water.

"What happened?" Madeline asks, shouting over the sound of sirens.

"I killed Daniel," I blurt out as the fire crackles around us.

She blinks at me, her lips parting slightly as if she's trying to process what I've just said. "What?"

I shake my head. "I don't remember anything from that morning. Nothing. I just... I just remember coming home and finding his body outside. I should go to the..." I let out a ragged sigh, the tears I've been holding back are finally spilling over. "I'm sorry... I'm so sorry."

Madeline cuts me off. "No. Listen to me. You didn't kill him. Whatever you think you did, it wasn't you."

Her words don't make sense. It's almost like she knows, but she's not saying anything. Or she's trying to defend me because she still has feelings for me and doesn't want to believe it.

"Then who the hell did it, Madeline?" My voice cracks. "Who?"

"It was me."

An explosion of flames shatters the roof. But I don't react to it.

My fingers hover over the back of my jeans, pulling the gun out of my pocket.

I point it towards her. My wife. The one who ruined everything she touched.

But I can't shoot.

Her stare only screams one thing—she's not afraid. Not even one bit.

Who the fuck did I marry?

FIFTY-SEVEN
CHARLIE'S JOURNAL

This is the last page of this journal.

I can't keep this secret anymore.

I will never forget what happened on the night of my birthday, how his eyes shut and never opened again.

I didn't want to believe what Daniel said. I thought I was imagining it for a minute, I thought I was just having a nightmare, just like Mom often has.

I should have done something. But instead, I stood there, frozen. Waiting. Praying he'd wake up.

But he never did.

That night, Sadie saw everything. Like she always does. She peeked through her window, half of her body hidden behind those ugly gray curtains.

And when she saw them moving the body behind a bush next to her guesthouse, she frowned. I don't think they realized she was spying on them, but I can see everything from my bedroom window, just like Sadie can see everything from hers.

I promised I wouldn't say a thing, so I wrote it down instead.

This secret is too big for me to keep.

Forgive me, Rose.

FIFTY-EIGHT

MADELINE

May 5, 12:00AM

"I have to tell her, Evelyn."

I had never heard him whispering in such a serious tone. Daniel is the only one who still calls me that.

"My name is Madeline now, you know that." I shake my head, gesturing around. "We already talked about this. Nothing is going to change even if she knows. It's just going to make things more complicated."

The lights inside the townhouse are all turned off. Tyler is sleeping, Charlie is probably on her phone underneath her blanket. Sadie's lights are turned off too, her curtains slightly open, but I don't see anything other than pitch black. We're standing by the edge of the pool, the lights inside the water glimmering on our faces.

"I'm her father," he whispers, pointing a finger to his chest, "I have rights."

I shake my head again. "It's been fourteen years and you've never asked about her before." I sigh. "Please, Daniel. Just leave it. You're going to destroy my life for one simple—"

"Mistake?" Daniel cuts me off, chuckling. "Maybe it was, but Charlie isn't a mistake. I want to be in her life."

"That's not going to happen." I shake my head, but Daniel has already stormed off.

He's walking towards the back door of the kitchen, his hands curled into fists. He pushes the door open.

I run towards him, my bare feet hurting from stepping on pointy little rocks. "Stop!" I whisper, cutting in front of him.

His eyes search mine. "Do you realize what you're telling me not to do?"

"Listen, I understand," I put my hands together, pleading with him, "but I love Tyler, okay? Very much. I can't lose him. I don't have anyone else."

He swallows, raising his eyebrows. "Too bad for you."

Daniel pushes my body aside and I can feel the color draining from my face. He steps quietly through the living room, going in the direction of the stairs.

I thought he was different from the Johnsons. I thought that being a "half-blood" would save him from having the same fearless, commanding type of attitude. But he's just like the rest of Tyler's family.

It's always their way or nothing.

But it doesn't work like that with me.

I open my kitchen drawer, taking out a big, sharp kitchen knife. I rush towards him, his hand is on top of the handrail, he's about to take the first step up. The sharp edge of the knife pinches the skin of his lower back through his shirt.

He freezes instantly.

"Get out!" I order.

Daniel turns towards me slowly, his hands raised to the ceiling. The blade now points at his stomach.

"Put the knife down," he whispers.

"I will. Once you get out of the house and promise to never show up again."

He chuckles again, dissolving my final reserves of patience. "You're not going to do anything, you're just pretending to be strong enough to—"

Daniel's words fade out as soon as he hears someone rushing down the stairs. Her blonde hair is tightly braided.

Charlie.

I hide the knife behind my back, turning my body so she can't see what I'm holding.

"Mom?" she calls. Charlie reaches the end of the stairs, frowning. "What's going on? Who is he?"

Daniel's lips part and he steps closer to her, glancing from head to toe. "Charlie."

I put a hand on his chest and push him back. "Daniel, go home," I repeat.

Charlie moves to my side. "Who is this man, Mom? What's going on?"

I swallow, I don't want to answer. She doesn't need to know. But Daniel has other ideas.

He places both hands on his chest. "I'm your dad, Charlie."

Charlie's face flushes red. She turns to me quickly, taking a step back. "Mom?"

I swallow, closing my eyes. This is my worst nightmare. "He is," I say reluctantly. "It's the truth."

But Charlie doesn't seem to believe me, she shakes her head frenetically, raising her eyebrows. "No. No, it can't be true. I... I don't know this man."

"It's okay, Charlie. Nothing will change, honey."

Charlie's eyes dart back and forth between us, her breath coming in shallow, panicked gasps. "No, no, no!" Her voice cracks, growing louder with each word.

She backs away, stumbling over the kitchen rug. "This isn't right! This... this is wrong. You're not him! You're not my dad! My dad is upstairs, sleeping!" Charlie's fists clench and her face contorts with a fury I've never seen from her before.

"Charlie, listen to me—" I start saying, but she cuts me off.

"Why are you doing this? Why are you lying to me?" she shouts, spinning towards him, her eyes wide with disbelief and terror. "You're just a stranger!"

Daniel takes a step forward. "Charlie, I swear I'm not lying. Your mother and I... we were seeing each other for some time. We were just friends, but things happen. I—"

"Shut up!" Charlie covers her ears with her hands, closing her eyes.

My heart sinks to see this.

I have no idea how to stop her pain.

It's all my fault.

"Charlie, you have to trust me. I know this is hard, but you —" Daniel tries again, but Charlie won't let him finish.

"I want you to disappear!" Her face flushes with rage and before I can stop her, she shoves him with a force born of panic and the need to make him go away.

But the push is too much. Daniel stumbles backwards, his body twisting before his head slams against the sharp edge of the counter. The sound of bone striking wood is deafening. He falls to the floor, unconscious.

Charlie stands there, breathless, her entire body shaking, while I'm about to fall to the floor. Her hands fly to her face, pressing hard against her temples as if she can push the reality back into place.

What has she done?

She didn't mean to hurt him. She never meant to hurt him. Charlie would *never* intentionally hurt someone.

"Go to the living room, Charlie, and call Rose," I say, trying to stay calm.

She sobs. "But—"

"I said, go!" I repeat, flashing her an urgent look. After a few seconds, she does what I said.

I rush towards Daniel, my heart hammering in my chest. My fingers press over his wrist. There's no pulse.

Did Charlie kill him? What if he wakes up?

I still have the knife, and I do what any mother would to protect her daughter. I stab him in the stomach.

I twist the knife around. Blood stains my floor, soaking his shirt quickly.

I swallow. *It's all my fault and I have to protect Charlie.*

If the police find out, they will take the only thing I care about. My daughter.

And if things ever go wrong, I want them to throw *me* in jail, not her.

My heart pounds louder and louder. The smell of blood makes me want to throw up.

Rose's car wheels come to a stop outside my home. The front door opens, her bag drops to the floor as soon as she sees the monster I've become.

She covers her mouth with her hand. "What... what happened?"

"Charlie, she... she pushed him. He was already dead before I stabbed him. I need to protect Charlie, Rose. Please. Please help me. I don't know what to do," I sob, trying not to make too much noise. The last thing I want is to wake Tyler up.

"Okay, okay..." Rose takes off her jacket and tosses it on to the couch where Charlie is sitting quietly, her gaze fixed on a point in front of her. "Charlie, hey." Rose bends down to her, trying to catch her attention, but Charlie's gaze remains distant. "I need you to listen to me, okay? Listen to me." Rose snaps her fingers in front of her and Charlie's head tilts slightly back, her eyes finally meeting Rose's.

"You're going to go upstairs now, get into bed, and try to get some sleep, okay?"

"How... how can I?"

"I know, I know it's hard, but you have to promise me you

will never, ever talk about this with anyone. This never happened, okay?"

"O... Okay," Charlie whispers.

"And never mention Daniel's name. Tyler is your dad. Understood?"

Charlie nods. Rose pulls her into a quick hug, gestures for her to go upstairs, then rushes towards me.

Rose's eyes glance at every inch of Daniel's body.

"He's—"

"I know," she responds. "I know. We need to move him. Now."

I swallow, glancing around us. "Where?"

"We can move him next to the guesthouse, behind the bushes, and leave the knife somewhere else. Anywhere but here. In the morning, I'll make a call at work to close the road for maintenance or something. Just to give us some time to figure it out."

I wipe my tears away and nod. I can't let my emotions take over. Every minute is crucial.

I have to get away with this.

We push Daniel's body out of my house, leaving a trail of blood that needs to be cleaned urgently. My fingers hold on to the knife until we reach a hidden corner of the guesthouse, behind some bushes.

Rose's breath comes out in wisps. "Push the knife through Sadie's back door. She'll think someone is threatening her, and she'll be next." Rose swallows, glancing around. "We also need to delete the footage from the camera at the front of your house."

Dazed, I do exactly as she says.

"Great. Now let's clean the mess inside."

May 5, 06:45 AM

Three drops of scopolamine fall into Tyler's coffee.

My plan has to work. When the police find the body, they must focus on anyone else other than me or Charlie.

Tyler won't remember a thing. I'll send him a message from a burner phone I bought with his credit card, telling him to meet Daniel at his place before work. There are cameras all around his building. And then, when the police investigate Daniel's death, Tyler's memory loss, and his proximity to the victim a few hours before he died, will make him the prime suspect.

I don't feel as bad about Daniel's death. He wasn't who I thought he was. He was a Johnson, like his father, like Tyler. *The world is a better place without fake people.*

After all, you need to unmask people to find out who they are right away or you might end up building a life with a stranger.

Outside the bedroom window, I glance at Sadie shaking Daniel's body, glancing around. But as soon as she steps into the back door of the guesthouse, she must have had a change of heart.

She returns and pulls the dead body to the back of the guesthouse, when no one can see it. Yet.

But the difference between me and everyone else is that I know how to keep a secret. And I will protect Charlie's—no matter the cost, even if it means someone else will take the blame.

People can think I'm a terrible person, but at least I'm not a terrible mother.

EPILOGUE
MADELINE

One Month Later, The Day of Our Anniversary

Perception can shift reality. Our minds build situations into the shape we choose to see.

But this time round, it hasn't worked out for me as well as I thought.

The floor of this place is designed like a chessboard with naked white walls caging me into this tiny room. You must be a good player to make it out of here. I spend most of my time crafting an exit strategy in my head, knowing that one move could change everything.

It's funny how time can strip away your illusions. Just when you think you have a grip on things, it reminds you how little control you ever had in your life.

For instance, my husband got *exactly* what he wanted. His company didn't collapse as I thought it would, his fraud was cleared, he had our house rebuilt, and he got to choose the exterior aesthetics and furniture without my input. Today is the day of our fifteenth anniversary, meaning he's probably at the bank right now, requesting the money of the inheritance.

I wonder if he thinks about me sometimes, if he still loves me despite everything, or if he's already arranged a meeting with his lawyer to talk about our divorce?

Honestly, whatever he chooses to do with his life won't affect me here, and in a way, I like that I don't have to share the same space as him. But on the other hand, since he got the judge to believe—or probably paid him off, *again*—that I was too mentally unstable to be thrown into prison, I'm well aware that I'm nothing more than a marionette, and he has full control over my life.

When the police and firefighters arrived to investigate and rescue us from the fire, I understood that my life, as I knew it, was over. Detective Rynn saw Tyler with a gun in his hand, but his hand was trembling, and he dropped it to the ground as soon as he made eye contact with her. He was terrified she might think he had done something bad.

That's when he revealed everything. Tyler told the authorities I was the one to blame, and not only was I charged with the murder of Daniel Johnson, but they also found out about Liam Wilson.

The only time Tyler came to visit in the last few weeks, I remember him saying, "They were going to figure it out anyway, Evelyn. I had to tell them. It's thanks to me you're here now instead of in prison. I hope you understand that I did what I had to do for you. You're unwell."

I used to hate that I have to be called by my old name here. It's one of the rules, and you can't bypass any rule in this place. But I got used to it—it actually makes sense. *Why should I be called Madeline if the life I was trying to build with that name has been shattered? I might as well go back to being Evelyn.*

The second bell of the day rings loudly, pulling me out of my thoughts, but I stay still, lying on this thin uncomfortable mattress, staring at the ceiling.

Is there anything better to do anyway?

I know that if I don't show up for lunch, the nurses are going to come check on me and eventually drag me into the room with the other psychos, but I'm not hungry. I'm never hungry in this place. I've probably lost so much weight here that when I see myself in the acrylic mirror—no glass allowed here—I don't recognize myself.

Rose is coming to visit this afternoon with Charlie. I'm so glad I have Rose. I honestly shouldn't have reacted the way I did when she expressed her feelings for me, because she's the only anchor I have and the only one taking care of my daughter. When Tyler figured out that Charlie wasn't his, well, he didn't want her around, so Charlie is staying with Rose, at least until I get out of here.

I can't help but pray every day that Charlie won't act out again, like she did when she sent her journal to the police. She was feeling so guilty that she couldn't take it anymore and wanted to reveal the truth about what really happened to her real dad.

I had to convince Detective Rynn that whatever was written in that journal wasn't true, that Charlie hasn't done anything, and that I had killed Daniel, like I confessed over and over. With the "help" of Tyler, who said that I had confessed to him, in the end, she believed me.

I can manage being a hostage in a mental institution. I've been to prison before, when I was a teenager, so this type of environment isn't new to me. I'm not scared. My only fears are about Charlie, but I'm thankful she has Rose by her side.

There's only one—or should I say *two*—minor issues in this place: familiar faces that I have to see every single day.

Turns out, the mother of the man I allegedly killed works here as a nurse, and she brought someone in to work with her who couldn't wait to see me miles away from my husband.

Both of them want the same thing: revenge.

Am I too lost to save myself this time?

Not if I play the game right. *And thankfully, I'm always one step ahead.*

Huge thanks for reading *Who Did I Marry?* I hope you enjoyed reading it as much as I enjoyed writing it! If you want to join other readers in hearing all about my new releases and bonus content, you can sign up for my newsletter!

www.stormpublishing.co/sara-pucci

If you enjoyed this book and could spare a few moments to leave a review that would be hugely appreciated. Even a short review can make all the difference in encouraging a reader to discover my debut psychological thriller for the first time. Thank you so much!

This is the first psychological thriller I've written, and I was really excited to dive into different characters. What inspired me to write this book was witnessing how impactful it is to grow up in a toxic environment where you feel unsettled, without the same sense of security that comes with growing up in a healthy family.

Thanks again for being part of this amazing journey with me and I hope you'll stay in touch—I have so many more stories and ideas to entertain you with!

Sara x

ACKNOWLEDGMENTS

Writing this book has been an incredible journey, and I have to thank a few special people who have believed in me since day one!

I'd like to thank my best friends Vanessa, Anna, and Federica for being my biggest fans. Your support has meant more than words can express.

A special thank you to my editor, Kate, for believing in me. Your guidance and kind words helped me shape this story into something I am truly proud of.

There are countless authors who have inspired me to pursue my dream, but the one who stood out and pushed me to fall in love with the psychological thriller genre is Freida McFadden.

Lastly, to all the readers who choose to dive into this story: thank you for your time and for allowing my words to enter your world.

I hope this book keeps you on the edge of your seat.

www.ingramcontent.com/pod-product-compliance
Lightning Source LLC
Chambersburg PA
CBHW010428170726
48283CB00011B/3114